**Abby North** has been a dreamer for as long as she can remember. She inhaled books as a child, and now immerses herself in the characters and worlds she creates.

She has a weakness for strong, capable heroines, and brooding, complicated bad boys, and loves to deliver the message that ultimately love and honesty can overcome even the biggest obstacles – after a little emotional angst, of course.

She is inspired by everyday people from all walks of life and loves to spend time in busy cities people-watching, as well as the quiet countryside listening to the birds and watching her dog live his best life following scents and running through the long grass.

# King of My Scars

Abby North

Revised new edition November 2025



Made in Stuttgart with ♥


This is a revised new edition of Holding Aces previously published 2014 by Nikki Groom.

**KING OF MY SCARS**

ISBN: 978-1-91834-303-8
E-Book-ISBN: 978-2-38619-134-3

Cover design: Nadine Jindal (nk_Coverdesign)
Book jacket design: Nadine Jindal (nk_Coverdesign)
With the use of motives from
stock.adobe.com: © RONY, © NpicArt
shutterstock.com: © detchana wangkheeree, © nadezhda F, © Sjoerd Smit Photography

Typeset by dp DIGTAL PUBLISHERS Ltd.
Printed by IngramSpark

# PROLOGUE

I had to leave. It was bad this time.

Each time it happened, I stupidly forgave him. I knew it wouldn't be the last time, and not to my surprise, each time after that it was worse.

I'm not even sure if I felt the physical pain anymore. I was numb, inside and out. A shell of the person I once was.

But this time ... this time he had gone too far. I had needed medical attention. His kick to my left side had broken two ribs, one of which had punctured my lung. My kidneys were bruised from his fists slamming into me repeatedly, and my wrist was broken from the impossible angle he had twisted it.

Until now he was careful not to mark my face or anywhere that someone could see. Each time it happened, he whisked me away for a weekend to 'make things okay' and let the bruises fade, and each time he took a little more of my soul.

My mom had her suspicions; I could see it in her eyes, and her gentle probing questions without asking directly for fear of accusing him of something he may not have done.

But she knew.

I wanted to tell her, someone ... anyone. It was a lonely burden, an elephant sitting on my chest. He had worn me down so far that I didn't have an identity. Functioning on a daily basis but not feeling.

I was his.

Nothing more, nothing less.

He was a powerful, well-respected businessman, so no one would ever believe me, and even if they did, he would pay them off and it would all be forgotten. Initially, I found it unbelievable that money could buy the conscience of a man, but it had become such a familiar occurrence that nothing surprised me anymore.

He had taken me to a private hospital and visited every day, the devoted fiancé. He had cried when he told the nurses how I was attacked in our home by an intruder, and I had cried at my helplessness.

I had ten days in that hospital with no fear and no pressure to conform because he couldn't do anything to me while I was there. It was the longest I had been away from him in five years, and it was the best thing that could have happened to me. Every day my confidence built, and I found a little more of the girl I once was. Only now, the girl had grown up. Now I was a woman, and I knew what my future held. The fire in my belly was small, barely a spark, but it was there, and I knew that if I stayed, that tiny glow of hope would be extinguished, and very possibly so could I.

So I did the only thing I could do ...

I ran.

# Chapter 1

I thought I was pretty tough. I've learned to adapt and grow with each situation I've been faced with and have suffered in far worse ways than I am now, and survived it.

But I'm living a lie.

Unhappily married to a man I don't love, answering to a name that isn't mine, and not being able to see a way out because, after all, I'm responsible for my own actions and it feels so tangled I can't see past it.

I chose to run. I chose to hide. And now, I don't know where to go from here.

I want to go home, but I don't know if I can. I want to be me, but I don't know how to find my way out of this mess.

My legs start to pound harder on the treadmill as the thoughts and possibilities battle their way through my mind. I welcome the burn through my thighs as I push forward, and my lungs fight to take in more air, a welcome distraction, my *only* distraction from the false life I'm living.

It's not a bad life—arguably better than the one I ran from. I'm also not ungrateful. But I'm not happy. Is the goal in life to survive ... or is it to thrive? I miss my mom; I haven't seen or spoken to her since I left Boulder City, and I miss my friend Lottie, the only true friend I've ever had.

I regret the fact that I let Jonny push those closest to me away, let him destroy my life. He's the reason I've lived with a false name for eighteen months. He's the reason for everything bad that has happened to me since the day I met him.

I now live in a beautiful house in LA. I'm married to a wealthy music executive, Aaron Jamesson, and I have the world at my fingertips. Money buys a lot of things, a lot of distractions, and it makes it easier to conjure smoke and mirrors, but it doesn't fill the hole in my heart.

At first, Aaron seemed to be everything Jonny wasn't. We had a fun courtship and a beautiful wedding. He offered me a friendship which I welcomed, and gave me the opportunity to start over with a new life and a new identity, something which I never thought would be possible. Being honest with myself, I used him to stay under the radar, to make it harder for Jonny to find me. I reinvented myself to save my life, created a persona much different to my own and agreed to things I wouldn't have otherwise. Like having a baby. God, the thought makes me break out in a cold sweat. I know it won't be long before Aaron starts to wonder why we're not pregnant yet, and I don't know how to delay the inevitable.

I've lived a life as Natalie Jamesson and tried to keep as little of my true self from creeping in as possible. For a long time, I didn't feel bad. The freedom of leaving my past behind outweighed the guilt that lurked on the periphery. How can you feel guilty when you've forgotten how to feel?

It's the same story that battles through my head every day.I never come up with a solution but I can't see a way out and again I find myself being unhappy. I just take each day as it comes and hope it works out somehow, leaving fate to find its path and hoping for a little luck along the way.

I finish up my workout, grabbing my towel and draping it around my neck as I switch off the lights and come out of the gym room. The front door slams and Aaron's loud voice carries through the foyer, his agitated tone making me feel a little uneasy. Since we came back from our honeymoon, where a small part of me started to think we might be able to be genuinely happy, things have gone downhill and proven that I should have kept my heart locked and my head on straight. That tiny band of gold around my finger has changed things, changed Aaron. Something shifted the minute we touched back down in LA, and from my experience, if something doesn't feel right in the first instance then the chances are it probably isn't.

"I've told you I don't fucking have it at the moment ... No, the earliest I can get it to you will be next Friday ... Fine." He abruptly hangs up the call and stands just inside the doorway, running his hands through his hair. His stress is almost visible, and I don't know if it's worth trying to talk to him when he is in this kind of mood but ignoring him will definitely make things worse. He glances up to find me looking at him.

"Hey!" I say cheerily before I walk over and reach up on my tiptoes to kiss his cheek. The strong smell of alcohol coming off him indicates that he's had more than one drink with his lunch. He's been drinking a lot lately, but whenever I mention it, he dismisses my concerns.

"How long have you been standing there?" he snaps.

"Um, only a couple of seconds. I just had a workout and finished up as you came in. I'm just going to take a shower, then I'll be down, okay?"

"Fine." His tone is flat, completely indifferent, and it throws me. It shouldn't make me feel so disappointed, but it does.

"Uh, just gimme ten," I mumble.

"Sure." The monotone answer makes me feel further deflated. I stupidly look forward to him coming home because a very naive part of me thinks each day he might be different, but today is no different from yesterday and all the conversation he can manage is monosyllabic. Dread crawls through my senses and I push away the feeling that I've been here before. Wouldn't I just be better off alone?

I turn and take the stairs two at a time, hoping he'll have mellowed by the time I come back down. Stripping off my sweat soaked clothes in record time, I fling them into the corner of the bathroom. Why do I even let him make me feel like this? Maybe a couple of years of marriage was too much to hope for; we've only just made it twelve weeks. I release the clip that has been gripping my hair in place and run my fingers through my long blonde locks. I haven't had it cut or colored since the wedding and it hangs nearly to my waist.

I turn the shower on as hot as I can stand it and step in. The multiple jets pummel my overworked muscles and I close my eyes as the burning water stings my skin. It's bordering on painful, but the feeling is a welcome distraction from the workings of my mind. Tipping my head back, I close my eyes and let the water flow down through the lengths of my hair.

A cold hand on my waist makes me jump, and I snap my head up and my eyes open to see Aaron standing in front of me. Judging by his lack of clothes, he's joining me in the shower whether I like it or not.

"Baby," he says softly, "I'm sorry I was blunt with you ..."

My whole body tenses as his hands work their way around the curve of my hips and settle on my ass, pulling me closer to him as he plants kisses along my shoulder and collarbone. His arousal presses against my stomach as his hands slide along my wet skin. As much as I crave the physical closeness that we used to have, I don't want him. Not now, not like this. His recent behavior has pushed me away and the distance grows further with every second that passes in his company. My pre-marital guarded self is returning slowly and surely, and instinct tells me I have to brace it to survive.

I roll my shoulder away from him and step back. "Not now, Aaron."

His hands stop their exploration of my body, and he pushes me away from him a little, holding my shoulders with his hands and crouching to look directly into my eyes.

"What do you mean, not now?" His hard stare makes me shiver, but I square my shoulders and refuse to be ground down.

"I mean exactly that. Not. Now." I punctuate the last few words through gritted teeth so he fully understands that I will not be persuaded otherwise. I push his arms away and brush past him to get out of the shower, but his fingers grip my elbow tightly before I make it out.

"Not now? You're denying me? I'm your husband for Christ's sake. How are we ever going to get you pregnant?"

I hate how selfish he's being, acting like I've ruined *his* plans. Well, he's not the only one who is angry. I'm angry for letting him in, for letting my guard down, and most of all I'm angry at myself for falling for this shit and getting into a crappy situation yet again.

I put my hands on my hips and lean my body toward him, brave in my rising anger. "What about me? What if I don't want to get pregnant, huh? Did you think of that?"

His face pales and his grip on my arm tightens. Shit, did I really just say that? *Shit, Shit, Shit ...* I instantly regret voicing those words out loud. His expression tightens changes, his stance changes and suddenly the space we are in feels so small.

I feel small.

"What did you just say?" He comes closer so his face is only inches away from mine; his tone is lowered and his pupils are so dilated with rage that I momentarily wonder if he's taken some kind of drug. I've had this feeling before, and it's not one I had planned on revisiting, but here I am with the nervous adrenaline flowing through my body and making my legs shake, unable to find the courage I need to get the hell out of here. Aaron's moods have been unpredictable of late, and I've been putting it down to him having a bad day, or the stresses and strains of work demands. I've been falling back into my old ways, making excuses for his snappy retorts, his unreasonable moods.

"You don't want to have my baby?" he questions.

"Aaron it's not like that." I let out an exasperated breath. "I'm tired, you're tired, and you've clearly had a bad day. So please, let's just go and get dressed and have something to eat." I sound desperate and I fucking hate it, but right now I *feel* desperate, I will do anything to fast forward from this conversation and the tension that has rapidly filled this space. I just want him to let go of me so I can get out of here.

"We've been trying for a baby for three fucking months." He grates the words out, his voice tight and strained and his teeth clenched. He's still holding onto my arm, and his fingers are gripping me so tightly that I'm sure it will leave bruises.

Then his expression changes as though a thought has just plunked into place, his grip loosens and his brows pull together in a deep frown. He backs out of the shower, and in the time it takes me to put on my robe, he is pulling everything out of the cabinets and tearing the place apart. Creams and lotions are hitting the floor all around us, smashing and leaving a slippery mess.

"Aaron, what the hell are you doing?"

He doesn't answer as he continues to empty the cupboards and drawers until the bathroom floor is covered. He kicks some of the things out of the way as he pushes past me, out of the en suite bathroom and into our bedroom.

"Where are they?" he roars, rushing to my dressing table.

"What are you talking about? Aaron, stop it ..." I try to grab his arm to make him stop, but he jerks it away, pulling out the top drawer and emptying the contents on the floor, and it dawns on me what he's looking for. We both see it at the same time.

Shit.

His eyes fly up and lock onto mine.

I can't move. Can't speak. I know he knows.

We both dive for the box at the same time, but he's quicker than me and picks it up, snatching it out of my grasp. He opens the tab and pulls out the half empty packet. He looks at the little white pills, calculating how many there are as I'm rooted to the spot, nervous for his reaction the longer he stays silent.

"You fucking bitch!"

I flinch involuntarily at the sheer volume of his voice, then brace for a further onslaught. He flings the pills on the floor and in two strides he's in front of me, his face just inches from mine. "You lied to me, Natalie." He's so close I can feel his breath on my lips. "You let me think we were trying for a baby, yet all along you've been taking your fucking pills."

I look down, to avoid eye contact with him and try to think of a way to diffuse the situation a little, but there is nothing I can say to make this any better.

He roughly grabs my face with one of his hands and lifts it so I'm forced to look at him. He squeezes my cheeks, his thumb and forefinger digging into my cheekbones, and I wince with the pressure. "I've been working myself into the ground to provide for you, to pay for all your nice clothes and your expensive lunches out with the wives so that we can have a family together, and this is how you repay me?"

"Aaron, please, I—"

"You what? Explain why you FUCKING LIED TO ME!" He yells the last words in my face, and I slam my eyes closed to try and block it out.

"Aaron ..." I can feel my bottom lip start to tremble as images of what may happen next fill my mind. I know what's coming. I've been here before.

His fingers release their pressure on my jaw before my head snaps to the side, the back of his left hand connecting with my cheek and stunning me. It takes a couple of seconds to comprehend what he has just done. His wedding ring leaves a sharp sting, and my cheek starts to burn. I instinctively put my hand up to touch my face as my eyes meet his.

"Fuck." He releases the word on a breath. His eyes are wide, and his mouth is gaping open in shock. "Natalie, oh god ... I didn't mean to, I don't know why ..." He reaches out to me, and when I recoil, the tears well in his eyes. "Please, Nat, I'm so, so, sorry."

"Get. Away. From. Me."

I start to walk backwards, my hand still covering my cheek in disbelief. I could see it moving in this direction. But I'd told myself that not all men were like Jonny, that not all men got mad and hit out. But it's happened again.

I back into the bathroom on shaky legs, slamming the door behind me and sliding the bolt as fast as I can. I tighten the belt on my robe, then scrape my wet hair into a messy pile on top of my head and secure it with a band. My cheek stings when I touch it, making me wince. I'm bleeding.

I rush to the mirror to take a look. Underneath my left eye is already starting to swell and my cheek is covered with an angry red mark. I know from experience that this color will only deepen until the blackness of a bruise covers it. There is an inch of broken skin along my cheekbone, and the blood is starting to trickle down the side of my face.

"Natalie ... please, let me in. I'm sorry, baby. I'm so sorry ..." he begs.

Hearing his pitiful voice through the door brings back memories. Only this time it doesn't fill me with fear. It makes me determined.

This is *not* going to happen to me again.

I know he probably feels terrible, and if I gave him the chance, he would apologize a thousand times to ease his guilt. He would beg and plead and promise that it would never happen again. He'd make it up to me with jewelry and a weekend break.

I know.

I've been here before.

But I don't feel sorry for him. I know I lied, but I didn't deserve that.

"Go away," I manage to say, still staring at my reflection.

"Nat, just let me in ..."

"I said, GO AWAY!"

I hear his footsteps walk away, and the loud bang of the bedroom door slamming makes me jump. My legs suddenly feel very weak, and my head is spinning as a wall of tears builds in front of my eyes, threatening to spill at any minute.

The fear, the shouting, the feeling of helplessness ... it's emotional overload and too much for me to take. I lower myself to the floor in a heap and curling up in a little ball, I tuck my knees tightly to my chest and wrap my arms around them. Then the tears start to fall freely, and I let them, not holding anything back. I begin to acknowledge that the last three months have been chipping away at my self-imposed armor and reduced me to the girl I used to be all too familiar with, the place I thought I'd never go again, the life I tried so hard to avoid. I might have changed my name, my identity, but the path my life is taking feels very familiar.

I don't know how long I've been crying for, but when I lift my head up and open my eyes it's dusk outside. My shoulders are tight and my chest aches from my body wracking sobs. When I stand up and straighten my body out, every muscle is protesting and my head pounds as I look around me at the evidence of the earlier argument. Flicking on the light switch, I survey everything with a stark realization. Everything feels so much worse in the dark but looks so much worse in the light. Resting my hands on either side of the bathroom sink, I look into the mirror, staring at my reflection and acknowledging the feeling of resignation that is setting in. My eyes are swollen and red and it stings every time I blink. There are trails of black mascara that have mingled with blood and dried in smudged lines down my cheeks. This is a face that I have seen many times before, a distant, broken look that I hadn't ever wanted to see again.

I can't stay here.

I can't stay married to Aaron.

Deep down, I never truly believed this would be a permanent arrangement, and I was stupid and weak for letting myself think that what we had could possibly become real. Jesus, the guy didn't even know my true name ...

Happily ever after was never a possibility.

I know what I have to do.

It's fight or flight and we have been fighting for far too long.

Unknowingly, Aaron has given me an out. He's given me the perfect reason to leave.

Splashing cold water on my face soothes the heat I can feel surrounding my eyes. I've cried out every last tear left in my body and there is nothing left to give. I feel nothing now. I'm empty, devoid of feeling any emotion other than annoyance at myself for letting this happen again.

The cold water awakens my skin and spurs me on to what I know is the next step in rebuilding my life.

I clean up the cut on my cheekbone and wince at the sting that comes from my touch. It's superficial and will heal fairly quickly. It may not even leave a visible scar.

Just an addition to the invisible scars I carry.

I open the bathroom door quietly and slowly, taking in the mess that surrounds me. I listen for any signs that Aaron might be here, but there is nothing but silence and a heavy air around me. I look out of the bedroom window and note that Aaron's car is gone. Relief washes over me. I know I might not have long to get out of here, but it's better than facing him. I throw on some clothes, drag a big suitcase from the top of the wardrobe and fill it with as many essentials as I can: handfuls of clothes, a few toiletries, and my sketch pads. My life, thrown together in a suitcase and packed up in five minutes flat.

I wheel the suitcase to the bedroom doorway, willing myself to stay strong and forcing my feet to keep walking. I walk faster and faster until I run down the curved staircase, the suitcase hitting every step with a thud as I drag it behind me.

When I reach the foyer, I pick up my purse. I don't know how far away I can get with my credit cards before Aaron puts a stop on them to cut me off, or a trace on them to find me, but I have a separate account that Aaron doesn't know about. I think deep down I knew it wouldn't work out, so I kept my backup quiet while still putting a little away in savings.

I take off my rings and leave them on the side table next to the front door so he will see them when he walks in. If he didn't already know that our sham of a marriage was over, he will when he finds my rings there. I snatch up my keys, fling the front door open, grab my suitcase and flee. Pressing the button on the key fob, my Porsche Carrera blips, and the lights flash to indicate it's unlocked. I bundle my suitcase across to the passenger's seat and jump in.

The wheels spin out of the drive and kick up a cloud of dust and dirt behind me as I glance in the rearview mirror at the house I am leaving behind.

It is beautiful, but it was never home.

# CHAPTER 2

After driving for a couple of hours, I can feel my eyes closing, and I don't want to risk falling asleep at the wheel, so my safest option is to stop somewhere for the night and take it from there.

I pull off the highway and into a motel. It looks rundown, but it's the last place Aaron will come looking for me. He'll expect me to go to a high class hotel, with full room service and every luxury available. But I guess he never really knew me. Maybe I don't even know myself.

I shut the door behind me and glance at my room for the night. A solitary single bed, one pillow and a small pile of sheets and blankets. I haven't slept in a single bed since I was seventeen.

*I feel like I'm constantly going backwards …*

The patterned carpet is psychedelic patterns in what I can only guess should have been red and yellow but now looks more like shades of browns, and threadbare in the places that suffer the most footfall. An armchair in the corner and a nightstand next to it are the only other furnishings and they are well worn and used. The lamp on the night-stand has no lampshade, making the light harsh and casting obscure shadows around the walls. I actually think this room might not have been updated since 1975.

I drop my suitcase and throw the keys onto the armchair in the corner. It takes four steps across the small dingy room to the bathroom door and I close my eyes as I push the handle, afraid of what I might find in there. Squinting them open, I turn on the light and I'm met with a very old bathroom suite but it's clean and I'm pleasantly surprised. I shut the door again and let out a long exhale. As I sit down on the bed, the springs groan and protest with my small weight and a stale musky smell invades my nose.

I glance at my watch. 10pm. I'm exhausted emotionally and my body has made its way down from the adrenaline high and feels twice as heavy to move as it should. I have no idea where I go from here, and my head is too weary to decide right now. Sleep, I need sleep. I'm hoping all will become clearer in the light of day.

I make the bed up with the surprisingly clean sheets and climb in fully clothed. My face throbs from the cut and I instinctively bring my fingers up to my cheek, touching lightly underneath the wound and recalling the events of the night. I never thought it would come to this. I just wanted to feel settled, like I belong somewhere. I just want to let my guard down and not have to keep up some sort of pretense.

If this is what my life is going to be like on the run, maybe it's time to think about taking some of my old life back. The scenarios running through my head exhaust me as I drift off into a surprisingly deep sleep.

I open my eyes just a fraction and snap them shut again. When the sleep mist clears and I work out what day it is and why I'm here, I groan. I don't know what's worse, my dreams or reality. I sit up and swing my legs out of the bed, cringing a little as my bare feet hit the not so clean carpet. I take a deep breath, stretch my arms above my head and go for a shower.

The scalding water beats down on my body, and with every minute longer that I'm in here, things become a little clearer. I have to satisfy myself that I haven't lost the girl I was just because I have a different name. Natalie isn't a fictional person; she's me. I'm still me.

I'm sick of this.

Running.

Fighting.

Always looking over my shoulder and having to think before I speak for fear of revealing who I really am.

This is my life and I'm taking it back.

I dress, put on some makeup, and then pack up my things. After leaving the keys at the front desk, I head for my car. It's crazy that my front seat is more comfortable than the bed I spent last night in; comfort really does come at a price.

When I turn on my cell, it's flooded with incoming messages from Aaron.

His messages start off frantic when he's realized I've packed up and gone. He's obviously sorry, telling me to call and to let him know where I am, telling me how important I am to him, how he loves me. However, he doesn't take long to change from worried, apologetic husband to angry and demanding.

When I've listened and deleted all of the voicemails and texts, I ring the one person I actually want to speak to, hoping that her number hasn't changed in all the time that I've been gone.

My insides shake with anticipation and excitement as my fingers fumble with the numbers. The familiar warm voice answers on the other end of the line.

"Hello ..."

I'm overwhelmed with emotion at hearing her voice. "Mom?" A sob rises up from my chest and escapes my mouth.

"Baby girl, is that you?" she asks in disbelief.

"Yes, Mom, it's me ..."

The floodgates open and we both sit there, on opposite ends of the line, crying tears of happiness at hearing each other's voice. It doesn't matter that I've spent most of my childhood looking after her, picking up the pieces after each failed marriage and being her strength when she was weak. It wasn't until I had spent so long away from her, unable to contact her that I realized we had always been each other's strength.

*She's the only family I have.*

"Where are you, my girl? Are you okay?"

"I'm fine, it's just ... I've missed you so much, Mom."

"Darling, every day I've hoped you would call. I knew why you didn't, but that didn't stop me from wanting to hear your voice."

"I would have called you sooner but ... you know ..." I'm so choked up I can hardly speak.

"I wished every day that you would." Her voice hitches, full of emotion.

"Mom, please don't get upset."

"I'm sorry, darling, but not knowing if you were happy or even where you were ..."

It was hard for me to be away from her with no contact and I'm just glad that she has her husband, Brent. I knew she was in safe hands with him. I killed me to think how she felt seeing her child go through all that, only to be left not knowing where or how I was.

"Well, there are few things that I need to get worked out, but it isn't going to be like this for much longer, I promise you that." I sound more determined now, even to my own ears.

"Why? What's going on? Do you need my help? Is there anything I can do?" She speaks fast wanting to do something after feeling helpless for so long.

"I just need to know ... have you seen *him*?" I can't even bring myself to say his name out loud. That name would feel like poison to my tongue.

"Jonny? No. He came to the house once after you left. He was angry, frantic, and he yelled ..." her voice trails off.

"Mom?"

She sighs. "He beat Brent up. He thought we knew where you were."

My stomach sinks. I didn't think it would put them in that position. I didn't think about anything. I just knew I needed to leave. "Oh god, Mom, I'm sorry, I'm so sorry. Was Brent okay?"

"Yes, he was sore for a few days, but it was mainly superficial. I think he realized we didn't know anything. We haven't seen or heard from him since."

"Nothing at all? He hasn't been around Boulder City?"

"Nothing at all. No one has seen him."

"What about his offices?" I ask desperately.

"I'm not sure, darling, I was just pleased we had seen the last of him. You want me to find out, I can do some digging?"

"No, no, it's fine. I don't want any waves made ..." I trail off as I think about what to do next. "Mom, I know this is going to be hard, but can you forget we've spoken today? Just don't say anything to anyone, not even Brent."

"But he'd be so happy that you've been in touch ... are you coming back? I really don't think there'll be a problem anymore, honey ..."

"I don't know. Honestly, I think he will probably have just moved on but until I know how the land lies, I want to be safe. I want you to be safe. You know how it was." I say this, but she didn't know the full extent. I kept so much from her. "I want to come back, I really do, but we'll see. Please, just give me a few days."

"Okay, if you know what you're doing."

"Not yet I don't, but I will."

"That's my girl."

I smile. She always said that to me as a child and she's right. I am her girl, even at twenty-six years old.

"I love you, Mom. I'll call soon, okay?"

"I love you too. Stay safe."

When the phone disconnects, I sit there for a whole minute and look at the screen. Just a short conversation with my mom and everything seems so much clearer. I have to work out a way to go back, a way to be near to her. She is my only family, and she feels like my calm in the storm. I've wasted enough time running away, and I'm not the person I used to be. I'm stronger for everything I've been through, and with family in my corner I'm sure I can get through anything life throws at me.

Where to go from here? I've been driving in the direction of Boulder City knowing I can't go there just yet, but I need to be close. I take a deep breath and dial the only other number I know off by heart, hoping it hasn't changed since I last called it. When she picks up, I smile.

"Hello?"

"Got time for a dirty martini, party girl?" I open our conversation with the greeting we always used to use. Her usual reply doesn't come though.

Radio silence.

"Lottie?"

"Almost two years ... it's been two fucking years since you called me ..."

"I know," I whisper. "I'm sorry ... stuff happened."

"Don't give me that shit. Your control freak motherfucker of a boyfriend happened."

"Lottie—"

"No, don't you 'Lottie' me. He didn't like me, so you chose him." My heart breaks a little that she thinks I would do that.

"It wasn't like that."

"No? So how was it? He got bored and now you want your friend back?"

"Lottie! Stop being a bitch, you know it was never like that," I say before dropping my voice to a whisper "He—"

"He what? What did that motherfucker do?" Her tone changes to protective. She's the stereotypical redhead—sharp, hot headed and fierce!

"I need some help, Lottie, and you're the only one I trust to help me."

"Don't change the subject, young lady! What did he do, and what can I do to help? You know I'd do anything for you, babe," she adds softly.

*I've missed* her straight talking.

*I've missed* her loyalty.

*I've missed* her friendship.

"I've missed you, Lottie." I hope she can hear my smile down the phone.

"I've missed you too," she says quietly before taking a breath. "Right. Now that we've got the sappy shit out of the way, are you gonna fill me in?"

She hasn't changed one bit. Straight to the point, no messing.

"Yes, but not over the phone. Do you know of anywhere close to Boulder City that I can stay? A hotel or something?"

"Stay with me," she states.

"I can't. I mean, I just don't think it's wise. Not yet."

"Okay." She pauses. "My boyfriend's brother owns a hotel on the Vegas Strip. Head there. I'll sort it and text you with details," she says firmly.

"Perfect. I owe you one, Lottie."

"Yes, you do. Call me when you get there. I'm heading over there in about an hour anyway, so I want to know the minute you arrive."

“I promise.” I know she is going to have a fit when she sees my face, but there’s not a lot I can do about that now. I’m just pleased she hadn’t been around to see me before I left Boulder City. “And, Lottie... can you put it under the name Natalie Jamesson?”

“Natalie who now?”

“Just... I’ll explain everything when I get there.”

We say our goodbyes and hang up. After speaking to the two people I hold dearest to me in the whole world, I’m happy. I turn the music up and open the windows, letting the wind blow away some of the weight that has been holding me down. I smile to myself and sing along with the music.

I’m going to Vegas.

After three hours on the road, I finally pull into Las Vegas. I’d lived fairly nearby in Boulder City for quite a few years and had come here occasionally, but it wasn’t a place I’d frequented. Aaron had been taken here by the boys for his Bachelor Party, although he had remained tight-lipped about what went down that weekend. “What happens in Vegas stays in Vegas.”

I take a deep breath and remind myself why I’m here.

Move on. Move forward.

I follow Lottie’s directions to the hotel. It’s huge with beautiful fountains outside and a gleaming glass frontage. There is sparkling gold lettering above the entry that reads 'The Kingdom' and I momentarily wonder if they send someone up there to polish it every day it's that shiny. The valet takes my car, and a bellhop greets me at the door, taking my case and walking me to the reception area. It's stunning. The floors are highly polished marble as is the main reception desk, and there are huge arrangements of bright green foliage and pure white fresh flowers. Everywhere you look there are subtle accents of gold—the desk has a gold trim. The tall ornate pedestals either side have gold flourished indentations. It's the kind of place Aaron would take me to for a weekend getaway.

I turn my attention to the friendly receptionist. I'm just about to speak when I hear a familiar squeal and I'm tackled from behind by a five foot redhead who has her arms wrapped around my neck and is squeezing me so hard I might pass out.

She lets go and bounces in front of me. "I'm so freaking happy to ..." Her beaming smile freezes and drops as her brows knit into fierce hard lines and her tone changes to angry. "What the fuck happened to your face? Talk ..." she says, putting her hand on her hip.

I smile at her softly. "Can I get out of these clothes first? Then we'll go get a drink ... please." I don't want to discuss this right here, and I really do want to freshen up.

"Fine. Come on, I'll see you up to your room."

My room is on the second floor and is beautiful. It has floor to ceiling windows, which are dressed in crisp white drapes with a gold trim. It's simple, but elegant and not overdone. I leave my case in the bedroom where the colors of white and gold are carried through, and I freshen up in the marble bathroom before Lottie and I head back downstairs to find an outside table at one of the bistros. We are served immediately, ordering drinks and a light lunch.

"Okay, spill it," Lottie says, putting her elbows on the table and clasping her hands under her chin.

"It's not really that bad," I say, waving my hand as if to prove my statement is true.

"You always were a crap liar."

And just like that, the brave face I have managed to put on for several very long years starts to fall away. "It's all such a mess." My words come out as a whisper, not wanting to really acknowledge how much of a disaster everything is, but knowing I have to get it all out in the open. I wouldn't tell my mom without it hurting her too much to know what I've been through, but I know Lottie is strong enough to handle it.

Her hand gently covers mine, and my throat aches with all the things I want to say, but I don't know where to begin.

"Start from the beginning, babe. I have all day ..."

So I tell her everything, from the day I fled Boulder City to this moment here and now. The elephant that has been sitting on my chest is lifted, and the hurt and pain I feel lessens.

"So does he know where you are, this Aaron guy?" Lottie curls her lip as she says his name. She might be small, but she can be pretty fierce.

"No."

"And he hasn't tried to contact you since you left?"

I shrug. "He's my husband, but seeing as he married a fictional person, I'm not even sure the marriage is legal."

"Are you going to let him know that you're not going back? I mean, you're not going back, are you?"

"No! I don't plan on going back, but I don't plan on telling him anything either. How would I explain all of this shit? I disappeared once, and I can do it again."

"I don't want you to disappear." She pouts. "I've missed you."

I nod gently, reciprocating her feelings. "I just don't know where to go from here."

"We'll figure something out. I know people, who ... know people."

"What do you mean?"

"You need help?" I nod. "Well, I'll help. You need info, I know just the guy. If it means keeping my best friend safe, then I'll pull out all the stops."

"Thanks, Lottie. I'm sorry I didn't come to you before. I just couldn't drag you into it all like that."

"Look, I know why you did it, but you're my friend, my *best* friend. Actually, you're more like a sister to me, so no more going it alone, okay?" She makes me laugh by following her *mushy shit* as she'd call it with a stern voice and a telling off.

"Okay, enough of my drama. I want to hear about *you*. Your boyfriend owns this awesome place?"

"Noooo, my boyfriend's brother."

"Tell me more." I lean forward, wanting to hear how happy she is.

We continue to chat, eat and laugh. It's great to do "normal" but before I know it the day has run away with us, and Lottie has to leave for her shift in one of the local bars. I leave her in the foyer with a tight hug and a promise to call tomorrow to formulate some kind of plan. I don't know what she has in mind, and I have no idea where to begin, but it feels like it might just all work out okay. Loneliness is hard on the mind when you have so many obstacles in your way, but when you have a friend like Lottie who is willing to hold your hand the whole way through, it suddenly feels easier. It actually feels possible to make some kind of sense out of this jumble I call my life so far.

I make my way to the elevator, and although my mind feels lighter, my legs feel heavy. The last twenty-four hours have exhausted me, and my head is racing with all kinds of thoughts and possibilities. The ding sounds on the elevator, bringing me back to reality from my daydream and when the doors open, I instinctively step forward, my feet thinking before my brain, and walk straight into the person exiting. My hands fly up to correct myself, landing on a hard, wide, chest, and I look up to apologize.

Time stops.

I take in the features of the guy in front of me. This guy is not botoxed or surgically sculpted, but he is chiseled—all natural.

His hands grasp my shoulders to steady me, strong but gentle at the same time. He must be about six foot two as he stands a head above me, and is dressed in a slate gray suit, with a crisp white shirt which is unbuttoned twice, giving me just a peek of his flesh at my eye level. As my gaze slowly travels upwards, I notice his dark hair is damp and falls gently across his forehead.

His lips curl into a sexy little grin, and that simple movement breaks the trance-like state I seem to have put myself in. I blink twice and shake my head.

"My apologies, miss ...?" he asks huskily. The vibration in his voice ripples through my body and down to the tips of my toes. Every follicle reacts by standing on end and my skin tingles.

"Uh ... Jameson. Miss Jameson," I manage to stutter, earning a low chuckle from him. I give him a nervous smile before I side-step to let him pass; he might be attractive, but I am not interested. But he doesn't let me move away from him as easily as I would have liked. He makes it almost torturous instead by sliding his hands down my arms, and letting his thumbs trace the inside of my elbows, finally breaking contact when he gets to the very tips of my fingers. It isn't sleazy or disrespectful, but I know it's more than I can allow myself to want right now.

It's only once he's not physically touching me that I can breathe, and my brain returns to some kind of normalcy. For a moment, I question my sanity. Men have only ever brought me trouble, but I've never had someone make me feel so mesmerized and so nervous at the same time. Clearly, I'm tired, possibly hormonal, and definitely emotional. It's been a long, tumultuous few days, few years, and I'm clearly not in control of my reactions.

I force my feet to scuttle forward and stop just inside of the elevator, pressing the button to my left repeatedly with my back still facing the door. Wanting so badly to turn around, but not actually being able to let myself, I continue to face the back of the elevator, head down, willing the doors to shut and get moving. As the door closes, I rub at my bare forearm to calm the unusual reaction across my skin.

*What the hell just happened?*

# Chapter 3

Sitting back in my hotel room on my own, I'm restless. I only have a few of my belongings with me, nothing familiar to distract me, and no routine to adhere to. Having spent time with Lottie, I'm craving familiarity, and being on my own now makes me feel lonely and unsettled. Hell, who am I kidding?

*I am* lonely.

*I am* unsettled.

The only difference now is that I'm hyper aware of it.

For the first time in as long as I can remember, I know what I want. I know how I want life to be, and sitting here, staring out of the window at the bright lights of Vegas, it frustrates me that I can't make it happen right now. I want to start my new life. I want to start living days full of fun, independence, and a hopeful future, but I can't do that if I'm sitting here waiting for it to happen.

I jump up, rummage through the few clothes I did pack and throw on an evening top and skinny jeans. I smooth some extra foundation over my bruised cheek, then touch it up with a sweep of blush. Grabbing my clutch, I head for the door.

As I walk through the foyer, the bars and clubs have come to life. There's live music playing and I find myself smiling. I love music; it's the one thing guaranteed to get a response from me. Tonight, the choice of either staying in a lonely hotel room, dwelling on the last twenty-four hours, or having a few drinks and letting loose is easy. I have no one to please, no one tapping their watch because I'm later that I said I'd be, and if I want to sleep in late tomorrow ... well, I can do just that.

There is a choice of bars, each fitting to a different mood, and tonight I'm drawn to the bar called *Heaven and Hell*. I'm pretty sure I've visited the latter several times, so maybe I can find a little piece of the other for the evening.

The bar is decorated in rich reds, golds, and clean white accents, giving it a fresh, but luxurious feel. It has large, cozy booths with leather seats placed around the perimeter, and the dance floor is down a few steps from the booths with two small stages for dancing.

The music is loud and energetic when I enter. The bass is vibrating across the floor and up through my body. Some of the servers are dressed as devils in ruby-red, skin-tight body suits with sparkly horns and tails, while the others are dressed as angels in white, tight, body suits with glowing halos above their heads.

*Heaven and Hell*—I like it.

I order a very colorful cocktail and find a tall stool at the bar which also gives me a great view over most of the club. As it starts to get busy, the people crowd in, and the dance floor fills up. I've always felt safer surrounded by people, so the noise and the gathering sea of bodies suits me. The podiums have been occupied by angels and devils dancing, so I watch for a while, fascinated at their ability to look so at ease with being on display.

The first drink goes down easily and I remind myself not to let that fool me. I'm not really a big drinker, so I have little tolerance. I gesture to a male devil, and he checks his horns are on straight as he heads my way. He doesn't wear a tight-fitted suit like the female servers but red fitted trousers and a red sequined shirt that has a deep V to his navel. The horns are a nice touch.

"What can I get ya?" he says with a dazzling showbiz smile.

I take a second to scan through the cocktail list, baffled by the extensive concoctions. "Surprise me."

I watch, entertained by his performance as he pours and twists, spins and shakes, and I can't help but smile at his show. He then splits the cocktail shaker and pours my exotic looking drink into a sugar-dipped glass complete with a white and gold umbrella.

"Please put it on room 144—"

"Let me get that for you," booms a voice from behind me.

I turn to find a middle aged guy, about five foot eight, not unattractive but not sexy either. He wears a multi-colored shirt and the buttons are undone to the middle of his chest, which is sprouting a carpet of dark chest hair. It is not a good look, and his lopsided smile makes me a little uneasy. He pays for my drink without waiting for my answer and the bartender moves off to serve another person.

I feel cornered. Uneasy. Breath tightening in my chest.

"Thank you but you really didn't have to do that." I smile politely in the hope that this guy gets the message.

"Come on, can't a guy buy a beautiful lady a drink?"

"Here, let me pay you back." My tone is shorter this time as I turn my body away from him to find some money in my purse.

"That's not necessary. Room 144, was it?"

*Oh god, he heard my room number.* Panic rises in my chest. Maybe I'm not ready to confront the big wide world after all.

"No, you must have been mistaken. Now if you'll excuse me ..." I place my drink on the bar and stand to leave, but he grasps the top of my arm with enough pressure to make me stay where I am.

"I definitely heard you say 144," he says, moving in close. "That's the same floor as me, so what do you say we make some sweet music of our own, eh?" He nods his head toward the door, and I'm paralyzed; unable to transfer the words from my head to my mouth, and the rest of my body refuses to work.

"I don't think so," a deep voice says, startling me. "I definitely heard the lady say no."

My eyes fly up to the source of my rescue—the guy from the elevator. His large hand is holding the guy by his shoulder, and I can see by the uncomfortable way the man is holding himself that he's applying some pressure.

"I can assure you, the lady is not staying in room 144, and as of now, you will not be staying in this hotel." His tone is professional but very assertive.

"B-B-But I was just asking to ..." the guy stutters and visibly shrinks.

"You have thirty minutes to pack and leave. I will not have my guests harassed in any way. You are not welcome here. Now, please leave."

He releases the man's shoulder, draws his shoulders back slightly which instantly makes him look taller and more menacing, then gives him a sinister smile which confirms he means business. His fists are balled at his sides and his eyes are hard; he hasn't broken his stare at the sleazy guy or even looked in my direction. Thankfully, the guy seems resigned to his fate and leaves, muttering expletives under his breath but not putting up any more of a protest.

My rescuer follows the sleazeball with his fixed gaze until he is satisfied that he has exited the club. He turns to me, and his eyes soften when he presses a hand to my upper arm.

"Miss Jamesson." He dips his head as he speaks.

"Yes." My voice comes out quiet and childlike.

"Are you okay?"

I nod my answer, unable to form words at this moment.

"I sincerely am very sorry. It's not something that happens frequently here, I can assure you."

"It's fine. I ... uh ... I have to go." I turn my shoulder as if to move past him, and he extends his arm to block my path but doesn't touch me again.

"Please, Miss Jamesson, I would like to offer you a different room for your peace of mind. You're booked in for a week with us, is that correct?"

"I, uh..." Lottie hadn't told me how long she'd booked for me, but all I want to do now is leave and stay somewhere else. But what would that achieve? Besides, oddly, I actually do feel safe at this very minute.

"Then please allow me to change your room in way of an apology." There's something so sincere about his offer, and I realize that sincerity has been sorely lacking in my life the last few years.

He holds out his upturned hand, a simple gesture and one that feels so intimate. Maybe it's the alcohol running through my veins, or maybe it's the fact that the sleazy guy reminded me how vulnerable I really am. Lottie wouldn't have told me to come here if she didn't think I'd be safe, and I'd trust her with my life. So I place my small hand in his. He gently curls his fingers around mine, squeezing reassuringly as he leads me through the sea of people and out of the club.

When we enter the hotel foyer, he gently releases my hand and places his large palm in the small of my back. He stops in the middle of the foyer and shrugs off his suit jacket, I turn toward him, confused as to why he's stopped.

"You're cold." It's a statement, not a question, and he's frowning, as if he really is concerned that I might be cold. "Here ..." He places the jacket around my shoulders and comes to stand in front of me, buttoning it twice like a parent doing so for their child. He's caring for me. I steal a glance at him as he fastens the buttons; he has flawless, olive skin and full lips. When my eyes meet his, my breath hitches. His eyes are deep chocolate-brown but have gold flecks that glint in the light. He is the epitome of handsome.

His gaze lingers then travels to the broken and bruised skin on my cheek and his brows crease even further. He opens his mouth to speak but closes it quickly again and shakes his head ever so slightly.

"Come."

He gestures with his head toward the front desk and once again holds out his hand for me to take. A giggle escapes me, and I wiggle my hands out from underneath the jacket and wave them at him. Of course, I can't take his hand as he's fastened me securely into his clothing. A genuine smile appears from him and a deep chuckle follows.

He places his hand gently between my shoulder blades and walks across the beautiful marble floor, stopping at the main desk.

"Wait here, okay? I'll just be a minute."

I nod as he moves around the side of the large desk and lets himself into the office behind. I look around and observe the people coming and going. I must look ridiculous standing here in an oversized suit jacket buttoned up so I can't move my arms.

It dawns on me that I know nothing about this man. He obviously works here ... a manager maybe? I'll ask Lottie. Her boyfriend will know who he is. What I do know is that my judgement is shot to pieces. I don't know his name, he's a total stranger, but I let him hold my hand? Maybe I'm past caring what happens to me. Maybe the worst has already been done, so nothing else could be as bad as that? My thoughts start running deeper, bitterness taking over and consuming anything good that I might have felt just moments ago. Because where there is good, there has to be bad, right?

He appears just minutes later and holds his hand up, showing me the key card to my new room. His smile is as wide as the ocean and it's hard not to smile back. "Let's get you settled," he says, leading the way to the elevator.

"Do you do this for all the girls that get hit on in your hotel?"

He stops walking and his jaw drops open a little. "What do you mean by that?"

It was a stupid question and I don't even know why I blurted it out. If I had been a little more assertive, he wouldn't have felt like he had to come to my rescue. Now I feel I've been ungrateful, and it frustrates me that I don't have the ability to see the good in people anymore.

"Nothing, I ... it's just ... well, this is a lot of trouble for you to go to, you know?" I'm trying to gesture with my hands, but the jacket is making it rather difficult, frustrating me further. "You're changing my room because a guy hit on me and I didn't deal with it like I should have been able to ... It's not even like I'm a VIP that deserves the special treatment, I have a basic room and only for a week. You don't know me from Adam, and I don't even know your name. Do you work here or something?" The tone of my voice gradually gets higher, and my words come out fast until I've run out of breath.

A low rumble bubbles up from his stomach, and he presses his lips together to stop the laughter escaping but he is failing miserably. It's infectious and I join him when I realize just how neurotic my little rant was.

"Okay." He holds my shoulders and bends a little at the waist to look directly into my eyes while trying to keep his laughter under control. "Do you know how funny and adorable you look trying to move your arms around in my jacket while your mouth is running away with you?"

I laugh. "I guess that makes me look pretty crazy, huh?"

He nods and smiles gently. "That's a lot of questions, so here goes. Firstly, my name is Denham King. I would offer to shake your hand, but ... you know ..." He tilts his head and smirks to himself, reminding me that I'm still unable to free my arms. "I'm sorry I didn't introduce myself before. I hadn't even noticed that we had skipped that part. Secondly ..." He takes a deep breath. "I own this hotel, so who I give rooms to is my business, and thirdly, please let me assure you that this is the first and probably the only time I've felt compelled to accommodate a guest so willingly. You looked like you needed to catch a break, and I wanted to be the one to help you." He looks down at the marble flooring and finishes his sentence with a shrug and a shy smile.

I stand there a little taken aback and silenced by his explanation while I try to take in all the information. He seems so genuine, and I want to accept his kind gesture as nothing more than that, a kind gesture, but the realist in me makes me skeptical of anyone being so thoughtful just because they want to and not because there's an ulterior motive. Lottie said her boyfriend's brother owns this place... is he...?

"Come on." He starts to walk toward the elevator. "I'll have the bellboy stop at 144 and bring your belongings to your new room."

"I would really like to pack up my own things and make sure I don't leave anything behind ... if you don't mind?"

"Of course, I'm sorry, I should have thought. Would you like to stop by there on the way up or ...?"

"It's fine. I'll pack everything up in a while. You don't have to show me to my room, really, you've gone to enough trouble for me, I am so grateful and—"

"We can stop at your room along the way, and then I *will* show you to your new room. It'll give me peace of mind that you haven't gotten lost or hit on by a middle aged sleazeball with questionable dress sense." He looks at me with a quirked eyebrow. "Besides, you'll need a special code for the elevator." He says the last words with a wink, and I scrunch my brows at him. Nonetheless, I put my trust in him, perhaps more than I should, given my circumstances, but I trust Lottie and she wouldn't put me somewhere I wasn't safe.

We stop at my old room and collect my belongings. Ever the gentleman, he waits outside while I get everything together. When I open the door to the room that I haven't even spent more than a few hours in, he is leaning across the doorway, one leg propped against the wall behind him.

He is casual, unassuming, and very attractive.

My negative feelings toward the opposite sex take a nosedive when I look at him. I watch him for several long seconds, taking in the shape of his strong jaw and containing the urge to draw my finger along his day old stubble.

"Will you let me take your case for you?" He smiles and holds out a hand. I look down at my case, all that I have.

Denham holds his hands up in mock surrender. "Relax, I'm not going to steal it, just carry it to your room."

Once again, I feel my tension slip away and I hand him my case. He should make me nervous but, strangely enough, he puts me at ease.

The elevator ride seems to take forever as we stand beside one another facing the door, close but not touching. An invisible electricity bouncing back and forth between our bodies. I feel his gaze on me, and when I give in to the craving to turn toward him, he snaps his head back around to look at the elevator doors like a naughty child who has been caught doing something he shouldn't.

The doors slide open, and we step out onto the landing. There's another huge vase of flowers directly in front of me like the ones in the foyer, and a plush cream carpet that looks deep enough to sink your toes in. I look at him in confusion when I see there are only two doors—one to my left and one to my right. Huge, imposing, dark wood doors with gleaming gold handles, but neither has a room number.

"Yours is to the left." He walks ahead, slipping the key card into the door and pushing it open. I walk over the threshold and let out an audible gasp. This isn't a room. It's a beautifully, elaborate suite filled with opulent details and spectacular views out of the floor to ceiling windows, which are more like a glass wall.

Luxury at its finest.

"What's this?" I ask, a tone of astonishment mixed with annoyance in my voice.

"It's your replacement room. It was the only one available, so I didn't think you'd mind."

"But I can't afford this room." Although I could stretch my money toward this kind of grandeur, I don't want to.

"It's a complimentary room, Miss Jamesson. You didn't ask to be upgraded, I upgraded you."

"Yes, but I'm not a charity case, I don't want you to feel sorry for me, and I don't need to upgrade to the penthouse just because someone hit on me."

"I think we had this conversation downstairs, and your mouth is starting to run away with you ... again."

He strides past me, taking my case through another door, and I break into a half run to keep up with him which isn't easy when I'm still buttoned into this damn blazer. I stop just before I slam into his back. When he puts my case down and steps to the side, I'm stunned at what I see.

"Whoa."

The room is exquisite. A king size bed draped in ruby-red silk sheets and sumptuous bedding is the centerpiece of the room—a masterpiece in intricately, hand-carved dark wood. Off to the side is an en suite bathroom with a sunken marble bath.

He turns to face me with a sincere look in his eyes. "Now, I would really like it if you were to stay here, but if you would like to go back to 144, I will understand." I open my mouth to speak, but he hushes me by holding a finger up. "I'm not trying to hit on you, win you over, get in your panties or make you feel inferior in any way. I'm just trying to do something nice for you because, well, because I can." He works the buttons open on the jacket I've been wrapped in but leaves it draped over my shoulders.

"Finished?" I say with a smile.

He grins. "For now."

"Thank you for being kind, not hitting on me, not trying to win me over or ... get in my panties." Even as a joke that was hard for me to say. I breathe and continue, "I would really like to stay in this room, but I cannot afford it, and I feel uncomfortable with your offer."

He shakes his head and rubs at his temples. "Fine, how about we make a deal? You pay the same price for this room as you did for the other. Then I'm not giving it away and you don't feel uncomfortable. What do you say?"

I shake my head at him. He's an insistent man and he makes it very difficult to say no. It's a good job I'm only here for a few days. I smile at him, and now that I can, I hold my hand out to him to shake on it. "Deal."

Our hands lock and electricity travels up my arm, setting the hairs on end. His hand encases mine with confidence and gentleness as his thumb moves slightly to rub the back of mine, sending tingles across my skin. I pull back and rub my hands together nervously, realizing that our handshake lingered just a fraction too long.

"Right, I had better get unpacked. It's been a long day."

"Of course." He reaches into his back pocket and hands me a card. "This is my personal number. If you need anything, just call. The concierge is at your disposal and the facilities are free for you to use whenever you wish."

"That's very kind, thank you, but I'm sure it won't be necessary." I take his card, giving him a smile, and he steps past me to leave.

"Wait." I spin around to catch him. "Your jacket ..." I slip it off my shoulders, handing it to him. "Thank you, you are very chivalrous."

I'm awarded by a flash of those beautiful, straight white teeth and a nod before he turns on his heel. I watch his long fluid strides, and as he moves through the apartment I can't help but let my eyes drift to his ass.

I almost let out an audible groan but stifle it just in time for him to turn and give me a knowing look before he leaves, closing the door behind him. I let out the deep breath I was holding and smile to myself.

For a day that started with so much uncertainty, it hasn't ended so badly.

# Chapter 4

Waking up in a different place for the third time in as many days is unsettling. I haven't ever been truly settled, never staying in the same place for more than a few years at a time and not really having any place that makes me feel like I belong anywhere in particular, but that hasn't stopped me from wishing for it one day. Confusion prickles my senses as I wake enough to recall where I am and when I glance at my watch, I notice it's nearly nine in the morning.

The extravagance of this suite makes for a lighter feeling than the motel I slept at last night though, and I am truly grateful when I set my feet on the carpet and they sink into the plush fibers rather than sticking to threadbare backing. I pull on a bright-white robe, and relish in the soft feel of it, blanketing me in luxurious comfort.

I make my way through to the living area and jump when I hear a knock at my door. I cautiously walk over to peek through the spy hole, and my body relaxes when I see that it's just room service with a breakfast trolley. I stand there for a minute, confused as to why he is there. I didn't order anything.

I open the door just a crack, and I'm greeted by a plump little man with a friendly face. "Mr. King requested breakfast for you, Miss Jamesson, where would you like it?"

*He what?*

It's such a thoughtful thing to do but not for the first time, I question his generosity. I feel uncomfortable for doing so, but experience has told me that you don't get something for nothing and I don't want to owe him. I don't want to owe *anyone.* "Um, I don't really know." My voice is unsure as I pull the door open to allow him in.

"How about I set it on the dining table for you, miss?"

"Okay, that would be fine, thank you."

He nods and wheels the trolley inside with skill, then sets everything down on the table with practiced precision. When he has finished laying the lavish meal out, he turns to me and asks, "Will there be anything else for you, Miss. Jamesson?"

"Goodness, no, this is more than enough, thank you." I shake my head to emphasize that I don't think I could possibly want for anything else.

"Very well. Please call room service if you require anything from the menu." He leaves with a friendly smile and a small nod.

The polished table seats six, but is set for one, and the cutlery is so well buffed you can see your reflection in it. The breakfast is fit for a king—pastries, fresh fruit, coffee, orange juice and a dish that is concealed with a silver cover. I lift it and I'm greeted with a plate of hot pancakes and bacon. Placed next to the feast is a gold embossed menu, listed with everything you could possibly imagine ordering for breakfast.

*How much do they think one person can eat?*

I didn't realize how hungry I was until I started to eat and now I'm not sure I can stop, but after devouring the pancakes and bacon, I grab a *pain au chocolat* and a mug of black coffee, and head for the balcony. I'm pleased when I find a sun lounger to relax on, so I sit and take in the most amazing view over the Strip, watching the rest of the world go by. The view reaches for miles as I watch the people going about their everyday life without a care in the world. Is this really the way it is? Or are they all running or hiding from something? I'm not naive enough to think that life is going to be a bunch of roses, but there must be an end to the constant stream of upheaval I seem to have dealt with all of my life. Surely it has to hit a plateau and run smoothly, even for just a little while?

When I have finished eating, I lie back on the lounger and close my eyes; after consuming all that food I'm feeling tired and sluggish. The Las Vegas sunshine is warm, and the feel of it touching my skin is comforting, but nonetheless my mind races with all the events of the last few days.

The shouting.

The slap.

The feeling of history repeating itself.

Oh god, this is one big clusterfuck.

I need to decide what's going to happen long term. It would be much easier to leave, start afresh somewhere else with a new name and a new identity where no one knows anything about me. But I'm tired of running, I don't want to leave my mom again. I don't want to leave

Lottie again, and I want somewhere to set down roots. I'm twenty-six years old. Time to face it head on and deal with it.

After a scorching hot shower, I'm feeling a little more human. I know where I need to start in order to put my life back together, and I'm not looking forward to it, but it has to be done. Delaying the inevitable won't help.

I slip on a pink matching underwear set—nice underwear is essential in making you feel empowered—followed by a black shift dress that hugs my figure and makes my long legs look even longer. A pair of black wedge heels completes the outfit.

I turn to look in the mirror. I'm not applying any makeup. The deep-purple bruising that has developed on my cheek only serves as a reminder of my past and I need to feel that anger and determination for the phone call I'm about to make.

I delve into my purse and take out my cell. No more missed calls from Aaron. Just a text from Lottie, asking about my plans for today. I'll call her later.

I'm not sure if he'll be awake yet, or even what state he'll be in, but I dial the number and wait. My hands are shaking and the nails on my free hand have left indentations where they are digging into the palm. My heart rate picks up with every ring he doesn't answer and I think it just about beats out of my chest when he eventually picks up.

"Nat?"

"Hello, Aaron." My voice is flat, devoid of feeling, but it doesn't take long for him to pull on my heartstrings and thaw my determination just a little.

"Natalie! Where the hell are you? I've been so worried. Come home. Please, come home."

"Aaron—"

"Nat, I'm sorry, I love you. Please just—"

"Stop, Aaron." I shake my head in frustration. "I'm not coming home. I'm not coming back," I say softly.

"What? What do you mean you're not coming home? We had an argument, all married couples have arguments. We can go to counseling, and I'll get help, whatever you want. We can work it out ..."

Just an argument? Is he crazy?

I pinch the bridge of my nose and screw my eyes tight shut in frustration. He doesn't see it, but then he doesn't know the full story so he wouldn't have known how deeply something like this would have affected me.

"Will you just stop? Please, Aaron ... come back to the real world. We didn't just have an argument. You hit me ..."

"I'm sorry." His voice drops to a whisper. "It'll never happen again. I don't know why ... I ... I've been under a lot of pressure lately, and—"

"You're right, Aaron, it won't happen again because I'm not coming back. I want a divorce."

"You want a divorce?"

"Did you not hear me the first time? I'm not doing this, I'm not living a life going back and forth like this. If it means being on my own, then so be it, but I'm not going to be miserable any longer. Our marriage has been a disaster from the minute we said I do. And you hit me, Aaron. You hit me! You can't come back from something like that. We can't."

The silence stretches out between us as I listen to his soft restricted breaths on the other end of the line.

"I really fucked up. Didn't I, Nat?"

I sit on the edge of the bed and my heart constricts at the defeated tone in his voice. I know I should hate him, but I don't. I certainly don't love him, but I don't hate him either. We shared some good times, and our honeymoon was one of the happiest weeks of my life, but it's all tainted with the twelve weeks that followed.

"Yes, you did." I swallow the lump that is forming in my throat and focus on the purpose of this phone call.

"Can you just come back so we can talk?"

"So you can convince me to give you another chance?"

"No, I just thought I meant more to you than ending everything we have over a phone call."

I sigh. "You did mean more to me than that, but you took away any love I had for you when you lost your temper. There's nothing more to work out. I don't want half of everything you own, and I'm not going to take you to the cleaners. With the gash on my cheek and the ugly bruising I'm looking at right now, if this goes to court it will ruin you."

I picture him on the other end of the phone, raking his hands through his shaggy surf hair as he does when he's agitated.

"I'll have divorce papers sent to you. I won't be asking for anything else from you, just a quick divorce with no publicity and no fuss. I don't want the Porsche. It's in your name anyway, so I'll have it shipped back to you at my earliest convenience." The matter of fact tone in my voice masks the multitude of emotions going through me right now.

"Nat—"

"No, Aaron, this is it, I'm not a contract that you can negotiate terms on. Please don't call me again. I'll find an attorney and they will be in touch." I hear him start to protest, but I cut him short. "Goodbye, Aaron."

I end the call. I have to.

It's the only way to stop this conversation going around and around in circles and risking me changing my mind because I feel sorry for him. I hate to think that my words are the cause of someone's hurt, but if he digs a little deeper, he'll see that it's not my words that have hurt him, it's his actions.

No sooner do I hang up, then it rings again.

Aaron.

I let it connect to voice mail. A second later, the shrill tone starts up once more. It's his last attempt at saving his marriage. If I were actually in love with him, I'd be impressed that he is fighting for me, but I know it's the shame and guilt pushing him to make things right. I dismantle the phone, removing the battery, and throw all the pieces in the bin.

And just like that, it's over.

I don't take any pleasure in ending our relationship, but I have already learned that if you don't get out early on then all you are doing is waiting like a sitting duck, ready to be used and hurt. The conversation could have gone back and forth all day and we still wouldn't have achieved anything. The minute he broke my skin, he hardened my heart. He won't give in and neither will I. No compromises. No alternatives. I'm putting myself first.

Having gotten that phone call out of the way, I decide to spend a few hours shopping. I put some makeup on to try and cover the bruising on my face the best I can, but it's come out fully now and is very noticeable. The clothes I packed are few and there's only so long that I can live out of a suitcase for, I'm going to need more than four outfits just to get me through the next week.

Four hours and countless shopping bags later, I return to the hotel, with a much lighter bank balance but a multitude of outfits from some great stores. I've enjoyed every minute of today's carefree shopping as I took the time to admire window displays and let myself browse as well as buy.

I enter the hotel through a different lobby to the main one. It takes me past some of the facilities I hadn't seen yet. A gym and day spa which I make a mental note to try and book into for a treatment tomorrow. Maybe I could book Lottie in with me and have a real girlie day. I've missed her so very much and the thought of spending some quality time with her makes me smile. Further along the walkway is a casino. I stop to look through the large double doors.

It has the trademark colors with cream walls, gold adornments and crimson carpets. Its tall ceiling makes it look huge and the flashing lights coming from all directions are mesmerizing. I have been to a casino once or twice with Aaron, but I don't really know what I'm doing. It is Aaron who is the pro and I can't even say I learned anything from him. He is a serious player and plays to win, poker mainly, sometimes blackjack, whereas I would do it just for the fun. 'The Promised Land' has been aptly named and makes me chuckle that people are actually led astray by the flashing lights and the guise of riches. There is only one winner in gambling and that's the bank.

"You're allowed in, you know. That is, presuming you are over twenty-one?"

I recognize the deep timbre of his voice and the vibration of his chuckle, and the sound evokes an acceleration in my heartbeat. I turn and face the source, already knowing who I will find. I am awarded with a full megawatt smile, he is clean shaven and smells divine. His crisp white shirt is open at the collar and his gray slacks fit his hips like they were made for him. Thinking about it, they probably are. I can't help the grin that spreads across my face.

"Good afternoon, Mr. King," I say with a genuine smile in my voice.

"Miss. Jamesson." He nods, his smug grin stretches across his cheeks and gives me the 'I know you were checking me out' look. "How are you finding your stay?"

"I'm enjoying it very much, thank you." His eyes haven't left mine and the corners crease making his handsome face softer. "I wanted to say thank you for breakfast this morning. It was very thoughtful of you. Extravagant, but thoughtful."

"Good, I'm glad you enjoyed it. Will you be visiting the casino this evening?" He nods his head toward the casino doors.

"Oh, I don't know. It's not really my thing," I say nervously with a shrug of my shoulders.

He leans ever so slightly toward me and his voice lowers to a soft growl. "And what exactly is your thing, Miss. Jamesson?" My heart rate spikes at the way his eyes burn into me, and my mind races with images of what my 'thing' could be. Every image involves him in one way or another, and I have no idea how he manages to do that to me.

"I ... uh ..." I seem to have lost the ability to form coherent sentences and I feel my face flush a little. He obviously finds my discomfort amusing as he's looking at me with a sexy as hell grin plastered across his beautiful face and an eyebrow quirked as if he's still waiting for my answer.

"I think the spa and salon would be more my *thing*. I'm not really a gambler. Anyway, I really need to be getting back to my suite, these bags are—"

"Please, let me take them for you."

"It's fine, I can manage, really." I start to walk away, needing to get out of this space but not really wanting to. In the few encounters we have had, Denham King sends my mind into a spin, but he also makes me feel alive in my soul, and I'm not sure I've ever really felt that before. The mix of emotions is not productive to finding the solutions to my current problems. I really have to keep a clear head.

"You are a stubborn little lady, do you know that?" he calls out after me.I stop and turn back toward him. He stands casually with his hands tucked into his pockets wearing that smirk.

"And you're very persistent, Mr. King. Do you know that?"

He looks perplexed as he frowns. "Hmm, I guess I am ... so will you? Let me carry your bags?" He jogs the small distance to catch me up and I laugh.

"Will it soothe your ego if I do?"

"Very much so."

"Fine." I shake my head with a small laugh. "You can carry them to the elevator. After that, I've got it covered, okay?"

"You've made my day," he says with a smile.

He takes my bags, sending little jolts of electricity through me when his fingers brush mine. What is it about him that does this to me? I flex my fingers when I'm relieved of the bags and their weight. My arms feel like they've been pulled out of their sockets.

We walk through the foyer and toward the elevator. "So, did you buy half of Vegas?" he says jokingly.

"Let's just say, I decided it was time for a change of image."

"Oh really? Well, your image looks just fine from where I'm standing." He winks and I bump his shoulder with mine.

"Are you always so smooth with the ladies?" I ask, loving the easy banter between us.

"Only the pretty ones with a *million* shopping bags ..."

"I do not have a *million* shopping bags. There may be ten, but not a *million*."

He slows to a stop as we approach the elevator. "So what brings you here to Vegas? Business or pleasure?"

"I ... uh ... I'm just visiting a friend."

Shit, I wasn't prepared for that question. There's something about him that makes me want to tell him the truth, but that's a ridiculous notion. What do I tell him? That I left my husband because he hit me when he found out I didn't want children and that I married under a false name because I was running from my ex-fiancé?

"I see." His eyes skim over the poorly camouflaged bruise on my cheek. "So do you have any plans for the rest of the afternoon, or has all this shopping left you exhausted?"

"No, no plans this afternoon, and shopping *is* tiring I'll have you know."

"You do know that the concierge can get you anything you need?"

"Yes, but I'd feel a little uncomfortable sending the concierge to Victoria's Secret." I start to take the bags off him one by one and he grasps his hands around the handles tightly.

"You mean to tell me there's a bag from Victoria's Secret in this lot?" He looks like the cat that got the cream and holds up the bags to the light one by one to see if he can see through them.

"No ... uh, yes, there is but ... oh, you know what I meant." I swat at his upper arm playfully but the moment my palm touches him I get the urge to keep contact and my fingers involuntarily squeeze to feel his bicep. I force myself to pull my hand away.

"I don't want someone else doing my underwear shopping is all. Give me those!"

He chuckles and hands the remaining bags over to me, then presses the button for the elevator and the doors glide open. I step in and turn to him scowling, but really I'm fighting a grin.

"Would you consider joining me for a drink this evening?" He smiles a lopsided grin and it creases one cheek, flashing a deep dimple.

"I ... um, I already have plans ..."

*Shit*, I hate lying. I really want to have a drink with him, but I can't, I just can't.

Disappointment flashes across his handsome face, but he nods and doesn't press me further. "Well, I hope you enjoy your evening, and if you change your mind ..."

"I know where you are." I press the button for the penthouse, type in the code and the doors start to close. His eyes don't leave mine until the doors close completely and I breathe out audibly.

My stay at The Kingdom is turning out to be an interesting one.

# Chapter 5

After hauling my *million* shopping bags through the suite and into the bedroom, I drop them just inside the doorway. I kick off my shoes and I'm sure I can hear my feet breathe a sigh of relief. No matter how used to wearing heels you are, a five hour successful shopping trip is going to be somewhat uncomfortable.

I sit on the edge of the luxurious king size bed, letting my shoulders drop, then rolling them in circles to try and ease the tension. I feel exhausted, so I let myself flop back, allowing every muscle in my body to relax. It feels like I'm being hugged by the deep, soft bedding and I shut my heavy eyes for just a minute, knowing that if I don't move in the next ten seconds I'll be asleep.

I don't move.

And three hours later I wake up with a jump.

I don't know what's wrong with me. I never fall asleep during the day. Hell, I struggle to sleep at night, but since I've been here, I've spent half my time sleeping. I know it's not the luxury and comfort that does it; I had luxury and comfort at Aaron's house. Maybe it's because I feel safe, like I can breathe and let my guard down. Maybe it's because I'm so close to home.

I stretch out my arms and rub the sleep from my eyes before hopping off the bed and padding to the bathroom to freshen up. I glance in the mirror—I look a mess. Yes, I've been through emotional hell over the last few days and I've just woken from a very deep sleep, but I look terrible. My hair resembles a bird's nest and my dark roots are far too long. My face is still very bruised, and despite the extra sleep I've had there are dark circles under my eyes. There's not much I can do right now about my hair, but I can certainly treat my body to a soak in the stunning bath in my suite. Even if it's a temporary fix, it'll make me feel better.

While the stunning porcelain bath is filling, I pour myself a glass of white wine and empty all of my new belongings on the bed. I survey my collection and smile. My mom always said I was a magpie, attracted to pretty and shiny things. The beginning of my new wardrobe is different to the simple, conservative clothes I've worn for the past year—sexy denim, sultry underwear and bright colored tops. It's about time I started living my life and having some fun.

New me. New start.

When I submerge myself up to my neck in the deep bath, all of my muscles relax and I groan in appreciation. The jasmine scented bubble bath is a perfect mix of fresh and exotic and I close my eyes, letting a feeling of calm wash over me as I listen to the water gently lapping as I move

The blare of the loud phone ringing throughout the suite makes me jump. By the time I've decided to get out of the bath, the ringing stops.

"Oh for goodness' sake," I mutter to myself.

It rings again, making me jump for a second time. I hop out and wrap one of the huge fluffy white towels around me. It's warm from being on the towel rail, just another nice touch that makes this place feel wonderful. I nearly slip over on the highly polished floor trying to run out of the bathroom, and I get to the phone just before it rings off.

"Hello?" I say, a little unsure and out of breath.

"Miss. Jamesson." That baritone voice, smooth like caramel, makes my body shiver even though I'm clearly not cold. "I'm sorry if I interrupted you, you sound ... out of breath." I detect a stiffness in his voice and then I realize what he may be thinking.

"Oh no, I ... I was in the bath and I missed the call the first time, and I wasn't expecting the phone to ring again, and when it did I had to run to catch it in time." *What is it about him that makes me act like a nervous schoolgirl?*

"You mean to tell me, you're standing there dripping soapy bath water all over my carpet ..."

"I'm not dripping water ... oh, maybe I am, I'm sorry. I'll have it—"

His laugh cuts me off.

"What's so funny?"

"I'm joking, but the thought of you standing there wet and covered in bubbles is no laughing matter." He sounds less humorous and I feel an edge that causes my skin to tingle.

"How did you know I had bubbles?"

"I didn't, it was a guess. A good guess though, and an even better mental picture."

I feel my cheeks flush. Coming from anyone else that would sound lame, but from him it sounds incredibly sexy. "Mr. King, were you calling for a reason?" I change the subject and tap my foot at him, even though he can't see it.

"Yes ... I wanted to offer you full use of the spa and salon tomorrow. You know, since it's more your *thing*."

"Why would you want to do that for me?" My tone is stiffer than I meant it to be, but I can't stop my instinct to be suspicious.

He sighs deeply. "Haven't we had this conversation already? Can't a man do something nice for a beautiful woman?"

His playful tone and the smile I detect in his voice softens me, and I actually believe that he wants to do something nice for me. That's the thing that scares me the most; they all start out like that, but then it ends badly.

"Not without expecting something else in return in my experience," I say dejectedly.

"Well, I don't want anything in return."

"Nothing?" I question.

"Nothing," he says with absolute certainty.

"I ... I don't know what to say."

"Say yes to the spa and say you'll have a drink with me this evening?"

I can picture the sexy smile he has on his face and after he's gone to so much trouble to accommodate me, I find it hard to say no. But he has just proved me correct—men can't do something nice without wanting something in return.

"No."

"No?"

"Yes, no ..." I'm not sure if he can detect my smirk in my voice, but I hold my ground.

"Why?"

"Because you said you didn't want anything in return, but then you asked me to go for a drink with you. You thought you could win me over by offering me a day in the spa and I would give in. Well, no."

"I didn't ... I ... It wasn't premeditated, I just—"

The way he stumbles over his words is cute. "Mr. King?"

"Yes."

"You're waffling ..."

I hear him laugh gently on the other end of the line, and it empowers me to know that I obviously affect him too. "Touche, Miss. Jamesson," he concedes.

"Thank you for your kind offer of the use of your spa, Mr. King."

"Well, , I sincerely hope you make use of it, and if you need anything at all—"

"I know where you are ..."

"Have a good evening, Miss. Jamesson."

"Thank you, Mr. King. You too."

I hang up the phone with a big grin on my face. Despite his proving me right with his inability to resist offering me a drink, there's something genuine about him and when he says he doesn't want anything in return, I believe him. You would think that my past experiences with the opposite sex would put me off for life, and I would have laughed in your face if you had told me one week ago that any man could make me laugh, put me at ease and accelerate my pulse like Denham King seems to do. I've never known anything like it, but it's fun, and exciting. A perfect distraction and the kind of light-hearted entertainment I need.

As I sit on the indescribably comfortable chaise lounge in my suite, I decide that I'm supposed to be starting over, wiping out the past and embracing the thought of the future, so that means facing things head on 'if' they happen. I'm in control of my own destiny and tonight is going to be just the beginning. I'm going to visit the casino, spend some money and maybe even win a little, and have a damn good time.

What do you even wear to a casino in Las Vegas? I finally settle on a black pants suit with flared legs and a black halter top. I'm lucky to be gifted with long legs, but this suit makes them look even longer, especially when I fasten a wide gold belt around my waist.

I sit for long minutes looking in the mirror, trying to decide how to wear my hair. I'm not happy with wearing it down since the ends look tatty, so I pin it up in a simple twist and pull down just a few tendrils around my face to soften the look. My eyes are smoky, my lips a deep red and I hope that the new foundation I bought conceals the bruising on my cheek. A gold watch and my favorite diamond bracelet that belonged to my grandmother complete the look. I feel confident. I know I look good and I feel like I'm smiling from the inside.

I pour a generous shot of Vodka from the mini bar and go to stand out on the balcony. The night air is warm and the daylight is starting to fade, I have a good feeling about things, about my future. Tonight is going to be fun.

I walk through the lobby, my heels clicking on the marble flooring and echoing around the high ceiling. As I approach the large doors to the casino, I'm greeted by two large doormen in sharp black suits who push the doors back for me and gesture for me to enter. They look smart, friendly and professional, but you wouldn't want to mess with them. They give off a feeling of authority and power and I'm sure they don't mess about when it comes to the crunch.

I scan the room and my eyes linger on the roulette table where a young woman is jumping up and down with excitement. She's obviously had a lucky bet and I smile to see her elation.

I head for the bar, not really knowing where to get started or even if I'm going to try my hand at lady luck, but observing the buzzing room from the bar with a delicious cocktail sounds like a great starting point.

The bar is relatively quiet and I find an empty stool immediately. The bartender makes his way over and welcomes me with a smile. Everything about his demeanor is friendly and he's cute but I'm guessing he's quite young—twenty-three, maybe twenty-four. He looks familiar, but I don't know anyone here.

"Good evening, beautiful. What can I get you?" The bartender asks.

"I'll have a dirty martini, please."

He looks at me with slightly narrowed eyes for a second and I frown in return. That was weird. "Sure thing, coming up."

He doesn't move very far to gather the ingredients that are needed and mixes the cocktail in front of me. "So what's a beautiful lady like you doing all alone in a place like this?" he says with a lopsided smirk and a twinkle in his eye. I roll my eyes at the cheesy line, although I'm sure it works on some of the women. I'll bet he gets his share just by flashing them his charming smile. "I'm just staying for a few days, visiting relatives."

"No husband?" he says surprisingly, glancing at my left hand.

"Nope, no husband."

His smile seems to grow wider and I really hope he's not going to chat me up. Yes, he's cute, but so are puppies and kittens. That doesn't mean I want one.

"You don't look like a gambler. You going to try your hand at poker?"

"I don't look like a gambler?" I say with a little laugh. "And what would a gambler look like?"

"There's something about you that tells me you're too savvy to gamble your money away."

"Is that a line you use on all your lady customers?" I quirk an eyebrow at him.

"Ha, not all of them. Only the very attractive ones," he says with a wink and I roll my eyes. "Voila, your dirty martini, Madame."

"Why, thank you, sir. It looks ..." I take a sip of the clear cocktail "...and tastes delicious."

"You're welcome." He leans his elbow on the bar top and rests his chin on his hand. "So what are you going to try your hand at?"

"She's busy. Get back to work, Spike."

I know who it is before I turn around, his commanding voice is unmistakable, but I turn anyway and find myself drinking in the sight of Denham King. His stance is protective as he glowers at the poor bartender. I follow his pointed stare behind the bar. Spike doesn't argue but flashes Denham a sharp look before walking away, shaking his head.

When Denham is satisfied that his unspoken message has been heard loud and clear, he turns to me with a grin and shows his dimple that is so cute I'm sure he only saves it for special occasions. He rests one hand on the bar top and one on the back of my bar stool so I'm effectively caged.

"Miss. Jamesson, what a pleasure to find you here."

"You scared the poor bartender off before I had the chance to pay for my drink."

"It's on the house." He chuckles. "Well, it's on Spike actually but he doesn't know it yet."

"He was just being friendly."

"Well, he can just be friendly to someone else then, can't he?"

"And what if I wanted to talk to him?" I raise an eyebrow.

"Do you want to?"

"No, but—"

"Well, that's settled then, isn't it?" He lowers himself onto the vacant stool next to me, tipping his chin and signaling to Spike to bring him a drink. He's arrogant, self-assured and I'm sure he's a man that always gets what he wants. But despite these things there's an attractiveness about him I can't explain. He's sexy, very sexy, and the way he angles his strong, toned body toward me makes me feel like I'm the only person in this room.

Looking contemplative, he traces my wrist with his index finger, running it along my diamond bracelet. The contact is unexpected and I try to hide my sharp intake of breath.

"Hmmmm ... diamonds," he muses. His eyes sweep across my décolleté, along my neck and up to my ears. "You should wear more diamonds. Their beauty and sparkle match yours."

I nervously moisten my now dry lips with my tongue. I'm uncertain how to react to compliments. In the past, they've been thrown around so loosely without any genuine feeling behind them, so it still feels alien to me.

"You're not used to such compliments?" His voice is low, almost a growl. "Then we will have to rectify that." He pauses, and I'm grateful when he changes the subject. "Are you here to play?"

I watch his lips move around the word play—soft, full and the most erotic thing I've ever seen. I blink twice and straighten my back.

*I really need to get a grip.*

"Roulette, yes." I say, skirting around the question as I'm not entirely sure of the direction it was meant. If I were just passing through Las Vegas, I would throw caution to the wind and give in to my feelings of lust, something I've not experienced before. But I'm planning on staying here and I do not intend on getting myself into any situations that could turn complicated.

I have only been with two men in my life, and both of them falsely took my trust before I ventured into anything physical. Denham King is different. He isn't hiding behind niceties or false promises of friendship. He is what he is, and I'm not entirely sure what to do with it.

"Just roulette? Have you ever played poker?"

"No poker. I like the simplicity of the little wheel. Just red or black, odd or even."

He nods, seemingly happy with my answer. Something tells me he's not a poker player either. He gives too much away in his eyes.

Spike brings Denham a drink. He's a scotch man, on the rocks, and he swirls the glass before lifting it to his lips. I watch as he takes a sip of the smooth amber liquid, his lips coated in a sweet, shiny glaze and his

Adam's apple dipping as he swallows. He's watching me watching him, and the corners of his lips curl just enough to make me realize this.

"Come."

He stands swiftly and clasps his tumbler in one hand, holding out his spare hand to help me down from the tall bar stool. I obey his gentle command without hesitation and place my small hand in his large, rough palm. He doesn't let go when I'm standing; instead, he pulls me tightly by his side and strides forward.

We weave through the small groups of people, and I can feel my heartbeat pick up as the anxiety kicks in. I still don't really know him, and I don't know where he's leading me. I try to wriggle my hand from his grip and slow my legs down, but he squeezes ever so gently and it reassures me enough to just go with it. I breathe a small sigh of relief when he stops at the roulette table. My crazy mind needs to be reeled in and stop thinking the worst at every turn. But old habits die hard.

Denham greets the croupier and guides me gently with a hand on my waist to one of the available seats. He stands behind me and leans down to speak softly. "You've played before?"

His breath tickles my ear and I swallow noisily. "Yes."

He nods to the croupier who is waiting attentively. Denham holds up one finger and a small stack of red chips is pushed across the smooth green felt toward me.

"Red or black?"

I spin my head around to him. "You want me to choose?"

"Yes."

"I don't want to lose your money."

"You won't. I feel lucky." He shrugs.

"Okay, I call red. No wait, black. Put one on black," I say, getting more excited by the second but also nervous with the pressure of gambling with someone else's money.

He steps forward and slides the entire stack onto the large square marked BLACK. I pull at his free arm in a panic, but I can't deny that this is exciting. "No! I said *one. Put one* on black."

He leans in so he's just millimeters from my ear and whispers, "I'm all or nothing, sweetheart. When I do something, I do it with everything I've got."

"No more bets," the croupier calls and the moment is broken.

We both look to the wheel as it is spun until the colors and numbers blur. The ball is tossed in the opposite direction to the spinning wheel and I watch for what seems like an eternity before it starts to slow. It rolls and bounces and I can hardly bear to watch. I don't know how much money is riding on this game of chance, but if will alone can make it land in a black slot we'll be hitting a home run. The crowd hushes and the last couple of bounces seem like they play out in slow motion; my heartbeat whooshes through my ears and the sound of the ball echoes around the table. It lands in a red slot, then jumps out at the very last minute, the 'Oh's and Ah's' sounding around the table adds to the tension as the little white ball finally settles in a pocket ...

Black!

"Yes!" I yell, jumping out of my seat and nearly knocking over our drinks in the process. Most of the other guests around the table are smiling and calling 'Yes!' and a few of them are looking downright relieved. I fling my arms around Denham's neck, it's an innocent gesture, one of elation and relief that I haven't lost all his money. I kiss his smooth cheek, noticing he's shaved and fighting the urge to nuzzle into him.

I don't know why I just did that. It just ... happened.

I go to pull back, but he wraps his arms around my waist and holds me even closer, just for a second, then turns his head so my lips just touch the corner of his. The innocence is sucked out of our moment and replaced by another exchange of smoldering looks. I pull back and he reluctantly releases me.

"I think I might keep you."

"What?" I snap my head up in his direction with a confused look on my face

"I think I might keep you. You're lucky. "

If only he knew. The bottom drops out of the happiness I was just feeling and I lower my gaze. "I'm not lucky. I'm trouble," I whisper.

He gently grips my chin between his thumb and forefinger and tilts my head so I'm looking up at him. "Well, in that case, I like your kind of trouble." His voice is lower so only I can hear. "I'll take my chances. I think the odds are pretty good."

My heart rate accelerates as he moves toward me and presses his lips to my cheek. I close my eyes and softly lean into him, and he lingers for a moment before pulling away, leaving my skin searing and my heart racing.

"You're all the luck I need. That's two thousand dollars you just won me."

My eyes widen and Denham chuckles. "Two thousand dollars? But ... you let me take a chance with a thousand dollars of your money?"

He nods and his smile widens. "Wait, you're kidding aren't you? You own the place it doesn't count, right?"

This just makes him laugh out loud. "It counts. Come on, Trouble. Let's play blackjack."

I shake my head gently, laughing at the craziness of Las Vegas, then I down what's left of my martini. "I think I need another drink," I mutter, and we detour to the bar.

After one more martini and several unsuccessful attempts to teach me how to play blackjack (mainly down to Denham making me laugh and distracting me with his handsomeness), I'm once again battling with the angel and devil who sit on my shoulders. I would like nothing more than to stay here for the rest of the evening and find out more about the man who is Denham King, but something is telling me that if I don't walk away now, this may venture somewhere that will be very hard to come back from.

"Would you like another drink?" he asks.

"No, I really should be going." I hop off the stool and straighten myself out. It takes all of my willpower to be determined enough to call it a night, especially because we are having so much fun.

Denham touches the tips of his fingers to my wrist and holds me in place. "Will you turn into a pumpkin?"

"Ha-ha. No, at least, I don't think so," I say, feeling a little sad that this evening has to come to an end.

"Then stay ..."

I look at his handsome face, his chiseled jaw, his soft inviting lips and his eyes, his deep rich brown eyes that I could lose myself in, his easy demeanor, his subtle protectiveness ...

"No, really, I have to go. Thank you for this evening. It's been fun and I'm glad I didn't lose you all your money." I stand to leave.

"I told you, you're lucky." I smile and shake my head gently. "Can I call you?" he asks with an air of confidence.

"You have my room number."

"No, I mean a cell. Your personal number."

"I, I don't have a cell." I frown when I realize how stupid that sounds. Everyone has a cell these days, and now he probably thinks I'm giving him the brush off. "I'm not lying, I mean, I'm not trying to just put you off so you don't call. You know I would like you to call, but I really actually don't have a cell. I broke it and ... well, I just haven't had a chance to get a new one yet."

"You're good at that," Denham says with a raised eyebrow and a cheeky grin.

"Good at what?"

"Waffling." He stands, offering me his hand and I take it without hesitation. "Come on, Trouble. I'll walk you to your room."

The swarm of butterflies in my stomach start when we're in the elevator. From the ground floor to the penthouse, we're alone and the air is crackling with sexual tension. By the time we reach my room, the butterflies are flying around so fast I feel like my legs are going to give out.

*He's just a man, just a man ...* I repeat over and over in my head. I have no idea why he makes me feel like this. It's an excited nervousness but unsettling all the same. Denham stands behind me patiently and I'm sure I look like a crazy woman as I mumble to myself under my breath while trying to find the key card in my tiny little clutch that isn't actually small enough for anything to get lost in.

"Got it!"

I exhale and turn to meet an expression that isn't instantly readable. When Denham steps forward, I take two steps back, bumping into the door and giving myself no way out.

"I had a great evening, thank you," I say nervously.

"Me too." His eyes never leave mine as he moves forward a half step more so our chests touch and rests his hand on the door frame above my head. I feel the wisps of his breath on my lips as he tilts his head toward mine and my senses go into overdrive. I can almost taste him. He lightly brushes his lips across mine, soft, inviting ... then his phone rings. We both jump at the intrusion, and I don't know if I feel disappointed or relieved.

Denham pinches the bridge of his nose and closes his eyes. "Damn ..."

"It might be important. You should really see who it is. Anyway, I should go." I turn and slip my card in the reader. The moment has gone, common sense has prevailed, and I really need to put a heavy, hardwood door between us for fear of what I might do if I stay where I am.

I step into my suite and leave Denham leaning against the door frame. "Goodnight, Mr. King."

I hear him murmur, "Goodnight, Trouble," before I softly close the door.

# Chapter 6

I wake to the sound of knocking. I have no idea of the time, but judging by the morning light it's still early. I groan as I hear knocking again and I jump out of bed, throwing on a robe. I open the door and see the plump little man with the friendly face again.

"Breakfast, ma'am."

I open the door wider, allowing him entrance and rubbing my hands across my face to wake me up. He wheels the trolley in, laying the table as he did yesterday and placing my breakfast down. There isn't as much food as yesterday—pancakes and bacon, a pastry and a delicious pot of steaming hot fresh coffee. The smells invade my senses and my stomach rumbles, reminding me I haven't eaten since breakfast yesterday.

"Thank you..." I take a look at his name badge, "...Anthony. That's very kind."

"Will there be anything else, miss?"

"No, no. This is more than enough."

"Very well." He nods and leaves with a smile.

I pour myself a coffee and realize that he left a package on the table along with breakfast. It is wrapped in crisp, white tissue paper with gold embossed edging and a little card tucked in the ribbon. I pull out the card and open it.

*Trouble, A beautiful woman traveling alone should not be without a cell.*

*Denham x*

Oh no. He did not just do that. I rip the paper off the box to find that yes, he did. He has bought me a cell phone. I turn the phone on and a message instantly pops up.

*Denham: Now I have your number and you have mine ...*

I giggle out loud and shake my head at his persistence. He's forward, I'll give him that, but he does it in such a way that isn't overbearing. His light-hearted banter has been just what I need these last couple of days, he hasn't pushed or pried and for that I'm grateful.

*Me: Do you always think of everything?*

It takes me the length of time to pour my coffee before a reply comes back.

*Denham: Yes*

*Me: Thank you, it's a thoughtful gesture, but I can't possibly accept it.*

As much as I know he'll be disappointed, I can't accept this gift. He has been far too generous already.

Although I feel like I know him, which in itself is unfathomable, he really is a stranger.

*Denham: You are an infuriating woman. Will you please just accept it as a gift? It would make me happy.*

I think about my reply before I send it. There is something about him that wants me to say yes because it will make him happy and that makes me smile. And part of me wants to run miles away from the complications that are sure to come from accepting gifts from strange men, but he doesn't feel strange to me. He feels calming, familiar, and most of all he makes me feel safe which scares the hell out of me.

I start to type a reply but can't figure out what I want to say, so I put the cell down on the table and sit to eat the delicious breakfast in front of me. I manage two mouthfuls before it dings again.

*Denham: You know it's impolite to return gifts?*
*Denham: Just call it your cut of the winnings from last night.*
*Denham: Pleeeeeease ... I'm making puppy dog eyes over here.*

How can I refuse?

*Me: Fine, but please, no more!*

*Denham: No more? As I told you about the spa yesterday it doesn't count, right? You have a massage booked at 10 xx*

*Me: Argh! Now you're infuriating!*

He is infuriating, but also thoughtful and very sweet, so I decide to go with it.

*Denham: I know ;) Enjoy your day xx*

*Me: Thank you for your generous gifts, Mr. King. And for breakfast x*

My finger hovers over the send button as I deliberate adding the 'X' at the end. It feels so intimate, but I also know that it put a smile on my face when I saw that he had added two. For goodness' sake, it's just an X. Now I'm just overthinking everything.

I hit send.

He makes me feel like a schoolgirl with a crush; the thought of him sends the butterflies in my stomach into overdrive and I'm not entirely sure why. I've never had feelings like this before. Maybe it's a crush. I've never had a crush before, I worked hard at school, not really taking any notice of boys, so my first real boyfriend wasn't until I was twenty-one and met Jonny. I was unsure of the direction my life was going in, and he won me over with lies and false promises, but I don't ever remember him making me feel like this.

I take my breakfast out onto the balcony and admire the view as I start to think about all the arrangements I need to make. I need somewhere to live, a job and I also need to have the car taken back to Aaron because there's no way I want to face him again. That chapter of my life is gone, over and done with.

Technically the marriage isn't valid, but I don't want to have to explain all of that to him, so it will be much easier to get a divorce and be done with it. That way he'll be blissfully unaware and can hopefully move on and have the family he's always wanted.

I don't know how many hours I've been here. I have no concept of the time of day as it has all gone by in an essential oil scented blur. I know it must be around late afternoon as I was brought a delicious lunch by the side of the pool and that was hours ago ... I think.

I had spa days with the wives in LA, but they never felt like this. Mainly because they were accompanied by a day of gossiping, back-stabbing and bitchiness which I always hated. I'm sure I'm the hot topic of their recent lunch dates. But all of that is behind me, and today has been relaxing and indulgent as I've been buffed, massaged and moisturized to within an inch of my life. My skin now glows and my muscles feel wonderfully relaxed.

My hair has also been cut, colored and styled. A good six inches off the length and taken back to my natural warm brown with just a few subtle highlights to enhance the layers. The makeup girls have done wonders with the bruising on my cheek, changing it from a nasty bluish-black to barely visible, and they have made my eyes look bigger and bluer. I can hardly believe the transformation.

I thank all the girls that have worked their magic on me and make my way back to my room. When I pass the main desk, I look for Denham but he is nowhere to be seen. I haven't heard from him all day and if I'm honest, I'm a little disappointed. When I get into the elevator, I type out a quick text.

*Me: Your spa is wonderful, I have had the most amazing day, Thank you xx*

I don't even hesitate with the kisses, I mean them.

When the elevator stops at the penthouse, I exit and turn to my door. I immediately turn back and look at the door opposite. I haven't seen anyone coming or going from that room, but the door has been left slightly ajar and I hear a soft sound that has me holding my breath and creeping closer. Someone is playing an acoustic guitar, soulful, enchanting laments, their fingers picking at the individual strings with meaning and skill. The playing suddenly stops mid-song and forces a sharp intake of breath from me. I rush across the landing to my door as quietly as I can manage, and fumble in my purse for my key card. I hear a woman yelling, a loud bang and the groan of guitar strings as it hits something. The sound makes me wince.

*Oh crap, it's a couple fighting.*

Conflict of any kind makes me feel uncomfortable. I rush through my door and close it quietly so no one knows I've been there.

Regardless of the occurrence across the hall, I've spent a couple of hours resting and feel so amazing after my spa treatments that I've decided to change and go out to eat.

I choose a little Mediterranean restaurant with a view over the spectacular fountains. A waiter seats me at a table in the corner of one of the sweeping balconies and I order a drink before taking in the surroundings. Wouldn't it be amazing to do this every night? To have this view and be surrounded by people who are visibly happy and enjoying their time in Vegas?

Before my food arrives, a large, bald man in a suit appears at my table. I recognize him as one of the doormen who were at the casino last night. He has a neutral expression on his face but is still intimidating. He leans down to my table slightly before saying quietly, "Mr. King would like to see you, Miss. Jamesson. If you would follow me, please."

I'm a little taken aback, but not surprised that he knows where to find me. Denham King is very persistent, but since I haven't heard from or seen him all day, I would really like to say thank you for my wonderful spa day. *Who am I kidding?* I'm excited at the thought of seeing him.

I stand and follow the gorilla out of the restaurant. He leads me down a corridor, and my heels sink into the plush burgundy carpet as we walk past closed wooden doors of dark wood with gold surrounds. Stopping at the third door, the imposing doorman knocks and enters.

"Miss. Jamesson to see you, sir ..."

"Thank you, Jack. Please show her in," Denham's deep voice beckons as the imposing doorman holds the door open for me to enter.

I am met with a modest office, not what I'd expect the owner of such an opulent establishment to have. His desk is set facing of the door with a few filing cabinets lining the walls. I can only see two chairs. One which I presume is his—a high-backed, black leather chair positioned behind the heavy set desk. The other is placed in the corner of the room for guests, I imagine. The lighting is dim, giving the room a cozy feel, almost intimate.

I step over the threshold and stop just inside the doorway. I'm frozen when I see him sitting at his desk, resting both his forearms in front of him, his hands clasped and putting an expensive pair of platinum and diamond cufflinks on display. His shirt is unbuttoned slightly, giving me a glimpse of a hard, sculpted chest. Rough and rugged, but handsome and sexy as hell.

"Come in and close the door, Miss. Jamesson." He smiles at me as he speaks, but it's not the warm, inviting smile I'm used to.

I close the door carefully and stand right where I am. I'm no longer excited to see him; he has put me on edge and the look he is giving me is unreadable.

"Good evening," I say, smiling sweetly. I refuse to show him that I'm nervous.

"Good evening, Nat-a-lie." He says my name long and slow as drawing the letters out, testing how they sound. His head is tilted slightly to the side, his eyes are narrowed, and his stare is intense.

My throat feels a little tight and I try to swallow the big lump that is forming. My stomach is clenching at the way he's studying my reaction to him, so I raise my chin a little and draw back my shoulders, trying to hide the nervousness that he's making me feel.

He swirls the last of his drink around his glass. The ice cubes clink, accentuating the silence in the room as he makes me wait for an answer. He drains the last of his drink and places his tumbler carefully on his desk then stands, pushing his chair back with his legs. He walks toward me, his gaze fixed and his movements slow and deliberate. He has an inquisitive look and it's making me feel like I need to be ready to bolt. He stops just inches in front of me and I instinctively back into the hardwood door. I place a palm flat on the door behind me, sliding it back and forth to try and find the handle.

"Hmm ..." he groans, musing his next words.

He's not touching me, but we're close enough that I can smell his intoxicating aftershave and the scotch on his breath. He raises his hand and strokes my cheek bone with the back of his fingers, inspecting the break in my skin. "Miss. Jamesson ..." He pauses and tilts his head the other way, focusing my attention on his rich-hazel eyes, the dim light making them look dark and mysterious.

"You're a very intriguing lady, do you know that?" He lets the question linger for a second before continuing "Tell me, who are you this evening, Natalie?" He lets out a small laugh and places his hands on the door, either side of my shoulders, and lowers his head to whisper in my ear. "Are you trying to con me? Is that what this is?" he questions. "I know about you ... Arianna."

His close proximity causes my body to react, but his words cause me to stiffen. I feel the strength of his voice on his breath as it travels along my skin, leaving goosebumps in its wake.

*Shit, he knows. How does he know? How much does he know? Lottie wouldn't have... If he knows, who else does?*

"Are you playing me?" he asks.

"No!" I shake my head vigorously, trying to convince him. I put my hands up to his solid chest to push him away, but he's too fast for me. He grabs my wrists, pinning them above my head and holding me against the door with his body. My breaths are hard and fast as I struggle against his grasp. His lips are just millimeters from mine, and all my instincts are telling me to run, but my body wants more. I twist my arms to test his grip. He's stronger, and his fingers tighten around my wrists.

"Don't try to run from me, Ari." It's a warning and the husky tone of his voice sends a shiver down through my body and settles between my legs, resulting in an ache there I've never experienced before. My lips part to let the heavy breaths escape and I can feel my heart beating out of my chest.

"Let me out," I demand through gritted teeth. I'm torn by the conflicting feelings that are being propelled through my body at lightning speed.

Fear.

Desire.

The feeling of a double edged sword.

"No," he replies sharply. I look at him in surprise, then his voice softens and he returns to the man I've become familiar with. "If I thought for one minute that you actually wanted to leave, I'd let you go."

He releases a low groan before he kisses me hard and fast. It is unexpected and his kiss is unforgiving as he explores every part of my mouth with his tongue which is still cold from the ice in his drink. He steals the air from my body, but somehow gives me so much more than he takes. I feel something shift. Something gives way.

My resolve? Maybe. My sanity? Quite possibly.

But there's a chance that it could be something deeper and far more superior to that. I'm intoxicated with his presence and his persisting lust.

He loosens his grip on my wrists slightly, I presume to test if I'm going to run, but I don't, I can't. The thought that he knows who I am terrifies me, but my body is on fire and I want him more than I've ever wanted anyone or anything.

He clamps both of my wrists in one of his big strong hands, running his other hand down the side of my face. His eyes don't leave mine as he drags his rough thumb over my bottom lip, and my body reacts involuntarily. I nip the pad of his thumb and he hisses in a breath through his teeth.

He leans into my neck. "Why are you hiding, Arianna?" he whispers before tugging on my earlobe with his teeth.

He takes his hand from my cheek, dragging his fingers along my jaw and down my neck leaving a trail of heat on my skin. He grabs my breast roughly and I gasp with the forceful contact. My nipples are pronounced through the thin fabric of my blouse and he pinches one, hard.

I cry out, arching my back toward him.

"You're avoiding my question." His hand doesn't stop kneading and pinching, his breath on my ear causing all the hairs on my neck to stand on end as he grinds his pelvis into me. Fuck, I'm not the only one affected here.

"I ... I'm not hiding ..." My words come out with ragged breaths.

"Don't run," he says before releasing my hands slowly, and I instinctively move to tangle my fingers in his thick dark hair. Both his hands move to my ass, squeezing and pulling me closer as he kisses me with a fierce tenderness I can't explain. I vaguely register him flicking the lock on the door as he walks us backwards, never breaking contact. He turns me as we reach his desk, and I hear paperwork flutter to the floor and glass smash as he sends everything flying before lying me down on the cold, hard surface, his body pressed tightly against mine. I have a desperate need to touch him, to taste him, to feel every inch of this man. I slide my hands in the waistband of his trousers and pull out his shirt. I let my hands roam freely over his torso, realizing I've wanted to do this since the very first time I saw him at the elevator.

He runs his hands down the length of my body and pushes them back up again, skimming my thighs and taking my skirt with them, exposing my lace underwear. "Stunning," he says before bringing his mouth to mine.

Tasting ...

Feeling ...

Testing ...

Our teeth crash together as the desire grows, and we both know it's impossible to stop this now. "Arianna," he says breathlessly. His chest is heaving and there are little beads of sweat gathering on his brow.

"Yes ..." I can barely form the word. I haven't answered to my real name for a very long time, but it feels natural coming from him.

"Tell me you want this ..."

It's a command, but I don't feel threatened. I want this as much as he does. I nod my answer.

"Tell me, Ari. I won't touch you until you tell me."

"Yes, yes I want you ..."

I hear a rumble in his chest before he slides his fingers into the corners of my panties and rips them off in one swift move. I gasp at the feeling of being exposed so suddenly, but I don't think I've ever been so turned on. I don't usually like the feeling of losing control, but within the last five minutes Denham King has almost stripped me bare, more than just physically.

He leans over and kisses me hard, making his way down my body with his hand and slipping his finger between my legs. Finding just the right spot, he works in circles, a relentless rhythm that brings me to the edge of release, then lets me back down again.

My head spins and I want more of him, I *need* more of him. I make quick work of his belt and slide my hand into his trousers. There are no boxers or briefs in my way and my hand makes contact with him instantly. He pushes into my hand as I free him and he groans as I slide up and down his thick length.

"Arianna, that feels ama—"

He is cut off mid-sentence by a rapid knock on the door and I push myself up onto my elbows. I know it's locked, but it's broken the spell that I was under and reality is screaming toward me at a hundred miles an hour.

Denham jumps up. “NOT NOW!”

“Sir, you might want to come out here for a minute.” It’s the doorman, and he sounds nervous.

“Just fucking deal with it, Jack.”

“Sir, I would but—”

“Shit, fuck!” Denham snaps. “This had better be fucking good, Jack.” He straightens and buttons up his trousers. His hair has that ‘just screwed’ look and his face is flushed. He holds my jaw firmly with his big hand and makes me meet his stare.

“Don’t. Go. Anywhere.”

I nod and he kisses me softly before striding to the door and turning to look at me. “I mean it, Arianna. Don’t move. I’ll be back in just a minute. Just let me sort this shit out.”

He runs a hand through his disheveled hair and swings open the door with the menacing stance of an angry bear. He is certainly not a man to be messed with. I hear yelling from down the hall before the door is slammed closed again.

I look around at the papers, shattered glass and my ripped lace panties discarded on the floor. I don’t know what just happened here, but I do know that I have to get out of here.

Does he seriously think I’m going to stay here like some whore waiting for him to come back and fuck me?

This is too much.

He is too much.

So I do what I do best. I run.

# CHAPTER 7

The elevator doesn't move fast enough.

When I reach my floor, I push through the gap before the doors are even fully open and run to my door, but my hand hesitates to open it. My heart skips and I briefly question my haste. I don't want to leave. I don't want to push him away. There's a full-out battle happening between my heart and my head.

How can I let him in? It's too soon after everything that has happened. I know I'm in a vulnerable position and he could win me over so easily. But where would that leave me in a few months or even a year? Would I be left broken and betrayed like my life pattern indicates so far?

I push forward and enter my suite. The air feels thicker in here now, no longer light and freeing, but dark and heavy with a feeling of foreboding. I need air. I need space to figure things out and The Kingdom is obviously not the place.

It's amazing how quickly things change. I hate running, I'm tired of it, but I don't see another way. I won't leave and not explain myself but right now I need to be far away from Denham King and his charms. I'll stay in another hotel and come back tomorrow to collect my belongings and explain everything over coffee, in a public place, with a table between us.

I collect a few clothes, some cash from the safe and replace my underwear that is still lying on the floor of Denham's office.

Once again, the elevator ride downstairs seems to take longer than I remember it doing before. My nerves jangle at the thought of running into Denham on my way out, so I exit the elevator and almost jog to the front desk to pick up the keys to my car. I don't want to wait for the valet, I just want to get going. After much discussion with the concierge at the desk about how it really is no trouble for the valet to bring my car to me, I insist that I'm more than capable of finding it myself and follow the concierge's directions to the underground car park.

The lot is cold and deserted, and all I can hear is the sound of my own footsteps echoing around the concrete walls. It's well lit, but still feels eerie. Shadows bounce off every corner and I find myself nervously scanning to find my car. When I spot it across the other side of the lot, I quicken my pace.

I get halfway across the open space before I'm halted by loud, fast, footsteps and yelling. I rush forward to one of the concrete pillars and hide behind it. My nerves are shot to bits and I just want to get out of here.

I poke my head around the pillar and see a man come flying around the corner. He's running as fast as he can, his head flicking from side to side as he scans the parking lot. I watch as he frantically presses a key fob, waiting for the car to blip and alert him of its location. It takes a few of seconds to process that I know this man. I don't recognize the panic on his face, but it's definitely him.

Aaron.

I rush forward when I see him stop at my car. "Aaron" I yell. He stops dead and snaps his head up. "What the hell are you doing here?"

"Nat." His eyes soften, then he pushes a hand across his face, trying to compose himself. "Nat, fuck ... I'm sorry. I just had to ... the car has a tracker, and I wanted to see you, and ..." He's out of breath and his eyes are still darting around the parking lot.

I hear more footsteps approaching and look around to find Denham, Spike the barman, and two huge doormen headed our way.

"Shit! Nat, I'm sorry. I need the car ... I'm sorry," Aaron blurts before flinging open the door to the Porsche, but I push my arm in the doorway to prevent him from closing the door. I want answers.

"What are you even doing here?"

"Arianna!" Denham yells as he approaches at great speed.

Aaron pauses and appears confused as he looks to both of us, then pushes his keys in the ignition. "I'll explain, Nat. Call me, please, and I'll explain."

"Aaron just—"

"I can't, I'm sorry."

His eyes plead with me for understanding before he starts the car with a roar and drives away at speed. The force of the car pulling away causes me to lose my balance and I stumble backwards clutching at the air and trying to find my footing. I'm caught by big strong arms as Denham pulls me to him and holds me tight to his chest.

"What the fuck are you doing down here? I told you to stay put."

"I—"

Our conversation is halted by the squeal of rubber and the most almighty crash. The deafening sound of metal hitting concrete bounces off the walls and Denham pulls me into his body, wrapping his arms around my shoulders until he's sure it's safe to let go.

We all turn simultaneously to see my Porsche wrapped around a pillar at the other end of the lot. I stand and watch in slow motion as everything that has just happened starts to sink in. Spike and the gorillas are running toward the now smoking car and Denham is still holding me tightly while watching it all unfold.

"Oh god, oh my god, Aaron!" I shout as I try to free myself from his firm hold. "Let me go! Fucking let me go and help him!"

"No," he grates.

"What do you mean no? Let me go!"

I struggle as his grip tightens to contain me. I give in and stop fighting just long enough for him to loosen his hold, then I break for it, running as fast as I can across the parking lot. I know Denham is hot on my heels, but I have to make sure Aaron is okay. What the hell is he doing here anyway? And why is he running from Denham?

I see Spike and Jack trying to pull Aaron out of the car. It looks like he's stuck as they pull frantically at him but to no avail. He has blood running down his face and is unconscious, making it harder for them to get him out. I try, but I can't get there fast enough. My legs slow as I near them, and Denham is right on me, grasping me around my shoulders and bringing me to an abrupt halt.

"D, man, it's leaking. Get the fuck out of here!" Spike yells while pulling frantically at Aaron.

Denham starts to pull me backwards, but I dig my heels in. "Get the hell out, Spike! Jack, I'm fucking telling you to leave it!" Denham orders.

"No!" I plead "You have to help him, please."

"Spike," he warns.

I know I'm being stubborn and difficult, but I need to know that Aaron's okay. He was my husband, is technically *still* my husband, and I don't want him hurt ... or worse. "Get him out. GET HI—"

I'm cut off mid-sentence.

Suddenly ...

Deafeningly ...

The car blows.

Shards of glass and debris fly through the air at lightning speed, but it all seems to happen like a slow rerun. I'm cloaked by Denham's body as he pushes me to the hard, unforgiving ground and shields me from the blast. We hit the ground with a thud, scraping the left side of my body as we land.

Then *quiet.*

After that comes the sound of crackling flames and a high pitched ringing in my ears. I'm hoping and praying that any minute I might just wake up from this nightmare. Ridiculous situations only happen like this in dreams, right? But it's not a dream.The weight pushing me down is very real.The crackle I can hear is my car burning.

Oh god. Oh god.

Is Aaron still in that car? Did they get him out? I scramble and fight against the weight holding me down, but it's no use.

I scream Aaron's name at the top of my voice until I can't even hear myself.

"Help him ... Get him out of there ..." I plead.

"Shh," Denham whispers. "It's okay, he's out. It's okay."

This is either a very bad dream or I'm having an out of body experience. My body doesn't feel like it belongs to me. My legs are heavy, my head clouded and the sounds around me are merging with each other, causing a muffled drone in the background.

The sound of ambulance sirens still plays in my head. The vision of Aaron's unconscious body being taken away as they worked to keep him stable.

I never wanted this for him. For us.

I know my legs are functioning, but I don't know how. It's an involuntary movement and the direction in which I'm walking is guided by the hand pressed to me. His large warm palm rests in the curve of my back as his fingers wrap around my waist, a source of warmth which radiates around the immediate area. Everywhere else feels cold, numb.

Detachment.

My way of dealing with trauma.

I'm good at it, I've had a lot of practice. I know what comes after this: tears, regret, then a strange sense of nothing as my mind blocks out the bad and moves forward.

I'm vaguely aware of the surroundings becoming silent as we exit the elevator on my floor. I instinctively step left toward my door, but he takes my arm and leads me right, unlocking the door and leading me into the opposite apartment. He stops briefly when we enter to turn on the lights, then shrugs off his jacket and takes my hand gently in his.

Suddenly, a new set of questions flood my thoughts. Why are we here and not in my room? If this is his, who was yelling in here yesterday? What does he want from me? Sex? More?

I can't think clearly, and I know I'm unable to make any rational decisions right now.

"Denham, I need—"

He presses a finger to my lips, silencing me, then shakes his head gently from side to side. "Shhh, he will be well looked after, and we'll call the hospital in the morning if that's what you want. There's nothing more we can do tonight." He's reassuringly calm. His demeanor is protective and I know I can trust him. I know he won't expect any more than I'm willing to give.

I don't know how I can be so sure of that, I just am.

He leads me through the lounge and I already know where we are going. The layout is the same as mine, so it feels familiar. When we enter his bedroom, he comes to stand in front of me and kisses my cheek. His lips are soft, warm and gentle.

He starts unbuttoning my blouse, but his eyes are soft without a hint of the intense passion I saw there earlier when we were in his office. He's caring for me, and I let him.

He removes my blouse, placing it on the nearby chaise lounge, then runs his fingers around the waistband of my skirt, stopping when his arms are circled around my waist and he finds the zipper. His hands linger there for just a second and I feel his warm breath on my neck. I know he's waiting for my resistance, but when it isn't met, he continues to undress me.

When I'm standing in front of him in only my underwear, he crouches and runs his hand down my calf, slipping off my heels one at a time. I should feel exposed, maybe even self-conscious, but I don't. He doesn't look away, but he doesn't stare. He's not taking advantage of the situation in the slightest. On any other occasion, I'm sure this would be erotic and sexual, but right now I feel comforted and beautiful.

He folds back the covers on his big bed, then guides me to it, helping me in before covering me over. We have so much to talk about, but we both know that now isn't the time, so we say nothing. I know that once I start to talk, I won't be able to stop. I want to tell him everything. He deserves to know the truth after being so honorable and I know I have to start facing things head on rather than ignoring them if I want to move on with my life.

I watch in the moonlight as he removes all of his clothes, completely comfortable in my presence. It feels as if we've known each other for a lifetime. He pulls on a pair of boxers which is a thoughtful gesture, before he climbs into bed behind me and pulls the light cotton sheet up over our bodies. His front is pressed to my back, our bodies joined from top to bottom, shoulder to shoulder, hip to hip, ankle to ankle. I'm cloaked in his strong protective body and I don't feel vulnerable or threatened in any way. Despite the events of last week, I feel safe and content, and strangely enough, I'm okay with it. I'm not sure how long we lie here, not speaking, not moving, just listening to the sound of each other's breaths as he combs his fingers gently through my hair.

My strained thoughts disappear and I can feel my heart rate level out. I give in to the heaviness of my eyes and drift off to sleep.

It's still dark when I open my eyes, but unlike the last few days, I immediately know where I am. Denham's presence is calming, his smell is intoxicating and I know I probably shouldn't be feeling happy after everything that's happened, but I do. I'm strangely happy that it's led me here. In the few small hours that I've spent with him, he has shown me that I shouldn't spend my life second guessing my own shadow. He's actually made me begin to think that there's more to life if I can just open my eyes and see past the fear. I've seen more happiness in the last few days than I have in the last year.

As much as I don't want to move, I'm starting to feel physically uncomfortable. I look at the clock and notice it's 3.28am. I really need to pee, so I try to sit up but Denham's body tightens at my movement and he pulls me closer to him.

"Don't even think about it ..." he mumbles, his voice husky from sleep and making him sound even sexier than usual.

"Think about what?" Does he really not want me to pee?

"Running ..."

"Running? Denham, I need to pee." I laugh at him and he chuckles back.

"You're not going to try and disappear?"

"No, your bed is far too comfortable." I turn onto my back and his arm slides around my waist and pulls me closer so I'm facing him.

"You promise you'll come back?"

"I promise." I kiss him on the cheek and wriggle out of his hold.

"You know I'm faster than you? If you come out of that bathroom and make for the door, I'll be forced to take you down." I can hear the smile in his voice, and the threat makes me tempted to run. The thought of Denham tackling me to the ground is quite exciting.

Once I've done what's needed in the bathroom, I look in the mirror. My hair looks like a bird's nest, my mascara is streaked down my face and my foundation has worn off, revealing the still very purple bruise that covers my cheek. I know it's pitch black in the bedroom, but one look at me in the morning and he'll be bundling me out of the door instead of tackling me to the ground. The little voice hovering over my shoulder tells me that I couldn't be further from the truth. Denham King does not scare easily. If he did, I'm damn sure I wouldn't be here now.

I find a comb and tidy my hair the best I can, then find some tissue and remove the streaked makeup from under my eyes before splashing my face with cool water and using the soft hand towel that smells of Denham.

I remember the previous day and hearing a couple arguing. I scan the bathroom for any sign that Denham has a girlfriend, maybe even a wife. The thought causes a nasty taste in my mouth. He doesn't wear a ring on that hand, but he does wear one on the other hand—a gold band encrusted with diamonds. It catches my eye every time his hand moves.

I dismiss the thought of him being married. Everything about him is genuine, it feels different, and he's different. There are no female products in the bathroom. It's all male, and besides, he wouldn't have me sleep in his apartment if there were anyone else. I use his toothbrush to brush my teeth and pick up his aftershave to smell. It's him, a perfect mix of fresh and sexy.

When I climb back into bed, I bypass the side that would be labeled 'mine'. It's cold and uninviting. Instead, I curl into Denham, tucking my head under his chin and burying my face into his chest. He nuzzles into my hair and groans. "Better?" he asks.

"Yes, thank you."

"Good," he mumbles, stroking my hair.

"We need to talk ..." I say regretfully, I don't want to talk, I don't want to ruin the bubble that I have happily placed us in.

"Yes, we do, but not now. Now you need sleep. When we're rested, showered, fed and fully awake, then we'll talk."

"You're bossy," I state.

"I know."

"Are you al—"

I barely get the words out before his lips are on mine. His lips become more insistent as he pushes deeper and harder until we're both breathless. He rolls me onto my back so that we're chest to chest, his lips never leaving mine. His arms are either side of my head and I'm caged in with his body, but he's careful not to allow his full weight to rest on me. I trail my fingers gently up his back, feeling every ripple. He pulls his lips from mine and lets out a sigh.

"Arianna, we can't do this tonight."

"We can't?" I question.

"I let it go too far in my office, and I'm not going to let it go too far now."

His words hurt me, an actual physical hurt that I can feel in my heart. It also twists my pride. Stupid girl, he just feels sorry for me. Why would he want me? I'm broken, damaged and probably beyond saving. I push at his chest as I try to roll out from underneath him. His words contradict all his actions … well, maybe they don't. Perhaps my mind is playing games with me and I've allowed myself to see what I've wanted to see. Maybe I'm so damn messed up that I can't see things for what they really are.

"You don't want me. Ugh, I'm stupid, so stupid." My voice cracks at the words.

Denham grabs my wrists and pins them above my head, making me gasp. "Just stop and listen to me for a minute before your mind and mouth run away with you."

I'm panting hard from struggling to push my way out from underneath him. The small amount of light coming in from the window allows me to see his eyes fixed on mine. He's not hurting me, he's not even frightening me, as his grip is soft.

"You think I don't want you? Oh, darlin' I want you. I intend to cover every inch of you with every inch of me, but I want you to give yourself to me. I want your body *and* your mind. I won't be your rebound. I won't be a snap decision."

"I … I don't know what to say …" No one has ever been so open and the honesty in his voice cuts through my panic and runs straight to my heart.

He releases my wrists, but my hands stay there of my own free will. "Don't say anything, Ari." He brushes his lips across mine and kisses the tip of my nose, then lies on his side and pulls me back into him so we are as close as we possibly can be. "Go to sleep."

I'm so tired; physically and emotionally exhausted. The warmth and protectiveness coming from Denham's body is making me relax and I feel my eyes growing heavy.

"Goodnight, Mr King."

I smile at the sound of his gentle laugh. "Goodnight, Trouble."

# Chapter 8

When I wake, I'm alone. The bright sunlight is beaming through the window and I get the feeling it isn't early. I hop out of bed, throwing on Denham's T-shirt that's laying over the back of a chair. It smells of him and his aftershave.

I make my way out to the lounge and I don't have to go very far before I find him in the kitchen making coffee dressed in nothing but a pair of loose fitting, ripped jeans. Holy smokes. It's the first time I've seen his bare skin in the daylight and there's a lot to look at. His back ripples even when he moves just a fraction and my fingers itch to explore the sensual ridges.

When he turns, I notice he's on the phone but doesn't hesitate in holding out his arm for me to come to him. I cross the room, but seat myself on the opposite side of the breakfast bar from him and he frowns at me.

"I'm taking the day off ... I know ... yes, Jack is going to call if there are any developments ... well, do you think you can manage or not? Just because you're family doesn't mean I can't fire your sorry ass ... Okay, and Spike? I don't want to be bothered unless there is a nuclear threat or the building is burning, understand?"

He hangs up, slides his cell across the countertop and rests his elbows on the bar in front of me.

"Good morning," he says with a sexy smile and a twinkle in his eye. "Coffee?"

"Yes, please," I answer, trying to return his warmth in my expressi on."Is everything all right?" I need to know for my own peace of mind. "Is there any news about Aaron? Or Spike and Jack?"

"Jack and Spike are fine. Aaron was taken to get checked out as you know. His injuries are nasty but not life threatening. They should be keeping him in for a while though."

I nod, relieved. "I didn't know I had slept in, you should have woken me."

"There was no need to wake you. How do you feel today?"

I shrug my shoulders. "I don't really know. I guess there's a lot to figure out, huh?"

"Plenty of time for that. I've called down for breakfast, I hope you're hungry."

We enjoy fresh pastries at the breakfast bar, sitting next to each other, our bodies brushing together occasionally, stoking the desire that is still smoldering from last night. But he's right; there is a lot to talk about and the bright light of day makes things all the more real. I know I can't run from it this time. Part of me doesn't want to run. Denham has a way of making me feel safe and protected, and somehow, I know that I won't have to face things alone. This makes it more bearable. The other part of me wants to run for the hills rather than talk. Detach from everything bad, in the hope it will go away, then I can focus on everything good. But I know it doesn't work that way. The bad eats away at you until there's nothing left. A shell of what you once were and a mountain to climb before you can even think about getting it back. I want to get it all out and open up. But I really don't know how.

Denham's warm hand on my knee brings me back to the here and now. "You okay there? You zoned out ..."

"Uh, yes." I put down my mug of coffee and turn the bar stool to face him. "Can we please talk and get this over with? I'm not good at talking, I don't want to talk, but we need to, so let's do it."

I straighten my shoulders and take a deep breath to ready myself. He raises his brows, then his features soften knowing I need this. He takes both my hands in his and strokes his thumbs along the tops of my knuckles. "Arianna, I don't want to *make* you talk if you really don't want to. That's your choice. I won't ever make you do anything you don't want to do. But I'd like some answers and I'm sure you would too."

I nod in agreement. He helps me off my chair and I settle on the large, black, corner sofa in the lounge, I don't know why I'm so nervous but I can feel my heart beating hard in my chest as I sit cross-legged right in the middle, watching as Denham sits in front of me, mirroring my posture.

"Okay?" he says, far more positively than I'm feeling.

I nod and continue to nibble at the skin around my thumb nail. He continues to look at me, presumably waiting for me to start, and I continue to look anywhere but him, just wanting to fast forward to the part where this conversation is all over.

"I don't know where to start ..." My voice is small, barely above a whisper, but the room is quiet, so Denham answers me quietly too but with confidence.

"Just start from the beginning, baby ..."

Hearing that endearment makes my skin crawl. I let it go when Aaron used to call me baby, but this is different. I don't want to associate Denham with anything that taints my thoughts. It takes me back to a place I never want to visit again, but it's the place where I know I need to start this conversation from.

"Please, don't call me baby." His eyes widen at my request and I can see he is confused. "I don't like and I won't answer to it. The root of most of my problems is a man that used that word as an affectionate term for me."

"Arianna I'm sorry, I—"

"You didn't know, I know, but you do now and if you want me to stick around that's one of the only things I'll ask of you."

He nods, his expression neutral except for a few lines around his eyes that tell me he's tense. Well, that makes two of us. I'm a little afraid of what revealing everything will do to me. I might be a victim, but I'm also a survivor. I don't want him to think I'm some little woman who needs looking after because I'm not. I can cope perfectly well on my own. But I want him to know about my past; I want to tell him everything.

Cards on the table.

"How about you start by telling me how you know the asshole that blew up your car yesterday?"

"He's my husband." I let that revelation linger in the air for a little longer than I should, the silence swallowing me. It's clear it isn't the answer he was hoping for.

"Arianna, I'm going to need you to elaborate ..."

"Okay, we got married twelve weeks ago, I left him on Friday and came here."

Realization shows across his face and his eyes flash to my wounded cheek. I see his shoulders tense and the muscles in his neck flex as he lifts a hand to my face. "He did this to you?"

"Yes." I lean into his touch, but I don't need the physical distraction if I'm going to get through this story. I straighten my back and his hand falls away as he sighs.

"We argued, he hit me, I left."

"He called you Natalie."

I nod. "He doesn't know any different."

"You want to tell me about that?"

"You're not going to like it."

"That may be, but I need you to tell me all the same."

I look down at my hands folded in my lap and continue to pick at the skin around my nails. I suck in a deep breath before I begin. "I left Boulder City a little over a year ago. I was engaged to a very violent man. He hit me, often, and the last time he beat me so badly I needed to be hospitalized for nearly two weeks. I knew then that I had to get out and the only way to do that was to disappear and start again, so I went to LA, changed my name, and started over. I met Aaron and fell into a comfortable relationship. I never loved Aaron, but up until we got married, he was good to me."

I shrug. Admitting this makes me feel guilty. "It was easy and I hadn't had 'easy' for a long time before that. Then, something changed, he changed. I couldn't go through that again."

When I look up, Denham's face is set in hard lines, his lips tight and a deep line creased his forehead. "I told you, you wouldn't want to hear it ..."

"Arianna ..." He sighs. "I'm sorry, I never thought—"

"You never thought that would be my story? No, there was a time when I didn't think so either."

"What about your ex fiancé? He never tried to find you?"

"Oh, he tried, but I didn't leave a trace, I just vanished. Even my mom didn't know where I was. I haven't seen her since I left. The first time she had heard from me in almost two years was last week."

"Do you know where he is now? If you give me a name, I could find out. I have contacts."

"His name is Jonny Ellison. I think it's been long enough now that he just stopped looking. But—"

"I'll have my guys ask around discreetly," he reassures me.

"Is that how you found out so much about me?" I look at him quizzically.

"I didn't find out as much as I wanted," he says with a sly grin. "I could only find out that you previously went by another name. Lottie was tight lipped about how she knew you, and I knew there was something she wasn't telling me. When you slammed into me at the elevator, I knew I needed to know more about you. I still do." He shrugs his shoulders and looks a little bashful.

"All you have to do is ask. I'd rather tell you what you want to know, than have you dig things up that might not be true." I pause. "So ... can I ask you something?" I say, looking up at him.

"Sure, anything you like," Denham replies honestly.

"Why was Aaron running from you last night?"

He sighs and takes a steady breath. I can see him thinking carefully about his answer before he finally speaks. "He ripped me off, Arianna. You want to know the whole story?"

I don't really want to know anything else that could fill my head with more fog than is already there, but I need to know in order to try and piece together this puzzle, so I nod and he continues.

"He came here about fourteen weeks ago, first of all with a group of friends."

"His bachelor party." I say more to myself than Denham. I'm nervous about where this is going.

"Yes, they were loud, rowdy, but nothing we haven't seen before. Do you know how long the bachelor party went on for?"

"A week," I answer. "He was gone for a week."

"He might have been gone for a week, Ari, but the large group was only here for two days. After that, he was on his own ..."

"But ..." my mind races to catch up with the bigger picture but I can't make sense of it all.

"He found a chink in our armor and a partner in crime with one of our croupiers. They exchanged $175,000 of counterfeit money for chips, played, won and walked away with over half a mil in genuine cash. I've been trying to find him and piece it all together, but he's proven to be very elusive. Then he turned up last week, and you know the rest."

"I don't understand ..." I murmur.

"What's not to understand? He's a con man."

"No, I don't understand why he did it. He's very wealthy. He has hundreds of thousands in the bank ..."

"I don't have an answer for that, Arianna. I'm sorry."

I nod and let the thoughts running through my mind try and find some sort of order, but without knowing all the facts, it's impossible.

"When we were ... in my office last night, Jack spotted him on the CCTV and came to get me straight away. That's why I had to leave so urgently."

"Oh, I had no idea about any of that ..."

"We tried to talk to him, give him a chance to put things right, but he caused a scene in the casino and made a break for it. After that ... well, you know the rest."

"I just can't get my head around any of this. It doesn't make sense. I don't—"

"Look, I know it's hard for you, you've had so much upheaval, but trying to make sense of it when you don't know all the facts isn't going to help at this time. I have my men on it. I have feelers going out in all directions and I'm pulling out all of the stops to get this sorted. Will you trust me to do that and try not to worry?" He searches my eyes with such compassion and honesty that it's impossible to argue. "I'll tell you the minute I know something."

"Okay," I agree. "But I want to know everything you can find out, even if it's something I can't do anything about, okay? I need to know to be able to put it all together."

"I give you my word." He leans forward and places a chaste kiss on my lips.

"So," Denham says, breaking the heavy feeling in the air. "Do you know what you're going to do long term? Will you stay in Vegas?"

I feel myself relax after letting the heavy stuff out into the open and the change of direction in our conversation is welcome. "I'm not sure. I just wanted to see my mom and Lottie, they're all I have, and I don't relish the thought of having to start over somewhere that I don't know anybody again."

"Then stay here."

"Yeah, I think that's where my thoughts are heading. Vegas is pretty cool, but I'm going to need to start looking for a job and someplace permanent to live."

"That's what I said. Stay here."

"Here?"

"Yes." He nods with a serious expression and a little sparkle in his eye.

"I can't stay here." I laugh nervously, not wanting him to say anything impulsive. "We've only just met, and I can't afford to stay in the penthouse suite you've put me in. Hell, I can't even afford the most basic room you have for any longer than a few weeks."

"Before you start waffling, I have an idea ..." He looks at me with raised brows.

"Go on ..."

"What if I rent you the penthouse for a very reasonable rate, same rent as an apartment downtown. But not until you've found a job that pays enough. It's not used for guests. It's mine for my personal use so I wouldn't be losing any money and you'd have somewhere to stay. It'll be nice to have you up here. This floor gets lonely, you know."

I look at him for what feels like long minutes, but in reality it's probably seconds. It seems like the perfect solution, logical even, so why am I trying to find something wrong with this idea?

Do I want to live in a penthouse suite? *Hell, yeah!*

Would it make me feel so much safer living here? *For sure.*

Can I keep the barricade around my heart intact if I'm living across the hall from Denham King? *Probably not.*

Denham's excited expression has worn off with the length of time it has taken me to answer him, replaced with a concerned look. "It's only an offer. You're not obliged and I won't take offense if you say no. I like the thought of knowing you're across the hall and that you can call me if you need me. I want to know you better, Arianna, and whether it's under this roof or another, I'd still like to spend some time with you."

I smile at his soft kind words. Once again he has managed to slow down my panicking heart rate with just a few gentle words. He's too good to be true and that's what worries me. But I can't deny him. I know he's not like the others. I'd even bet on it. I don't fear him physically, and for now that's enough for me to put my trust in him.

He takes his hand away and places it on my knee. "Look, why don't you go shower. Think about it. Take all weekend if you need to. If you then want to find somewhere else to stay, I'll help you."

"I don't need to think about it." I smile. "I'd love to rent the penthouse from you, but I want a proper contract and you need to ask a reasonable rent. I'm not accepting charity."

"Okay. So that's it? That's all of your conditions to stay?" He smirks.

"Yes. What can I say? I'm easily pleased ... Thank you for being so understanding. You must think I'm crazy."

"Yes."

"Yes? You do think I'm crazy?" My eyes widen and I laugh. If anyone else had just heard our conversation, they would think I was crazy too.

"Yes, and funny and beautiful ... and sexy."

I let out a nervous laugh and look into my lap, but his fingers come to rest under my chin and tilt my head up to meet his eyes. I watch his whole face change as the smile creeps across his cheeks and turns into a full-out grin. He leans into me ever so slowly, his eyes not leaving mine other than to glance at my lips, and I watch as his lips part slightly before pressing them to mine. He pushes his hands up into my hair, pulling me closer into him as his tongue moves slowly, tangling with mine. A groan escapes me as he explores every inch of my mouth.

My hands find their way to his chest and I take full advantage, running them over his hard muscles contained behind smooth, flawless skin, then I pull away, wanting to go further but knowing I need to prove to him my head is on straight. I know that I have a few things to work through and my mind is working in a lust filled haze right now.

"Arianna ..." he says breathlessly between kisses.

"Yes ..."

"I was going to tell you not to stop, but we need to stop."

"I know." I force myself to leave his lips and rest my forehead on his.

"Can I take you out today?" he asks, giving me a hopeful look.

"Out where?"

"A date."

I smile. "You want to take me on a date?"

"Yeah, I think we've had enough of the serious stuff for today. I told you I want to get to know you and the perfect place to start would be with a date."

"Okay," I answer, trying to contain my smile and play it cool.

"Great!" He jumps up off the couch and holds out a hand to pull me up too. "Go and get that sexy ass of yours showered and dressed, and I'll pick you up in an hour."

"You wanted me to stay, now you're practically pushing me out of the door."

"That's because the sooner you go, the sooner I can come and pick you up." He turns me by my shoulders and points me in the direction of the door.

"An hour and a half ..." I call over my shoulder.

"An hour. And I'll let myself in whether you're ready or not."

"You're bossy," I tell him as I open the door and smile at the look on his face. Kind, relaxed.

He returns my smile with a wink. "I know."

# CHAPTER 9

One hour.

One freaking little hour to get ready for a date that has me more excited than Christmas did when I was a kid.

I'm still haunted by many unanswered questions about the events of last night., and it's a mission to balance everything out logically in my head. I know I should probably be demanding answers from Aaron and finding out what the hell went on, but a big part of me wants to enjoy my date with a handsome man and just pretend that everything is normal for an afternoon. I'm not stupid enough to think that it will all magically go away but I don't know how to deal with it all and ignorance is bliss as they say.

Normally an hour would be plenty of time to get ready if I were getting ready for work, or lunch with Lottie, but in less than fifteen minutes I have a date with a man who has captured my attention in inexplicable ways. This means I have to shave everywhere, moisturize everywhere and take time over my makeup for that perfectly natural look. Thank god for the spa day yesterday.

My hair has to be blow dried and not left to dry on its own to turn into a ball of frizz, and this alone takes at least a quarter of my time up. Not only that, I have to choose something to wear. I don't know where we're going, so I have no idea what to dress for and despite my recent shopping trip, I still have a fairly limited wardrobe.

With minutes to spare, I'm dressed and ready to go. I'm going all out girlie with a summery floral skirt, a sheer tank, and cute, white, peep-toe sandals that are a touch higher than I remember them being in the store, but complete the outfit perfectly. I'm not sure if I'm wearing the correct attire for my impending date, but I'm sure Denham will tell me otherwise.

After rushing around like a lunatic for the last hour, I perch on the edge of the couch, bouncing my knee like a frog on speed and trying my hardest to stop myself overthinking this and being nervous as hell. *It's just a date, it's just a date*, I keep telling myself but it doesn't help to calm the nerves. What if he's decided after our chat that he doesn't want to take me out on a date anymore? Even worse than that, what if he has changed his mind about everything and doesn't want to know me at all?

He's under my skin, already.

His loud bangs on the door break me out of the internal pep talk I'm trying to give myself and give me no more time to speculate. I jump up and grab my purse, checking my reflection in the mirror on the way to the door one last time.

"I'm giving you to the count of three, then I'm coming in, ready or not." His muffled voice from the other side of the door makes me laugh and any earlier worries vanish, leaving a childlike excitement in their place.

I pull open the door to find him leaning on the framework with one hand tucked behind his back. His eyes travel slowly up my body, lingering on each curve and taking in every inch of me. I'm not used to being savored as though I'm on display, but I get the feeling that the more time I spend with Denham, the more I need to get used to it. He knows what he likes and he isn't afraid to show it. The grin that creeps along his face is contagious and I find myself smiling right back at him.

"Arianna, you look ... stunning. This is for you." He hands me a single red rose.

"Thank you, kind sir. Such a gentleman." I smell the pretty perfume from the rose and then place it in the middle of vase of flowers by the door.

"Nothing less for you, Trouble."

I giggle at his affectionate nickname and ask, "Where are we going then?"

"It's a surprise," he says, holding out his hand for me to take. "Let's go."

We're seated in a private corner of the Eiffel Tower Restaurant. The view is spectacular and the company is just as enchanting. So far, Denham hasn't let go of my hand for more than a few seconds and insists on holding at least one of them across the table. His thumb moves in slow, lazy circles along my knuckles and with each movement I find it a little harder to concentrate.

Not only are we in 'Paris', but Denham has spoken to the waiter and ordered wine for us in French too. "I'm guessing you have a lot of talents I know nothing about ..." I raise an eyebrow at Denham.

His eyes lock on mine and he moves closer to me across the table. "Stunner, I have a whole load of talents and I plan on showing you every single one." His voice is deep and dusty and not only do I hear it, I feel it.

The waiter interrupts our heated exchange. "*Monsieur, madame, vous avez choisi*?"

"*Mes excuses, s'il vous plait vous donner un peu plus de temps*?"

"*Bien sûr, monsieur.*"

The waiter returns to his station and I have no idea of the exchange they just had. "You do know that I have no idea what you guys just said to each other?"

"No idea at all? Well, that information could be kinda useful." He waggles his brows at me and it earns a giggle that I can't stifle. That's the kind of action that could really turn you off because it can really look pervy on some guys, but I'm that smitten with Denham King that I can't think of a single thing he could do that would put me off him. I'm pretty sure he could pull faces at me all night and all I would do is laugh.

Unless it's the face he's making now.

The 'I can see straight to your soul' look. The 'heated, strip you bare, emotionally and physically' look.

I may as well be sitting here in my underwear. I feel my cheeks flush as tingles spread all over. He's devouring me. He turned me down in the early hours of this morning, but he's making it clear that it wasn't due to lack of desire. His withdrawal is him being chivalrous. I'm out of my depth and totally unsure how to handle a man like him. A man honest in his actions as well as his words.

"So," I say, needing a break in the intensity, "what do you recommend?" I pick up the menu and study the words as if my life depends on it.

He hooks a finger over the top of my menu and pulls it down so I can see his eyes. "Will you let me order for you?"

I study him for a moment. He's asking me to put a little trust in him. "Sure, but I don't eat mushrooms."

"You don't?"

"Nope ... or snails."

He chuckles "No mushrooms or snails. Got it."

After ordering what sounded like *loads* of food, we settle into comfortable conversation about where we grew up, how many different places I've lived and outline the dynamics of our families. This didn't take long for me as I have no aunts, uncles, brothers or sisters. Just my mom.

"So, Lottie said you have a brother, do you have any more brothers or sisters?" I ask, wanting to know everything about him.

"Yes. You've met my brother, and I have a sister named Tara."

"I've met your brother?"

"Yes." My confused face clearly shows I have no idea who he is talking about, and he frowns. "Yeah, Spike."

"Spike is your brother?"

"Yeah." He frowns. "You didn't see that?"

"I didn't, I—" I haven't really been paying attention to anything. "So your mom named him Spike?"

"No," he says, shaking his head. "No, he's called Preston but no one calls him that. He was born with a mohawk of black hair, so I called him Spike the day he came home. It's kinda stuck ever since."

"Now that I think of it, he does look like you. He's younger, right?"

"It's that obvious, huh?" he says with a smirk.

"No! Sorry, no, I didn't mean it like that. I just—"

"I know. Yes, he's twenty-seven. And Tara is twenty-three."

He looks at me intently and I study his face. I'm not surprised Preston is twenty-seven, he looks his age, but Denham ... I'm having a hard job placing his age. He doesn't look old, but he's wise and his eyes show that he isn't a young nave twenty something.

"And how old are you, Denham?" I say quietly, softly looking up at him from under my lashes.

"Don't you know it's rude to ask a person's age?"

I know he's just kidding with me from the smile in his eyes. "Well, I'm guessing you know how old I am from your little findings, so it's only fair."

"Yes, I do." He smirks and then I sense a little hesitation. Maybe he's older than I thought and he's unsure about how I'll feel about our age difference. "I'm thirty-four."

I smile back at him and lean across the table to reward his answer with a kiss. It's gentle and lingers just a fraction longer than he was expecting. I'm hoping it lets him know that there isn't much that would deter me from getting to know him better.

"There's quite a gap between you and Spike ..."

"Yes, my mom and dad had trouble conceiving. It seems that when they resigned themselves to the fact that it wasn't going to happen easily for them, it happened. Then four years later, Tara surprised them again."

"It must have been fun growing up in a busy house, with other kids to play with ..." I wriggle one of my hands free to pick up my glass of wine."Yeah it was, plenty of arguing, especially between Spike and Tara as they're closer in age. That all stopped when Dad ..." His voice softens, and his fingers loosen from around mine but I tighten my grip which makes him look up into my eyes. "My dad died ..." his voice catches and it's clear that it's still painful for him.

"I'm sorry," I say. "We don't need to talk about it. This is a date, remember? Plenty of time for the serious stuff another day." It's clearly hard for him to talk about. I want to know everything about him. But I also know that this is our first official date and I want to remember it for all the right reasons and not the ones that could ruin the memory.

"I will tell you all about it, Ari. Just not today, okay? I want today to be about us, nothing else."

"That sounds perfect."

Over lunch, our conversation is light and easy. Denham makes me smile and he's very affectionate with little touches here and there that make my whole body hum. The wine he ordered to drink with our meal is going down very well, and before I know it we're finishing the bottle. Well, I mean, I think *I've* finished nearly an entire bottle. Come to think of it, Denham still has half a glass and I'm sure it's the same half he started with.

I'm feeling fuzzy around the edges, so I excuse myself to go to the bathroom. As I straighten myself out and reapply my lipstick, I decide I'm only going to have water from here on in, hoping the fresh air will do me good when we leave. I can't remember the last time I was tipsy like this; I've kept control of myself and my sensibility for so long, yet I didn't even notice I'd let that guard slip.

When I return to the table, I see that Denham has ordered a dessert for two. Ever the gentleman, he stands before I'm seated. "Everything okay?" He frowns and holds a hand out for me to take.

I smile wide and nod. "Yes, I just ... I didn't realize how much wine I had drunk ..." I look away, feeling a little ashamed.

"And that's a problem because ...?" He bends his knees until his eyes are level with mine.

"I don't want you to think I make a habit of this," I whisper.

"A habit of what Ari?" He laughs.

"You know ... getting drunk on a first date. I mean, I'm not drunk, just a little tipsy, but it's the first, first date I've been on since ... well, since ..."

"Arianna ..." He says my voice so softly but it still stops my train of thought.

"Yes ..." My voice is just as quiet only it feels small.

His lips meet mine, gently at first but then with more pressure as he moves into me. The rest of the world falls away and as far as I'm concerned we're standing alone at the top of the Eiffel Tower. When Denham breaks away, reality comes screaming back to me as the rest of the diners start to cheer and whistle at our very public display.

How does he do that? He makes it feel like we're the only people in the world. I've never been one for public displays of affection, mainly because Jonny used to use them to pretend to the world how happy we were. But Denham isn't Jonny, he's the polar opposite. I might be so embarrassed that I want the ground to open up and swallow me whole, but that doesn't mean I didn't enjoy it. I quite like the fact that Denham isn't afraid to show all these people how he feels toward me. It's a genuine gesture.

He's everything I've never had and all I could possibly want.

"You ready for dessert?" he asks with a smirk.

I nod and take my seat. There is one glass bowl placed in the middle of the table filled with what looks like chocolate sundae and my mouth starts to water just looking at it.

Denham scoops some onto a spoon and looks at me expectantly. "Open ..."

"What?"

"Open your mouth, Ari, and close your eyes."

"I ..." I'm lost for words again.

"Please," he asks hopefully.

And just like that, my eyes close at his gentle request. It feels weird to close my eyes in the middle of the restaurant and not know what to expect or when to expect it. It's another test of my trust to a degree, albeit a small one. I make true to my promise not to open my eyes, but the sounds around me have my senses on high alert.

"Keep your eyes shut," he orders in a soft, husky tone.

The first touch of the cold ice cream makes me shiver. He sweeps my lower lip, wetting it just enough that my tongue instinctively moves to taste it. The sound of a low growl from Denham confirms that it isn't just me enjoying this. He moves the spoon from one side of my lip to the other before gently allowing the sweet ice cream to slide off and on to my tongue. It's delicious and I groan in appreciation. I might have my eyes closed, but I can feel Denham watching me and the waves of heat coming from him.

"Is that good Ari?"

"Mmmm yes, very."

I feel him come close to me again. This time the spoon is replaced with his thumb as he runs it across the length of my bottom lip, tugging gently and wiping away the remaining melted ice cream. As hard as I try, I can't control my reaction to his touch and I open my eyes.

He holds my gaze, his eyes burning holes into me and dips into the chocolate sauce with his index finger. He lifts it to my mouth, bold, unabashed and waits patiently while I hesitate briefly to part my lips. This doesn't feel like two people sharing a dessert, it feels like a slow, torturous, delicious foreplay, one that has me fidgeting in my seat and wanting to throw caution to the wind and give in to him completely.

"Taste ..." he insists quietly before gently slipping his finger into my mouth.

I close my lips over his finger and swirl my tongue around it, keeping my eyes locked on his. I suck gently until all the cream is gone and I just get a taste of Denham. His gentle insistence makes me feel like I can do anything, and I feel bold from his reaction to me.

"Fuck," he hisses, pulling his finger out and straightening himself in his chair.

I smile knowing that while it certainly affected me, I can get away without it visibly showing, but he can't and this is a far too public place to be taking this any further.

"You're killing me, Stunner," he breathes out.

I laugh softly. "I know the feeling ..."

He smiles, warming me from the inside and making me feel more alive than I've ever been. "Eat up," he says, handing me a spoon.

After leaving 'Paris', we wander along the Strip with Denham's arm wrapped around my shoulder and my head nestled into him like we're made to fit. The fresh air clears the fuzziness that is lingering from the alcohol and I'm beginning to think that this could be one of my favorite places to be, tucked in close to his warm chest and held fast by his strong protective arm, surrounded by a bubble of happiness. It's comfortable, but it's easy to feel comfortable with him. He makes it that way.

I look up at him and smile. "Denham, where are we going? Have you forgotten where you live?"

"No." He chuckles. "I haven't forgotten where I live, and just to correct you, you live there too now, remember?"

"I haven't forgotten. So where are we going then?"

"I don't know ... anywhere." He shrugs and pulls me closer into him. My arms move further around his waist until we're squeezed together tightly. "I don't want our first date to end, so I thought we'd just keep walking."

I don't want it to end either. So far it's been amazing. "You know if we keep walking, we could end up in Mexico."

"Wouldn't be far enough," he states.

"I'm not sure I could walk that far in these heels."

"Your feet hurt?" He looks down at me, his handsome face marred with a frown.

"No, not yet, but if we walk to Mexico they will."

"I'll carry you." He stops in the middle of the sidewalk and turns me so I'm flush to his body, pulling me closer with his hands on my hips. Even when I'm in heels, he's taller than me. I angle my head a little to look up at him. I'm close enough to see every whisker, every crease in his handsome face.

"I might be too heavy."

"Arianna, you'd never be too heavy. I'll always be strong enough to carry you."

I don't think we're still talking about Mexico; the look in his eyes tells me it couldn't be further from his thoughts. I watch his lips part as he moves closer to me. They touch mine with the pressure of a butterfly—a sweet, sweet kiss, full of promise and I've never been kissed like this before. His sincerity steals my breath away. He presses harder then pulls away and I feel bare. My lips immediately miss his."Breathe, Arianna. I love that I make you breathless, but if you stop breathing every time I kiss you, I'm going to stop kissing you."

I laugh and take a deep breath. "Okay, I'm breathing." I pull my shoulders straight. "Where to now? Mexico?"

Before I can blink, I'm scooped up in Denham's arms. I let out a squeal as I wrap my arms around his neck and he marches back in the direction of the hotel.

"I can walk. Honestly, my feet aren't hurting, I promise."

He stands still and looks at me. "I know, but I want to carry you." He places a gentle kiss on the end of my nose and continues to walk down the Strip. I know this is Las Vegas and crazy stuff happens here so we probably don't look out of place, but it still feels kinda weird. I'm so used to keeping up appearances that it feels strange to let go without a care.

"People are looking at us like we're crazy," I say.

"You care?"

"No, but ..."

"But what? Are you happy? I don't mean in general but in life. I mean right now, this very minute, being carried along this street, are you happy?" Denham stops walking again and waits for my answer.

I look deep into his eyes and answer him honestly. "Yes."

"Well then, who gives a shit what these people think? I'm happy, you're happy. What else matters?"

He's right, I know he is, but years of careful actions leave it hard for me to think any other way. He's exposed me in so many ways, and now he's doing his best to strip me of my insecurities.

"Arianna, it's been three days since we first met and I don't know about you, but this feeling ... well, I've never felt like this before. When I'm with you, you're the only person in the world that matters."

Well, shit. He's voiced every word that's going on in my head but was afraid to admit. He's intense, self-assured and very convincing, and he's doing irreparable damage to the walls around my heart, but it feels right. So right. Even in the beginning of my previous relationships it was never like this. It's all too much and I can't think straight.

"I think we should head back. I can walk now." I wriggle and twist my legs to make Denham let go, but he just holds on to me tighter.

"What's got you looking so frightened, Stunner?"

"Denham, put me down," I sigh. I don't want our amazing date to take a negative turn, but my self-preservation is starting to kick in.

"No," he says flatly.

"What do you mean no?"

"I mean I'm not letting you go, not until you tell me what's going on in the pretty little head of yours. I'm sorry if my words are too soon or too much, but I can't be anything but honest with you, Ari."

I look into his deep brown eyes and see nothing but pure intentions and genuine, heartfelt honesty. I may be way off the mark, but I can't fight it. I'm already out of my depth, but it feels so goddamn right. The thought of not spending more time with him stabs at my heart, but I can't keep going back and forth like this. It's not fair on him and it's making me dizzy.

"Ari, I'm not going to apologize for the way I feel. It is how it is. I won't force anything on you, but I won't let you run from it either."

He gently lets my legs fall until they touch the floor, but his eyes haven't left mine. I'm not sure if he's waiting for me to speak or looking for the answers in my eyes. He takes both my hands in his, pulls them up to his chest and holds them tight. "I don't know who you're thinking about but I'm not all those assholes that hurt you before. I'm not them." With those few words, he confirms that he can, in fact, see into my soul.

There is no hiding from this man.

"Okay."

"Okay?"

"Yes, I know you're not them. You've been different from the very first day I met you. It's hard for me to say this but ... I trust you. I have no idea why, there's no explanation for it, I just do." He lets go of my hands and wraps me up in his large frame, pressing me to his chest and resting his head against mine.

"Are we done with the serious stuff?" he says after a few minutes.

"Yes."

"Good, not that I wasn't serious about everything I said, but this is our first date, and I want to have some fun." He turns his back to me and bends to crouch. "Hop on."

"You're crazy!"

"I know," he says, turning and giving me his most playful smirk. "Come on, hop on."

"You have a thing for carrying me ..."

"No, I just have a thing for you. Being able to carry you everywhere is a bonus."

I sling my purse strap over my head and brace my hands on his shoulders. I feel his muscles bunch under my fingertips, ready to take my weight. "You ready?" I ask.

"Do it," he says impatiently.

I take a leap, wrapping my hands around his neck and my legs around his waist. His hands instantly grip around the back of my knees and he holds me tight. I've never had a piggyback before. Not even as a child. He playfully starts to wobble from side to side.

"Jeez. All that lunch you ate is sitting heavy." He chuckles.

"I knew I'd be too heavy. Just let me down, I can walk!" I try to get him to let me go by wiggling my legs, but he grips tighter.

"Not a chance, sweetheart."

He breaks into an all-out run, spinning me around in circles and feigning his inability to carry me. I laugh and scream nearly all the way back down the Strip until we reach the fountains outside The Kingdom. Denham slows down and walks to the edge of the biggest fountain.

I rest my head on his, still clinging on for dear life, but when he feels my body go slack and relax a little, he playfully tips me toward the fountain. I don't think he means to tip me quite so far and it throws him off balance. It happens in slow motion, both of us trying to regain our balance but overcompensating, and before I know it, we're plunged into the cold water of the fountain, falling in headfirst and coming up gasping for air. We glance at each other, stunned and soaking wet from top to toe as we sit on our asses in a fountain in the middle of the Las Vegas Strip.

I can't hold the laughter in; it's the kind of contagious laughter that makes your ribs ache and your soul dance. It feels great to laugh so hard, especially in such great company. The whole day so far has been amazing. The world that was weighing so heavily on my shoulders feels a little lighter now.

Lighter, but wetter!

# Chapter 10

Our little scene at the fountain attracts quite an audience. Either Denham has a thing for PDAs or he really doesn't give a shit what people think. He kisses my breath away and I have to bring myself back to earth and remember where we are before he helps me out of the fountain.

We walk into the hotel, holding hands and dripping fountain water onto the very highly polished marble floors, but Denham ignores the staff trying to catch his eye as he passes. I love that he has no interest in anything or anyone else but me.

I hear fast, heavy footsteps get closer as we reach the elevator and I jump when a person approaches us from behind and shouts, "Where the fuck have you been?"

We both spin in the direction of the sharp voice and I relax when I see that it's only Spike. Denham, however, does not relax at all. He drops my hand and I see tension ticking through his jaw and the muscles in his neck bunching up. He pulls back his shoulders, instantly making him look taller and more menacing, then narrows his eyes before pushing Spikes shoulder, making him take a step back to regain his balance.

"Apologize," he barks forcefully.

"What the fuck, D?"

"Apologize to the lady. One, for scaring the shit out of her, and two, for speaking with such disrespect."

"I'm sorry D, but—"

"Don't apologize to me. Apologize to Arianna."

I watch him jigging around impatiently, trying to get out what's bothering him and clearly frustrated at being stopped by Denham. "Arianna, I'm sorry, I really am. I didn't think. But D, I've been trying to call you ... what happened to you guys anyway?" The urgency in his features is momentarily replaced by confusion as he takes in our dripping wet state.

Denham casts a look over his shoulder toward me and a cute grin breaks the hard lines that were set along his face. He turns back to Spike and speaks through gritted teeth. "I told you, I didn't want to be called. I don't want to know unless the place is burning down and I don't see a fucking fire."

Spike runs a hand through his unruly dark hair. "It's important. Gimme a couple of minutes?"

Denham looks back to me and I give him a gentle nod before he grips Spike's elbow and takes him to one side. I can't hear what they are saying, but Spikes face is deadly serious. Denham's shirt is stuck tight to him, the water making it hold onto every curve of every muscle in his back. A flush creeps across my chest and up my neck at the mere sight of him. I sigh in appreciation, and any awkwardness I was feeling about standing here in dripping wet clothes dissolves when I look at his fine form.

I see Spike nod at something Denham says and he glances over at me, giving me a tight smile before jogging off in the opposite direction to us.Denham walks back to me, taking my hand and threading his fingers through mine as he leads me into the elevator. His face is a mask of unease, and the tension is radiating off him in waves.

"Is everything okay?" I ask cautiously. I know it's a stupid question. If everything were okay he wouldn't be giving off such an uneasy feeling.

He punches in the code and the elevator starts to move. After a few very tense minutes, he takes a deep breath before turning to me. "Arianna, you said you trusted me. Do you?"

I nod. "Yes," I say with as much sincerity as I possibly can.

He walks me backwards, pinning me to the mirrored wall of the elevator. One hand holds me in place by my hip as the other tucks a stray hair behind my ear. I shudder as his fingertip traces my lobe and the air is sucked from this small space. His dark eyes are locked on mine and I watch as his lips part and he draws a ragged breath.

I thought I knew the rhythm of my heartbeat. The only reason it has ever wavered from the continual steady pulse is to accelerate through fear, driving adrenaline around my body to pull me through. No one has ever made my heart race with passion.

Until now.

Now it's beating faster, making my head spin with sensation and my body react with desire.

Denham slides his hand across the wall and turns the key, halting the elevator with a jolt which makes me gasp.

I don't care that there may be people waiting for the elevator that will have to take the stairs.

I don't care that the world could be falling down around us.

I don't care that this might be the man that takes down every carefully constructed brick that has been my heart's shield for as long as I can remember.

Because I *feel* it. Not just physically. The emotional connection of two lost souls finding one another. I feel every part of the man who might just be the one to save me from my self-imposed emotional isolation.

Denham's lips skim my neck, nipping at my throat and causing soft moans to escape from my body. He lifts me up until I'm resting on the handrail. My hips are level with his and I wrap my legs around him, pulling him in to me as close as I can, but it's not close enough. There are too many clothes between us. I want him.

Skin on skin.

My fingers work to undo his belt but his hand halts me. He rests his forehead against mine, his breaths ragged and uneven. "Not yet, Arianna, and not here," he says regretfully, kissing my cheek. "Not the first time. After that, definitely here."

I groan, knowing he's right, knowing I got caught up in the moment, but also knowing that I want this more than anything. I just need to convince him that my head is in the same space as his.

He starts the elevator again and we ascend to our floor. He looks visibly more relaxed now, but I'm worried about what had him so agitated. I'm not going to pry, though. If he wants to share, he will. He walks us to my door and opens it to let me in, and I watch as he scans the apartment, walking to the balcony doors and then to the bedroom.

"Denham, what are you doing?"

"Just checking."

"Checking for what?" I laugh, but the thought that he has to check my room makes me nervous.

"It's my job to make sure you're safe." He walks back to me and pulls me toward him.

"Is there likely to be anyone hiding in here?" Now I'm starting to panic.

"Relax, Arianna. I just wanted to make sure that room service wasn't here making your bed or cleaning the bathroom."

"Oh, okay," I say, confused and not in the least bit convinced about his answer.

"But also, if there were anyone else here I wouldn't be able to do this ..." He supports the back of my head and dips me backwards like they do in the movies for a long hard kiss. When he brings me upright, he runs a hand down over the curve of my waist and squeezes my ass, groaning into my mouth.

"I could get lost in you, Ari," he murmurs against my lips. "You're fucking beautiful, you know that?" My already pink cheeks heat even further and I look away, but his hand comes up to cup my chin, "Arianna, don't be shy, not around me, not ever. You. Are. Beautiful. And I will tell you every day, ten times a day so you believe me."

My heart doesn't stand a chance. It's exposed and bare for Denham to do with it what he will. I smile shyly at him, and he strokes my cheek gently with his thumb, kissing me softly on the lips.

"And as much as I would love to stay here and kiss every inch of your beautiful skin, I have some things I need to see to."

"Sure," I say softly. It'll give me time to get my head out of the spin that it's in and think straight. Not that I think I will feel any differently. It's a feeling I could get very used to. But so many things have happened that I just need time to process it and put it all in order.

"I'll be two hours, max."He makes for the door, my hand slipping from his and letting go of my fingertips at the last minute.

"Denham," I call after him. "I think you may want to get changed into some dry clothes first." I giggle.

He gives me a wink and a flash of that cute dimple I'm becoming very fond of, before leaving me standing here feeling like a schoolgirl with a grin on my face the size of the ocean.

Time on my own is good. I love to have the freedom and space to do as I please. As much as I enjoy Denham's company, I need to keep my head and build my independence once again. I've spent a long time being stamped down and overruled.

Life as it was three days ago is finished. I feel a jumble of emotions, and I'm not sure which one to deal with first. I'm devastated. I didn't want it to be over like this. I feel guilty. Not because he came here looking for me. No, I feel guilty for being relieved. I'm so damn relieved that I can put 'Natalie Jamesson' to bed and move on from that part of my life. And the guilt for feeling that way is making me sick. I also still have no information about how Aaron is doing. I can't cope with it. I can't deal with it right now.

I flick on some music as a distraction. I need all the answers and I need closure on everything before I can undo the jumble, but I don't have the capacity to do that right now, so I strip out of my wet clothes and take a quick shower before dressing in a robe and sitting in the middle of the huge bed.

I take the opportunity to look over my past designs and pull every sketch out of my treasured folder. It is worn and tattered around the edges, but it has come everywhere with me for the last five or six years. There are years of visions transferred to paper and there is so much of me invested in the kaleidoscope of designs. If there was one thing I would save in a fire it would be this. It's been my saving grace, my focus, my passion. It might have sat in a bottom drawer for many years while I lived with Jonny, but just knowing it was there, knowing that I could pick up the soft lead pencil and loose myself in flowing lines and stunning angles was a huge comfort.

When real life was tough to take, I would picture ideas and visions in my head—a ballroom full of possibilities, and fantasize about having my one dimensional visions brought to life. *One day.* That is how I detached from even the darkest of days and found a light.

*One day.*

Just a quick glance through and I feel myself inwardly smiling. There are only a couple of blank pieces of paper left, but I have so many ideas bouncing around in my head that I can't wait. I can feel every little grain in the paper as the pencil that feels so comfortable in my hand works over the page. Everything I've ever gained inspiration from is stored in a compartment in my brain, safely tucked away for future use. I get lost in creation, in a page of black and white soft lines and curves.

I get lost in the one thing that makes my heart happy.

A little noise breaks me out of my bubble and I naturally whip my head up toward the doorway. When I lock eyes with Denham, I smile. "How long have you been standing there?" I ask, then frown. "And how did you get in?"

"I knocked, you didn't answer. I thought I had better come and make sure you were okay." He shrugs.

"Oh, I'm sorry. I didn't hear you knock. I was—"

"Busy drawing?"

"Sketching. It's nothing really, just a hobby." I try and brush him off like it's no big deal, but he starts to walk toward me, so I scoop up all the papers and start to tuck them into my folder.

"Wait." He holds his hand out to me. "Let me see ... I want to see."

"I've never shown anyone ..."

I'm holding most of the designs tightly to my chest. There are still a few strewn around the bed that I haven't picked up yet, so Denham reaches forward and picks up one of my older designs. It's a favorite of mine—a beautiful silk ball gown inspired by a designer that I was lucky enough to meet when I was in LA. I can hardly believe I designed it.

"Arianna ..."

Self-doubt overcomes me, and even though I love it, I'm nervous about letting others see. "You don't have to say you like it." I reach up and try to take it from him, but he turns his body from me so I can't reach. "Denham—"

"Will you stop it, woman? I'm trying to look." He chuckles and I sit back on the bed cross-legged and nervous.

Why am I nervous? Why do I care what he even thinks?

"You did all of these?" He gestures to the remaining few pieces on the bed.

"Yes."

"May I see?"

He holds out his hand and I hesitate before handing him the pile of papers that moments ago were clutched to my chest. I watch as he flicks through the designs, taking what seems like an eternity to look at them all. His face has no expression and my stomach feels heavy. I've never shown anyone.

"Arianna ... these are ..."

"Awful?" I wince.

"God no. they're amazing."

"You really like them?"

"No, I don't really like them, I love them. I can picture you wearing each and every one." He comes to sit next to me on the bed, carefully placing the papers down. "Stop picking at your fingers and look at me," he says softly, turning my cheek with gentle fingers. "If we're going to spend more time together you have to start believing my words. Don't doubt me. If I say I love your sketches, then I mean exactly that."

He traces his fingers down my jaw and runs his thumb over my bottom lip. "If I say I love your soft lips, then I mean it." His words drip with desire as his other hand tangles in the hair at the nape of my neck, pulling me to him gently. "If I say I love the way your skin flushes when I pull you close, then it's because I can't get enough of your body." I watch as his gaze travels the exposed skin of my chest that my robe doesn't cover. "Never enough," he murmurs under his breath.

As his fingers tighten, I tip my head back a little, exposing my throat. He places lingering kisses down my neck and across my collarbone. Shivers of pleasure follow the path of his lips as once again he manages to make me feel awakened. I open my eyes when the kisses stop. Denham has an intense look on his face. Carnal, and so goddamn sexy.

"You have beautiful skin, Ari," he says.

I hesitate before saying, "Thank you."

He pushes us back so that I'm flat on my back and he has me pinned under his body in just a second.

"It's sexy as fuck," he says with a grin. "Do you believe me now?"

"You're fast!" I laugh.

"You didn't answer me ..." Denham wraps his fingers around my ribs and starts to tickle me.

I fling my legs wildly and start to buck my hips. "Get off me!" I squeal, playfully trying to wriggle free.

"You didn't answer. Do you believe me now?" he says with that delicious cocky smirk firmly in place.

"Yes, yes I believe you."

His fingers ease, but stay in place. "Even when I stop tickling you?"

"Yes, even then ..."

"Good. I only came to tell you I made plans for us this evening. I had no intention of pinning you to the bed and tickling you until you surrendered."

"No?"

"No." He frowns. "And now I'm aware that you're only wearing a robe. Do you even have anything underneath?"

"Nothing," I breathe out. It amazes me how fast our interactions change from playful to sexual. He shakes his head before hopping off the bed in one swift move and heads for the bathroom. I sit back up, tightening my robe and covering as much skin as possible, hoping that this will make it easier for him to concentrate on anything but my lack of attire.

When he comes back out, he smiles at me gently. "I'm going to sit over here until you go and get dressed. I can't sit on that bed with you knowing I could have you naked just by pulling the tie on your robe that's keeping it all together." He sits on the chaise lounge with his elbows glued to his jean clad legs.

"You managed last night when I was just in my underwear."

"I did not manage Ari, I coped. There's a huge difference. It was a long painful night made both equally better and worse by having you next to me. I never knew I had such self-control, but I can't promise how long it's going to last, so you had better get some clothes on that hot little body of yours before I break my own rules."

I slide off the bed, taking care not to flash too much leg, and walk toward him. I place a kiss on the top of his head. "You're so cute, you know that?"

"Fluffy rabbits are cute, Arianna. I am not cute," he says, keeping his voice purposefully low.

I pick up some clothes and smile to myself all the way to the bathroom. *He is totally cute!*

# CHAPTER 11

"Where are we going?" I ask as we stand side by side, fingers entwined as we wait for the elevator to descend. Denham had said to dress for dinner but remained tight lipped about what he had planned.

"It's a surprise."

"I don't like surprises ..." Surprises make me nervous.

"You'll like this one," he says with certainty, keeping his focus forward but I can see his lips curl at the corners.

"How can you be so sure?"

"Because, Arianna," he turns to face me with smug certainty, "we've only know each other for a few days, but it might as well have been a hundred years. I *know* you're going to like this."

Well, that shuts me up.

He steers me through the people in the foyer and we enter a beautiful restaurant. It's dimly lit, sultry rather than dull, and every table is intimately lit with candles. The room is filled with the gentle, sophisticated tone of someone playing a baby grand piano in the corner.

"It's beautiful," I remark.

Denham gives me a knowing smile and a wink. Yes, he was right. So far, I do like this surprise. We are greeted by the maître d' and he gestures Denham in the right direction. Denham whispers something to him and he nods in return.

"I have someone I'd like you to see ..."

I look up at him nervously "You do?"

"Yes."

He guides me in the direction of the private booths situated across the room and my heart starts to beat faster. When we near the booth, Denham slows and stands in front of me. He kisses my cheek, lingering a fraction longer than a peck, then stands to the side.

This can't be real. This doesn't feel real.

"Mom!" I cry.

"Arianna, my girl!" She leaps out of the booth and we both wrap our arms around each other.

I can't let go. It's been so long and I've wanted to see my mom for what seems like an eternity. I want to hold on tight and not ever let go. I have a lot of time to make up.

I look up through watery eyes to see Lottie, Brent, and Spike, seated at the table. In my excitement, I hadn't seen them initially.

"Lottie!" I release my mom from the tight embrace but keep her hand snug in mine. "What are you all doing here?"

"Denham called and said there'd be a free meal in it for us, so of course, I was all over that," Lottie jokes, and everyone laughs. One by one, I get a warm hug from all of them, even Spike who squeezes me like he's known me forever.

I'm ushered into the booth and sandwiched between my mom and Lottie. Denham sends little looks of happiness my way and his eyes dance. I smile wide, letting him know that indeed, he was right, I *do* love this surprise. This is by far the kindest thing anyone has done for me.

We eat, we talk and we laugh. It all feels normal, and I love it. Hope blooms in my chest that this isn't a one off. This is what I want my life to be like, spending time with the people I love.

Mom looks brighter than when I saw her last. Her hair is longer than I remember it being with beautiful soft waves the color of brown sugar falling just below her shoulders. She looks happy. Brent and my Mom only met a couple of years ago, and married after four weeks, so I hadn't spent a lot of time with him before I'd left and didn't know him very well.

Brent is her fourth husband. The previous three were good for nothing and didn't treat her as anything more than someone to look good on their arm. It seems different with Brent; he treats her with respect and gives her enough love to make her skin glow. I know from the look in my mom's eye when she looks at him that he takes care of her and makes her happy, so that makes him one of the good guys in my book.

I watch Lottie and Spike. They are like a couple of teenagers, so cute and carefree with each other. I know from experience that Lottie has no control over what comes out of her mouth, and it seems that she has found someone who not only accepts it, but loves her for it. I can see it in the way they look at each other. From our conversation at dinner a couple of days ago, I'm pretty sure they haven't declared their love for each other, but it's plain as day that they are smitten.

"So, darling, how long are you staying here? What will you do now?" Mom asks.

"Well, there's still a lot to sort out ..."

"Oooohh, I know," Lottie says excitedly, bouncing up and down on her seat "You can come and stay with me! Chica, we'd have a blast."

"She's staying here," Denham quickly interjects.

"Says who?" Lottie replies indignantly.

"Arianna, can you afford to stay here?" Mom inquires gently. "You can stay with us, or like Lottie says, you could stay with her."

"Thanks, Mom. You too, Lottie, but I can't come back to Boulder City. You know why. There's just too many bad memories there and once I've gotten everything sorted out, I want a fresh start. You know?"

"I understand," Mom says while Lottie pouts like a child.

I turn to her and laugh. "Babe, you're always here anyway visiting Spike. I'll see more of you here than I would at your place." She nods resignedly. "Besides, you should see my new room." I give her a nudge like an excited teenager, knowing that she will freak when she sees the penthouse.

"You have a new room? Why do you have a new room?"

My stomach drops. Just another situation that turned bad. I don't want to explain it all. "I kinda got moved," I say quietly, so quietly that the whole tables hushes.

"I moved her to the left penthouse," Denham says confidently. "That way I'm just across the hall, so she can shout if wants anything." I watch him as he handles the conversation then slides his eyes to mine and adds, "Anything at all, just ask."

I want to kiss him. I actually want to get up from the table and kiss him full on the lips in front of everyone, but Lottie bounces excitedly next to me, veering my mind off the track it was taking.

"The penthouse! You're going to be living in the penthouse suite? Ari, that place is awesome! The bed is so—" Lottie squeals and Spike interrupts, shoving her with his elbow.

"Lottie," Spike hisses through his teeth.

"Uh, I mean ... oh shit." Lottie flushes a shade of pink and hides her head in her hands as the whole table starts to laugh. Spike glances nervously at Denham.

"Spike, relax. You think I don't know? I live across the hall and your girl is not quiet." He emphasizes this with a small shake of his head.

"Oh god ..." Lottie groans and buries her head behind my shoulder. Spike has turned almost the same color as Lottie. They really are like a couple of teenagers. I glance at my mom and Brent who are trying to hide the fact that they are finding this funny too.

"Sorry, man," Spike says sheepishly.

"No problem, just don't do it again. Arianna is living there now so the penthouses are off limits, okay?"

"You got it." Spike's shoulders relax and he affectionately pats Lottie's knee, signaling that it's safe for her to come out of hiding from behind my shoulder.

"Arianna," Brent says quietly, leaning over to me. "I don't want you to worry about money. Your mother and I will take care of your hotel costs if it makes things easier for you."

The offer makes me choke up a little. He doesn't have to do that, he doesn't even have to offer, but the fact that he did makes me feel like I have him as part of my supportive family.

"That won't be necessary," Denham says harshly.

What was meant as a sweet gesture has created a suddenly very tense atmosphere. Brent tries to make his point. "Mr. King, your kindness is appreciated, but Alice and I can take care of Arianna, I wouldn't expect you to—"

"I know it's not expected. Arianna and I have an agreement regarding her stay," he says before looking at me pointedly.

I know what they are doing. It's the alpha challenge, a pissing contest. Even though I don't know Brent or Denham particularly well, I know them enough to say that Denham would win. It warms my heart that a few days ago I had no one fighting my corner, now I have a whole table full of people ready to argue over who gets to help me out.

"Guys, it's okay," I say, trying to diffuse the situation. "Thank you, Brent. If I need anything, I won't hesitate to call." I turn and look at the stern handsome face I have grown very fond of. "The same goes for you, Mr. King." I treat him to the same sexy wink as he has given me many times this evening and his expression softens.

My mom clears her throat. "So, Arianna ..." She looks between Denham and I. "What are your, uh ... plans?" I know what she's subtly trying to ask, but I can't reply because I don't have an answer for her just yet.

"Well ..." I look over to Denham who is waiting for my answer, and I smile. "I'm just going to see where things take me," I say without breaking his gaze. Seemingly happy with that answer, he flashes me his dimple. "There's a lot to be sorted out, finalized." I think about Aaron and my throat closes over. I swallow noisily, it's like someone flicked off the happy switch. "I have a lot to tell you about, Mom, but not tonight, okay?"

"All in your own time, my girl," she says softly and I rest my head on her shoulder.

Not wanting to bring the mood of the evening down, I straighten up, push up a smile and change the subject. "What I would like to do is get a job, earn some money and have some fun."

"That sounds like a great plan to me, darling," Mom says, taking my hand. Not wanting to be left out, Lottie takes my other one and squeezes. My smile then comes from the inside, up through my chest and across my face. I'm sure it touches every part of my body as an actual feeling rather than an action.

*This is what happiness really feels like.*

A waiter arrives at our table with a bottle of champagne and six crystal glasses. Denham flashes me a wink as he takes the bottle from the waiter. Skilfully twisting and letting the cork out with a soft pop, he pours the champagne into the glasses. He hands me the first one and purposefully brushes my fingers with his, before making sure everyone else has a drink in hand.

"I'd like to propose a toast." Denham clears his throat before proceeding "To Arianna, new beginnings and a happy future."

Everyone agrees and we chink glasses, then Lottie announces, "To my bestie. Thank god I got you back. All my other friends suck!" Everyone bursts with laughter.

It feels weird. Good weird. It's surreal to be here, drinking a toast to what's to come with my nearest and dearest and new friends that look set to be part of my future. It's a situation I never allowed myself to dream it could happen. For as long as I can remember, I've held very little hope for the happiness of my future until now.

I'm overwhelmed and I feel my eyes start to gloss over. For all of the days I've had that are worth forgetting, this is, without a doubt, one to remember. I wipe away the stray tear that is sliding down my cheek, and it triggers a hug response from the women either side of me. I'm squashed between them, their arms wrapped around me, and it's the best feeling a girl could wish for.

"It's just the beginning for you, Ari," Lottie murmurs.

I nod in agreement. I hope so, I truly hope so.

I feel a foot against my leg under the table and look up to find a gentle smile from Denham. I lift my foot to tangle with his and he breaks into a sexy grin. I want to kiss him. I want to kiss his handsome face and tell him how happy he's made me. I'm not even sure if words could explain how I feel about what he's done for me, not just this evening, but for the small time I've been here. He's healed some of the cracks. They may only be little cracks, but they're healing nonetheless.

I realize I've been holding his gaze and the intensity of our exchange starts to pick up. Neither of us wants to look away, but it's not appropriate for us to be looking at each other like this in company. He breaks first, pulling his shoulders up and downing the last of his champagne.

"Who would like more drinks?" he asks.

My mom loosens her grip around me and places a hand on Brent's knee. "That's very kind of you, Mr. King, but we really should be going. Leave you kids to your evening."

"Please, no formalities. Call me Denham."

"Thank you, Denham," Mom says with a genuine warmth in her voice. "It's been a wonderful evening."

"It's been my pleasure. You're welcome here anytime, both of you." Denham dips his head toward both my mom and Brent, but I don't miss the tightness in his smile when his eyes settle on Brent. The pissing contest is obviously not over yet. It's touching that they both feel like they need to take care of me, but I need to learn to take care of myself first.

We say our goodbyes and, of course, there is a disagreement as to who will pay the bill—Brent or Denham. Both insisted, but Denham won. Brent only relented after insisting he return the favor sometime very soon, which I have no doubt that Denham will not allow him to do.

I'm reluctant to let them all go home, not being used to having them so close at hand, but knowing I can see any of them at any time is enough for me to be content with them leaving.

When we arrive back at the penthouse, Denham and I find ourselves in the same place as we were two nights ago. I'm backed into the door with Denham's hands resting on my waist. I feel like a teenager on a first date, not knowing if the boy is going to kiss me or whether I should kiss him.

I should kiss him. I want to. I've wanted to all night.

It's not like we haven't shared kisses throughout the day, and we've both given them freely. Hell, we both shared a bed last night so kissing shouldn't be awkward.

"Denham I—"

"Arianna—"

We're both nervous for some strange reason and start to speak at the same time, halting each other in our tracks and breaking out into giggles.

"May I go first?" Denham asks. I nod. "Arianna, I know a lot of things have happened to you, and I know yesterday was hard for you. Hell, the last eight years of your life have been hard." He pauses, seemingly trying to steer the direction onto a more positive path. "I'm just trying to say that I know you have things to work out, but I've had an awesome day today and I really want to do it again soon, but only if you want to. Don't feel like you have to just because you're staying here because our agreement still stands even if you don't—"

"Denham ..."

"Yes, Stunner?"

"Shut up and kiss me."

I give him no time to think or answer as I close the distance between us. He meets me halfway, and our breath meets and mingles before he nudges my lip with his. I need no encouragement to open up to him. My tongue darts out to wet my lip and catches his at the same time. It elicits a deep groan from his chest as he covers my mouth with his. He kisses me with the fervor of a desperate man, and each time it's like we're kissing for the very first time, exploring each other like our lives depend on it and making every second count. I'm pressed tight against the hardwood door, his hands tangled in my hair and mine in his. His tongue sweeps the roof of my mouth and I think I'm going to melt.

This man can kiss.

Our breathing is hot and heavy, and the groans coming from my body are audible. I want more. Need more. Knowing we've already gone further than this is making me tremble with anticipation. I know it's going to be good.

"I need you," I whisper.

"And you'll have me," he answers, "but not yet. When you're ready."

"I'm ready. I am ready." I try to put as much conviction into the words as I possibly can, but I know there's a very small part of me that wants him for reassurance, for comfort.

"Ari, it's too soon. Everything that's happened, it's too soon for you to make decisions like this. I don't want you to regret it."

I get it. I totally get it. But I'm also surer than anything that it's something I wouldn't regret.

"Let's just get you properly settled, okay?" He cups my face with his hands and kisses my cheek gently. "Stop pouting, it's taking every ounce of my self-control to do this but you need it, Ari."

"Okay. I'll sort things out and prove to you that I'm ready. It's my mission."

"Good girl. Now go and get some sleep." He pushes off the door and frees me from being caged in-between his arms. He takes a key card from his back pocket and slides it in the door, pushing it open for me to enter. He tucks it back into his pocket and smirks at me.

"Just in case."

I open my mouth to say something, but I have no response. I know he won't misuse it or intrude when he's not wanted. I trust him.

He enters, flicks all the lights on and checks the apartment. Seeming satisfied, he returns to me just inside the door and kisses my lips. It's a firm kiss, but as platonic as he can make it. I can tell that he's trying not to start anything again, but it's hard to be near him and not feel charged.

"I'll see you tomorrow, Arianna. Go to bed."

He leaves with his trademark dimple firmly in place. I'm still smiling from the inside, and I don't move even when the door is closed behind me. Part of me expects him to come straight back in, but I know he has more willpower than this. I listen out for the sound of Denham's door closing, then I move away and head to bed.

I get undressed and slip on a tank and boy shorts before climbing between the luxurious ruby-red sheets. I'm bone tired and sleep takes me quickly, but the night isn't kind to me and my slumber doesn't last nearly long enough. A spectrum of feelings and emotions swirl in my head in such a jumble it's hard to make sense of them all. I toss and turn, trying to find some peace, but at 3am I finally give in and get up. The bright moonlight lights my way to the kitchen and I can just about find my way around the cabinets. I lift a glass from the top shelf but my hand catches on one of the other glasses as I take it out. As I panic in the dark to try and catch it, the glass I was holding slips out of my fingertips and falls too.

"Shit." I mutter.

Both glasses fall to the floor and smash into hundreds of little pieces all around me, the sound is deafening in the quiet of the night and it takes a few moments before it is still again. I can't move. I have bare feet and with only the moonlight I can't see where the glass lays.

Another loud bang makes me jump, and the front door flies open, bouncing back off the wall behind it.

"Arianna? Arianna!" Denham shouts frantically.

"Denham, be careful there's glass everywhere."

"Where are you?"

"I'm in the kitchen," I call out to him.

He flicks on the lights. "What the hell happened? Are you okay?" he asks, walking toward me.

"I'm fine, I just wanted some water and the glasses fell." I gesture to the floor covered in spiky shards.

"Don't move," he orders. He's dressed in loose fitting lounger bottoms—nothing else. I watch as he starts to walk toward me, the muscles on his torso stretch and ripple as he moves.

"Denham, no! Your feet ..."

He ignores my protests and navigates the large pieces of glass, but I don't miss his body tensing as the smaller shards dig into his feet. He puts his arms around my back and dips before sweeping his other arm behind my knees and swinging my legs up, holding me close to him.He walks back over the glass, being a little more careful now that he has me in his arms, and continues to carry me into the bedroom.

He places me down carefully in the middle of the bed and goes to the bathroom, closing the door without saying another word. He's hurt, and it's my fault. I give him a few minutes before I tap gently on the bathroom door.

"Denham ... can I come in?" I don't wait for an answer because I know he'll tell me he's fine even if he's not. I crack open the door slowly and find him perched on the edge of the bathtub pulling tiny pieces of glass from one of his feet.

He looks up at me with a tight expression. "It's fine, just give me a minute."

"It's not fine, you're hurt. You're bleeding." I walk to the cabinet beneath the sink, knowing there's a first aid kit there. I open it and pull out antiseptic wipes, then I rummage through my makeup bag and find tweezers.

I kneel down in front of him, taking his foot gently in my hand. "Here, let me." I wince when I take a closer look at his foot. There are several nasty pieces lodged under his soft skin. "I'll be as gentle as I can, okay?"

He nods and I watch him clench his teeth as I pinch one of the shards with my tweezers. I pull gently, not knowing if it's better to go slow, or get it over with quickly, but not wanting to cause any further damage also. When the piece is out, I wipe his foot with the antiseptic, pressing down firmly to stem the bleeding. He watches me intently, but I say nothing, not wanting him to stop me caring for him as he has for me.

After taking the last piece out and cleaning that too, I tidy everything away, then walk back to where he's still sitting silently on the edge of the bath. I wrap my arms around his shoulders and bury my head in his neck.

"I'm sorry," I whisper.

His arms slide around me and his fingers find their way under my tank to rest on my back. "Don't be sorry, you didn't do anything."

"It's my fault your feet are cut," I whisper, feeling guilty.

"Don't talk crazy, Arianna."

"Then why are you mad?"

"You think I'm mad? Ari, I'm not mad." He shakes his head softly.

"Then why the silent treatment?"

He shrugs. "No one other than my mom has ever cared for me like that. I don't think anyone has ever wanted to."

I don't know what to say to that. I'm sad for him that no one has wanted to look after him the way he has me, but I'm also glad that no one else has done that too. Selfishly, I want to be the only one who cares for him. I want to tell him that I'd do it every day if he wants me too, but I don't know where those thoughts are coming from and why. He's right. There is a whole tangle of things to think through, but I'm certain of one thing. He makes everything easier just by being around. I'm happy to let him take care of me, and I want to take care of him.

"Come on, Stunner, it's the middle of the night and you need to rest."

"Will you stay with me tonight?" I ask without hesitation.

"Will you sleep better if I stay?"

"Yes, the bed is too big when I'm on my own."

I love having a huge, plush bed to myself, but after having slept with Denham wrapped around me last night, my bed feels cold and lonely without him.

Denham turns all the lights out and we climb into bed. I wriggle until my back is flush with his front, and his arm pulls me in close, his fingers lacing with mine. Our even breaths synchronize and we drift into a very peaceful sleep.

# Chapter 12

I wake to the sound of a continuous dull thud. It takes a couple of minutes to clear the sleep fog before it dawns on me that I'm not dreaming and I can actually hear this repeated sound. I sit bolt upright, and try to figure out where the sound is coming from. It's not in the apartment, but it's close.

Denham is still fast asleep so I shake him by the shoulder to wake him up. He groans and stirs but shows no sign of waking fully, so I whip the covers back. "Wake up, Denham, there's someone out there." That gets him. He sits up fast and springs out of bed.

"I think someone is banging on your door across the hall, it's been going on for ages."

"That's it?" he grumbles. "Whoever is banging can wait. Or even better, they can go away."

I watch his stomach ripple as he runs his hands through his now mussed up hair. The just got out of bed suits him very well. In fact, he owns it. I let my eyes roam down the angular lines of his jaw, across his broad shoulders and then down over his sculpted torso. The lines of his body seem to lead me to that sexy V which draws my eyes downwards under those cotton lounge pants which I just want to ...

"Are you objectifying me, Arianna?" he questions.

*Oh god. Ground, just open up and swallow me whole.* "I ... um, I ..." I cover my now very red face with my hands and let myself fall backwards.

He climbs back in, and I feel him place his hands either side of my head as he straddles me with his legs and covers me with his body, pushing me into the mattress. He kisses my hands in turn so gently it sends shivers down my arms. "Look at me," he orders softly.

I shake my head from side to side. I'm mortally embarrassed. I have no idea what just came over me, and even worse, I'm fighting with myself not to uncover my eyes and finish my visual exploration of Denham's amazing body.

"I said, look at me."

I spread my fingers and peek through the gap.

"Arianna." He chuckles. "Take your hands away."

"I can't," I mumble and screw my eyes tight shut.

Peeling my fingers back one by one, he takes my hands in his, then rests them gently on either side of my head as he tangles his fingers with mine. There's no getting out of the firm grip he has me in.

"Open your eyes," he demands softly. I open them slowly and I'm met with his golden gaze. He has soft creases in the corners of his eyes that make his face more handsome somehow. "You want to look at me?"

*Oh, god ...* Yes, I want to look at him but I don't know how to say yes. "Denham," I protest and turn my head to the side in total embarrassment.

"Arianna, I don't know who taught you that you should be embarrassed, but whoever did it is an asshole." I turn my head slowly, making sure to look just at his face. "Don't be ashamed of your desires. If you want to look, then look. I work damn hard to keep in shape and I like that you want to look at me."

My eyes want to travel. They want to explore every inch. I don't even know why I'm protesting so much. Sex has always just been sex. Even with Aaron it was just sex between two people. There was no mutual appreciation. I think we did it just because that's what couples do. Don't get me wrong, it was good at the time ... I think. I didn't really have anything positive to compare it to. It was a physical exchange. Not one I craved or needed. There wasn't this electric charge I can feel thrumming through my body every time I even so much as think about Denham.

"Don't zone out on me, Stunner. It's me and you right now. Don't let it be anything else. No past. No demons. Just us."

For a moment, it crosses my mind that the knocking has stopped, but Denham distracts me again. He takes our entwined hands and places my palms flat on his chest. I feel his pulse accelerating under my touch and mine speeds to catch up."Close your eyes," he says softly. I hesitate for a moment. "Trust me."

I let my lids fall shut.

He covers my hands with his and guides them slowly over his skin ... over the curve of his pecs ... down the planes of his torso ... Silky, soft skin covers hard, granite muscle and every sense is heightened as the pads of my fingers tingle with sensation, feeling every bump and ripple. I let him guide my hands over his body, each second getting easier.

I want it. I crave it.

I hold my breath as he traces his V with the tips of my index fingers and a soft growl escapes from his lips. He stops, holding my hands still and breathes deep when we reach the band of his pants. I don't know if he's bracing himself to continue or willing himself to stop. I slowly open my eyes to look up into his face. His eyes are pools of inky black, pupils dilated so I can't see the gold flecks in his eyes. I watch his chest rapidly rise and fall as I wait on his next move, guided by him and not my embarrassment.

"So beautiful," he whispers. "It's gonna be so sweet, Stunner, and worth every second that we wait." He groans huskily.

"Still set on that waiting idea, huh?" I joke.

"It might take every ounce of my self-restraint, but yes. We're waiting until your mind is healthy and your heart is healed." He kisses me hard on the mouth and climbs off the bed. "So what would you like to do today?"

"You wind me up, tighter than a coiled spring, then you ask me what I'd like to do?"

Nervous tension.

Sexual tension.

*All* the tension from the past few days is building inside of me and it's starting to make me irritable.

"What's up? You don't have any self-restraint?" He snickers.

"You think this is funny?" I reply, my voice raising an octave. I hop off the bed and stomp toward him, poking him in the chest. "I asked you a question. Do you think that it's funny to frustrate me then make me wait?" I dig him hard in the center of the chest with my index finger a second time.

"Well ..."

I place a hand on my cocked hip and wait for his reply. His demeanor changes and the air suddenly feels chilly. I feel my skin prickle across my shoulders as his eyes hold mine in a hard gaze, then he takes a step closer to me, causing me to shuffle backwards until the back of my legs touch the bed.

"You think I would take pleasure in giving you any discomfort?" He snatches up my hand, making me jump. "You think I take pleasure in this?" He pushes my hand into his crotch and holds me there as I curl my fingers around him—thick, hot and hard.

Waves of pleasure push through my body and settle in my core. I don't think I've ever felt sensations in my body like this. I'm turned on and wishing there were none of his stupid rules, wishing there were no layers of clothing between us.

He lets go of my hand, dropping his head and taking a deep breath.I don't let my hand fall away like I'm sure he expects me to. Instead, I push my palm further into him, stepping forward and tilting my head so our cheeks are touching.

"I don't want you to be uncomfortable. I'm trying to prove to you that I'm not broken and I don't need fixing."

"What do you need, Arianna?"

"I need you to stop treating me like a fragile bird." The flimsy cotton of his pants does nothing to conceal his arousal as I rub slowly up and down his length. His eyes flutter closed, getting lost in the sensation, and his pelvis tilts as he pushes into my hand.

I move closer and speak against his lips, "Stop being a gentleman, Mr. King. I need a man."

His hand wraps around my wrist and pulls me away from his groin, making me gasp. "Don't push me, Arianna," he grits out "You are testing me ... Christ, you would test the patience of a saint, and I'm trying to do the right thing here, dammit."

He scrubs his hands through his unruly hair and pushes past me to the bathroom, then shoves the door hard with his foot. It slams behind him, the noise reverberating through the entire apartment so hard that I feel my insides rattle.

*Ugh*, I handled that terribly. I actually have no idea how to deal with feelings of lust and frustration because I've never had to. He's the only man who has ever brought it out in me. The only man who has ever made me feel desired. I desire him too. So much. He treats me with respect, but I've pushed him. I don't want him to do something he's not entirely comfortable with and it dawns on me that I've been unfair. In my wants and desires I've been selfish and thoughtless.

I head to the kitchen and make a coffee, but there's still glass everywhere and I have nothing to clean it up with. He needs space for a few minutes and I need to calm myself before I push him further away, so I take up my usual position on the balcony, I rest my elbows on the wall. As usual, the world walks on by, seemingly trouble-free. What if he doesn't want anything to do with me now? What if he finally takes my advice and decides it's best for him to steer clear? He could cut ties and never look back. But could I?

Maybe he's right. Maybe I am broken. Maybe I was never really whole in the first place.

I hear gentle footsteps behind me and I stiffen, bracing myself for the ache that I'm already starting to feel if he walks away. I close my eyes and when I can no longer hear his footsteps, I wait for the sound of the closing door.

It doesn't come.

Instead, bare arms snake around my waist and pull me in tightly as Denham nestles his chin in my shoulder and buries his nose in my hair."I'm sorry." His apology is barely audible, but no less sincere. "I wasn't trying to tease and frustrate you. I can't keep my hands off you, Ari. I don't *want* to keep my hands off you. But you've ..." He loosens his arms and turns me to face him. "You've been through so much, Arianna. I just want you to know what you're doing and not feel like it's what you *should* be doing. You have a choice, you always have a choice, and I'm going to make you see that." The lines of his jaw are still sharp and angular, but his features are soft. The look in his eyes is enough to get lost in and the little smile he is giving me hints that the best is yet to come.

I scold myself for immediately thinking the worst. I need to start ruling my past and not let my past rule me. "I'm sorry too. Can we start today over?" I ask hopefully.

"I'd like that. Can I cook you breakfast?"

"I don't know. Can you cook?"

"Smart ass. I'll have you know that I make the best pancakes and bacon. Now, go get some clothes on that hot little tush."

Denham steps to the side and swats my ass as I walk past and I squeal and jog to the bedroom, unsure if he's going to follow. I secretly want him to, but I know he won't. He'll be the gentleman and give me space to get dressed without the distraction of his impressive body and the risk of us hitting that damn wall he's decided to put up.

I throw on dark blue jeans and a white tank, then rake a brush through my unruly hair and tie it all up in a messy bun. I decide against putting shoes on as we are only going across the hall. "Okay, let's go, chef," I call out as I walk back through the lounge.

Denham is in my now favorite spot on the balcony. The morning sunlight dances across his broad shoulders and I take him in as he takes in the world below. His triangular torso is sculpted to perfection—the kind of body that makes your fingers itch with the desire to touch. If he stood still in the street, I'm sure he would have people stopping just to admire.

He turns and smirks. "Ready for breakfast, Stunner?"

I nod, and he steps into me, taking my hand in his and kissing my cheek before leading me through the penthouse. He pulls open the door with his free hand, strides through, then stops abruptly. I slam into his shoulder and look up to find a tall, skinny blonde propped against the wall by the elevator. She looks almost as surprised to see us as we do her, but she composes herself quickly and slips on a mask of confidence.

"Well, well, well ..." the blonde says, drawing the words out. "What do we have here? A little whore to keep you busy for a few days?"

Denham strides forward, taking me with him. His grip on my hand is tight, bordering on uncomfortable. "What the hell are you doing here?" he grates out.

"It seems we do have things to discuss after all ..." the blonde replies, starting to look smug.

"Like what? The only thing I'm discussing with you is which way you are going to leave this building."

"Denham, baby, that's not very well mannered of you. You haven't even introduced me to your ... friend." She looks me up and down, taking in our joined hands and curls her lip. The way she calls him baby makes my hackles rise and I'm consumed with jealousy that she uses an endearment for him. I'm also repulsed.

I've never felt such an intense dislike radiating from someone, the way it's coming from Denham at this moment. I know his grip on my hands indicates that he still wants me here, but I'm starting to feel really uncomfortable. "I'm going to leave—"

"No," Denham barks. "You're not going anywhere. Amy was just leaving." He steps forward and pushes the button for the elevator. He still has my hand, so when he moves I'm jerked forward. I wiggle my fingers to free myself of his grasp, but he tightens, not letting me go.

"Denham, you seem to have lost your manners. I don't know why you're getting so uptight." She speaks in a confident voice, but I don't miss the underlying unease.

The elevator doors open and Denham gestures with his head toward them. Amy stands in the opening, one hand braced on the side, her body slightly twisted to show off her long twig like legs. She's as tall as Denham, so she levels him with her slate-blue eyes. There's no softness there; just a hard, cold sneer.

"Call me ... lover," she drawls, the sickly sweet sound of her voice making the hairs on the back of my neck stand up. I've never taken such an instant dislike to someone. "This one you have here is pretty. Call me when you're starting to get bored with her, maybe we can have a three-way. It's been a while since we've done that, and I know how much you enjoyed it." She ends her words with a loaded smile before stepping back and pressing the button to descend. She manages to blow a kiss just before the elevator doors close.

"Fucking woman!" Denham yells. He pounds the elevator door with his free hand out of frustration, and I finally manage to wiggle my fingers out of his grasp, but he spins and reaches for me, his face softening. "I'm so sorry, Arianna, Amy is ..."

While he searches for the words, I fill them in for him. "Your ex? A bitch? Psychopathic?"

He lets out a strained laugh. "Yes, all of those things plus a few more."

"Was she the one you were arguing with the other day?"

"Yes." His brows crease. "How did you know that?"

"The door was ajar when I came back and I heard a guitar playing, so I stood to listen. Then there was yelling, and I didn't want to stand there and hear it all. It was none of my business."

I clasp my hands in front of me and wonder if I'm strong enough to deal with his complications. I have enough of my own without getting involved with a man who clearly has a very pissed off ex-girlfriend. Plus, there's the little mention of him being involved in a three-way. I don't know why that grates me, but it does. It's totally irrational that I don't want him to have had an experience like that, and it's even more irrational that I don't want him to have been with anyone else, *ever*, in that way. It's jealousy that I can't do anything about, but it's there and I've never had to deal with it before.

"I'm sorry she was here. She must have been the one banging on my door this morning. When you heard us arguing it was because I'd taken her keys. She's pissed at me for cutting her out of my personal life. I should have changed the code for the elevator ..."

I just nod. If she hadn't gotten up here, I might not have known about her at all, so best to get it all out in the open now. "You have any more ex-girlfriends I should know about?" I ask.

"None"

"Okay." I hesitate before continuing. "Was she telling the truth about you having a threesome?" I don't really know why I asked him that, but I want to know. I want to know what the chances are of him getting bored with me and needing more than I can give.

"Arianna." He sighs. "I'll tell you anything you want, but can we do it in my place ...with coffee? I don't really want to discuss this in the hallway."

He holds out his hand for me to take and I gingerly place my hand in his. He holds it tenderly and smiles to reassure me as we walk through his apartment. He seats me at the breakfast bar and says nothing until he's made me a coffee and changed into jeans and a black tee. It's such simple attire but really quite breathtaking on the right frame. *And he has the right frame ...*

He rests his hands on the breakfast bar. "Can we talk while I cook?" he asks.

"Sure, you can talk and cook. I'll listen."

I watch him move around his kitchen, silently collecting ingredients for breakfast. He puts some bacon under the grill and whisks a mixture together for pancakes. "I'm sorry you had to bump into Amy like that. I would have told you about her you know?"

I raise my brows at him and say nothing.

"Okay, here it is in a nutshell ... You know my dad died three years ago. Well, it was unexpected ..." He takes a deep breath before he continues. "He was shot. We never expected anything like that could happen to our little family and it chewed us up and spat us out. The Kingdom had debts and Dad was in trouble. Although I worked with him every day, I never knew the extent of the trouble we were in. I needed investors or it was going to be closed down. Amy invested. She is a silent partner in The Kingdom, and we were kind of together for a long time. It was comfortable, convenient."

He looks up through his dark lashes warily, bracing his arms on the counter. "If I had an itch, she scratched it. It was the same for her too. We used each other. It was unfulfilling, and was never meant to be long term. Before your crazy mind starts ticking away and coming to all the wrong conclusions, that is not what's happening here. You're not some meaningless distraction that I want to forget about."

I nod slowly, taking it all in and processing his words. It's a lot to process. I didn't actually need him to tell me what was happening between us, and I'm hyper aware that what is happening with us is not meaningless.

"Wow, that's a lot to take in," I say, a little stunned "So you're not grooming me to join in with one of your three-way sessions with her?" I look at him pointedly and he visibly shrinks.

"No! Fuck, I hate that she brought that up. Yes, we did it once, but like I said, she and I were insignificant." He comes around to where I'm sitting and grips the back of the chair, turning me so I'm in front of him. He pushes my knees apart with his legs and settles between them, then his hands cup my face and he tilts my head until we're looking directly at each other.

"I know you must think I'm selfish and shallow after this morning, but I'm not. I will not share you whether it's male, female or battery operated. I will be everything you need me to be and I'm damn sure I can satisfy you enough for you to never look any further." His determined explanation goes some way to reassuring me that I'm not a pawn in their twisted idea of a relationship. "We have something Ari. I don't know what it is, but there's something. Everything is different with you, and I don't intend to let that go. When I see that sparkle in your eye, and it's coming in my direction, I feel like I'm holding all the aces." He searches my eyes for a reaction to his honest words. "Does that scare you?" he asks sincerely.

"Yes," I answer honestly. "It terrifies the hell out of me. I've been in two relationships, and both have ended very badly. I don't want to be hurt again."

"I won't hurt you," he says resolutely, and I believe him.

He's right. This does feel different to anything else I've ever felt. I'm opening my heart wide and it scares me.The smell of burning breaks the moment.

"Shit!" Denham flies around the breakfast bar and pulls some very black bacon from the grill, then drops the pan on the countertop and mutters expletives.

Laughter bubbles out of my chest. "Breakfast smells good, chef."

"You distracted me! I can't cook breakfast with distractions."

"Me? I didn't do anything!"

"You look too good. You smell too good. You taste too good ..." His eyes narrow and he starts to walk slowly toward me. Every nerve starts to twitch as anticipation starts to take over and neither of us look away.

I'm determined not to break first, but my nerves get the better of me and I hop off the stool and run toward the balcony doors, laughing as I go. He breaks a split second after me, but with the length of his legs and obvious prowess, he's faster. I manage to get to the leather couch before I'm tackled and brought down, trapped under his body as adrenaline runs rapidly through both of us. Giggling and panting hard, we lie together in a heap of tangled arms and legs. I have no doubt that I will never be left wanting with this man.

He thrills me. He electrifies my senses.

*He warms my soul.*

# Chapter 13

After burning his attempt at breakfast, Denham reluctantly decides that we should go out and eat.

I'm slightly shaken by the surprise meeting with Amy this morning, and disappointed that if I want to spend time with Denham, I'm going to have to deal with a crazy assed ex-girlfriend who's sizing me up for a threesome. I find myself scanning the area surrounding us for any sign of her, and it doesn't take long for my doubtful mind to start working overtime and going downhill. It seems so much easier to stay upbeat when all around good things are happening but the minute something happens to break my happy bubble, all the doubts and negativity come screaming toward me and I can't makes sense of it all. By the time breakfast arrives, I've lost my appetite, so I drink my coffee and push my food around my plate. I automatically answer when Denham speaks but I can't disguise the fact that I'm distracted.

"Out with it."

"Sorry?" I query.

"You're distracted. There's clearly something on your mind and I'm sure that by keeping it all inside, you're making everything ten times bigger. Talk it out."

"Bigger? I'm not sure how it can be any bigger than it actually is." My voice rises past the acceptable volume for a restaurant, but I can't contain it. Denham slides his hand across the table, covering mine, but I snatch it away. "How dare you tell me I'm exaggerating. My husband hit me, hunted me down, and then almost went up in a ball of flames. I shouldn't even be here because my ex fiancé beat me so bad he nearly killed me. And to top it all off, I'm not the only one that has a psychopathic ex!" I spit the words out, fast, furious and out of control.

"Arianna—" he speaks calmly, but I don't let him continue.

"Don't you fucking *Arianna* me. I don't need this shit. I just—"

Denham is out of his chair before I can blink the wall of tears away. He lifts me up and wraps his arms around me, pulling me into him, and I don't try to fight him. I don't want to. He strokes my hair, letting me sob into his chest as I cry, letting it all out like a caged animal that's been given freedom for the very first time.

The steady heartbeat I can hear through Denham's chest and the rhythmic feeling of his fingers in my hair has the calming effect that I need and finally the sobs escaping from my chest become quieter, turning into little hiccups. I release my arms from the tight bundle in front of me and encircle them around his waist.

The tension releases in his chest and he brings both hands up to my face, running his fingers past my temples and through my hair. He secures his hands at the nape of my neck and dips his head to kiss my cheek. Kissing the path of my tears, he kisses my closed eyelids with such tenderness it pulls at my heart, then his lips press softly on my bruised cheekbone, lingering there a fraction longer as if needing more of his tenderness to heal. He continues until no part of my face has been left un-kissed.

"I'm sorry. I—" The words catch on a sob and I begin to wonder how I can balance being brave and sticking up for myself with allowing good things to happen.

"Don't be sorry." He nuzzles his head into mine. "You've been through a lot. I just ... I want you to know that you don't have to fight it all on your own. Don't try to fight the things in your head, Arianna."

"It's always been that way, I don't know any different."

His muscles bunch at my statement. "That's because you didn't know me. I'm truly sorry that you have had to deal with all that shit on your own. If I could take it all away for you, I would, but I can't. What I *can* do is help you *now*."

"I need to see Aaron," I blurt out of nowhere. "I need to explain everything to him." I don't know why I feel I owe him an explanation, I just do. I hate the lies. I hate living a lie. It's taken me a while to try and get my head around things and I think I need to make sure I have closure on the things from my past before I can fully embrace the future. "I'm sorry I made a scene."

"Arianna, look at me. Do I look like I give a fuck what these people think?" I shake my head. "Then stop apologizing for being who you are. You need to yell? Yell. You need to cry? Cry. If I ever find the bastard that made you sorry for every goddamn breath you take, then I'm going to damage him beyond repair." His voice has risen considerably and his shoulders have drawn back in taut ropes of muscle that are bunching under my fingertips. I feel a warm blanket fold around me at his words. He makes me feel protected.

"Can we please start today over?" I say hopefully.

He softens, kissing me on the forehead. "I have to do some work today. But I have someone I'd like you to meet first." He takes my hand and starts to lead me out.

"Denham, wait. I'm not dressed to meet people. I have no makeup and ... stop walking, will you?"

He stops and turns to me with amused expression.

"You look amazing as you are." When I open my mouth to protest, he holds up a finger to my lips. "Do. Not. Argue."

"I'm not going to argue, I promise." I take a deep breath before continuing as I know he's not going to like this. "Now that I've made a decision, I have to see Aaron before I can do anything. This is me taking control, okay? This is something I have to do to move forward ..."

The air lingers between us before he answers. "Fine, but I'm coming too."

"I don't think that's a good idea. I'm fine to go on my own—"

"I'm coming," he says firmly, leaving no room for arguments. "Let's go."

We hail a cab to the main hospital. It's a short ride, but there is a tight silence as both of us look out of opposite windows, deep in thought but with our hands still joined and resting on my lap. I know Denham doesn't want me to do this. He's protective—not overbearing or obsessive, but he actually wants to look after me. I have to do this, though. I have to see Aaron and get some answers. Some kind of closure in that part of my life so that I can begin to move on.

The cab pulls up and Denham pays him before exiting and taking my hand a little tighter than he did before, I'm not sure if it's a gesture of reassurance for me or him.

He strides to the main desk and commands attention from one of the nurses there. "I'm looking for an Aaron Jamesson," he asks sharply.

The nurse puts on a friendly face and answers confidently, "And who might you be, sir?"

Denham pauses for a moment and I take the opportunity to step in and answer. "I'm Aaron's wife," I say, dropping Denham's hand and placing both hands on the desk. Denham narrows his eyes at me and I can see that he's not happy about it—*at all.* I stare pointedly at him, imploring him not to make a fuss here. I know that being Aaron's wife will get me in to see him and that's the only reason I did it. Holding someone else's hand while professing to be married to someone else would not have been convincing. I don't miss the nurse glance toward my ring finger where, of course, she finds no wedding ring.

"If you'll just give me a minute." She taps on the keyboard in front of her. "I'm sorry, but it appears that Mr. Jamesson checked out early this morning. That's all I can disclose." She smiles a public service smile before going back to her work.

I'm disappointed. Not because I really wanted to see him, I wasn't looking forward to it in the slightest, but I feel lighter having made the decision to come here and face him. I feel stronger for taking control and doing something about my situation. Now, it's out of my hands and all I can do now is look forward.

I turn to leave and take Denham's hand. Both of us go to speak, but neither of us knows what to say, so we leave the hospital and walk for a while, swinging our joined hands and letting the air clear, letting our thoughts become more rational before either of us speaks.

Denham breaks the silence. "I'm sorry he wasn't there," he says unconvincingly.

"No, you're not," I say with a smile.

"No, you're right ... kind of." He smiles back at me. "I didn't want you to see him, but I knew you wanted to, so I'm sorry you didn't get what you wanted."

"I just wanted to straighten things out. Explain everything to him."

"You don't owe him anything," Denham says protectively.

"I owe him an explanation. I'm not who he thought I was. No matter what he's done, I should at least explain that to him. I'm also worried that he's in some kind of trouble. He's not a bad person, and though I never really loved him, I care that he's ok."

"Well, he's a big boy, I'm sure he can deal with his own shit." His jaw is set hard, and he's looking everywhere but at me.

"Hey, stop that," I scold, swatting at his upper arm playfully. "Stop acting like a child who doesn't want to give up his toys."

"You're not a toy," he grumbles. "And I most certainly will not give you up."

I laugh and shake my head. "You're being cute again."

"I'm going to ban you from saying that word," he grumbles.

"You're sweet." I stop on the sidewalk and wrap myself around him.

He strokes my hair. "Try again ...""Funny?"

"Hmmm ..."

"Sexy?"

"Now you're getting there." He chuckles. He kisses the top of my head, then rests his cheek there. "Arianna, if you need to find him then we will, but you must promise me that you're not going to try to do it alone."

"Okay," I mumble into his chest.

He strokes my hair then rests his hand gently on the back of my head. His chest rises and he releases a deep breath. "Would you like to start today over? From now?"

"Yes, I really would." I close my eyes and breathe in the warmth and safety of Denham's chest.

"Good because I have somewhere I'd like to take you."

We walk in companionable silence, hand in hand, fingers entwined, taking in the warmth of the morning sun. We stop at a boutique, and Denham looks down at me with a smile and a wink before we walk through the large, highly polished, glass doors.

A tall, elegant lady looks up from behind the main desk and a smile graces her perfectly painted features. Her long chestnut hair is tied up in a smooth ponytail that swishes from side to side as she walks toward us. Dressed in an immaculate, midnight-blue pantsuit, she exudes class. I feel extremely underdressed in jeans and a tank, and I'm cursing Denham in my head for letting me come here so unprepared. Hell, I don't even have a scrap of makeup on.

"Well, hello there. If it isn't my favorite King." She laughs. "Denham, it's wonderful to see you." She greets him with a warm smile and a kiss on both cheeks and I'm immediately jealous. It's irrational and unjustified, but I can't help it. I don't want him to be her favorite anything. I'm hoping and praying that these two don't have a history together because I'm not sure my emotions are under control enough to filter what comes from my mouth.

She turns to me with the same genuinely happy expression on her face. "And this must be the lovely lady you were telling me about."

Denham squeezes my hand and looks at me with what I can only describe as pride, and I feel the tension in my shoulders soften. "Beth, this is Arianna. Arianna, this is a very good friend of mine, and the person you can thank for my sense of style, Beth."

"Arianna ..." Beth clasps her surprisingly warm hands on either side of my cheeks and kisses me as she did Denham. I'm a little taken aback at her openness, but I don't find it offensive. Instead, it's warming and I find myself liking her already. "Look at that magnificent bone structure. Girl, have you ever done modeling?"

"I ... uh, no, I haven't, ma'am," I stutter.

"Oh please, no formalities. It's Beth," she corrects.

"Okay, Beth."

"You are every photographer's dream. Maybe a little shy, but we'll work on that."

Denham laughs. "Give the girl a chance, Beth. We've only been in the door two minutes and you're making plans already.""You know me, Den, no point wasting time. Always on the lookout for new faces," she says frankly.

"Well, Arianna is very interested in the fashion industry. I thought you'd be the best person to come and see."

"Oh! This is?" Beth says with wide eyed recognition, and Denham nods. "The one who?" Denham nods again in answer to her bizarre question.

"Oh, dear lord. Why didn't you say? Come with me, Arianna. We have things to discuss." Beth takes my spare hand and I look between her and Denham, catching a wink that he throws her way before letting my hand drop reluctantly. "Cancel any plans you had together. I want your Arianna for at least a few hours. Go on ... I'll call you when we're done." She makes a shooing motion with her hand, and just like that, Denham is affectionately dismissed.

He steps forward and kisses my cheek. "I guess I'll be back later when you're done whatever it is that you girls are doing."

I smile, not knowing what to say. Not really knowing what's happening but none of it feels bad, in fact, it all feels really amazing.

Beth wastes no time, marching me to the back of the shop. I try and take in the rails and shelves of designer clothes around me, but her stiletto covered feet are moving too fast and I'm trying to keep up. We go through a mirrored door and into what I can only guess is her stock room, filled to the brim with designer clothing. She grabs a dress off one of the rails and holds it up—floor length and cut on the bias with a plunging neckline adorned with tiny crystals that sparkle when the light hits them. It's beautiful. I reach out and touch the silk, running my finger along the delicate stitching on the neckline. Any woman who wears this dress will feel like a million dollars, I'm certain of it.

"You like?" Beth asks confidently, already knowing that I will.

"I love it, Beth, it really is a quality piece." *It probably has a quality price tag too.*

"Yes, it's a one off. I know the designer and managed to secure it." She hangs it carefully back on the rail before pulling out another dress to show me.

"Okay, tell me honestly, what do you think of this?" She holds out the next dress—blue, green and yellow in an explosion of patterns and swirls. It's illegally short and one of the most disgusting dresses I've ever seen, but how do I tell her that when I've known her for approximately five minutes. She owns a high class, designer boutique on the Las Vegas Strip and she's asking *me* what I think.

"Your face says it all darling. Be brutal ..."

"I ..."

"Just say the words that were going through your head when you pulled those faces not ten seconds ago."

I decide to be as tactful as I can. "I think ... the colors are a little too much for me. The patterns are garish, and I'm sorry Beth, I really, really ...hate it." *Oh shit.* I hadn't meant that to come out. She said be honest, and it was actually easier than I thought it would be, but now I'm standing here watching her flat expression, and not really knowing what to say or do next.

Beth suddenly dissolves into hysterics, holding onto my shoulder for support as she roars with laughter. It's contagious and I laugh with her. Before long we're both holding our stomachs and wiping tears from our cheeks.

"You're hired," Beth says as she calms her giggles.

"What?"

"Oh, I'm sorry, Arianna. Would you like a job?" she offers more seriously.

"You're offering me a job?" I ask in disbelief. She nods. "Yes, I'd love a job!" I have no idea what job she is offering me. For all I know, it's the job of errand girl or coffee maker, but I don't care. I know I would love to work here.

"Good, I need a buyer, someone with class and style, but most importantly I need someone who isn't going to blow smoke up my ass. If you don't like the clothes, I want you to tell me. Got it?"

"A buyer?" Shit. I know what I like, and I have a pretty good understanding of the fashion world, but I don't know if I'm good enough to make decisions like that. I have no experience and...

"Denham said you would do this."

"Pardon me?" I question.

"He said you would, and I quote, 'Talk to yourself in your head'. What are you worried about?"

"I ... I'm not sure I'm experienced enough to be given such a responsibility."

"He said you'd do that too ..."

"Do what?" I question, slightly irritated at having to guess what she's talking about.

"Put yourself down."

"I—"

"Listen to me, Arianna. I won't feed you any bullshit if you give me the same respect in return. Speak to me. I want your input. From here on in, you need to believe in yourself and trust your instincts, understand?" I nod. "Good girl."

"Did Denham tell you to give me a job?" I query. As much as I think it would be a sweet gesture, I want to make my way on my own. I want to do it myself.

"There you go again, doubting your ability. He most certainly did not tell me to do anything. I would *never* hire anyone on his say-so, or anyone else's for that matter. If you work here, you've earned it on merit alone. My instincts haven't let me down yet and they're telling me that you and I will get along just fine."

She doesn't look like the kind of person who would take an uncalculated risk. She takes no prisoners and makes no apologies for it, but I feel at ease with her. She's similar to Denham—no pretense and no ulterior motive. What you see is what you get. It's far easier to be yourself when you know you don't need to change to please someone. If I had trusted my instincts up until now, I never would have married Aaron and I would have left Jonny long before things got really bad.

"But he did tell you about me?" I know I shouldn't pry, but I can't help it.

"Yes, we're good friends. Denham has been there for me through some tough times. When he told me about this beautiful young woman he met, I just had to meet you. So, tell me ..." Her voice softens as she brings her perfectly manicured hand up to touch my bruised cheek with her index finger. "Is he sorting this out?"

"Yes," I whisper.

"Good. Denham King isn't your average asshole, Arianna. He's one of the good guys. Let yourself go, just a little bit. You'll soon learn that he'll always be there to catch you." She smiles kindly and removes her hand. "Now, what do you say to coffee?" It breaks the intensity and I am so grateful. "And then it's time for the fun part. We need to get you dressed for your new role."

"I'd really love that, Beth." I answer with genuine enthusiasm and awe for how this day is turning out.

After five hours at the boutique, I am loaded down with bags. Denham seems to be running late, so I decide to go back to the Kingdom alone. I have a problem accepting gifts; every gift I've ever received in the past has been tainted with guilt and used as a method of persuasion, or given as a gesture of apology. But Beth has told me that the bags are not full of gifts, and to consider it a uniform of sorts. Needless to say, I don't think Beth has any other motive than to employ me and make me work my ass off. She has convinced me that I need to look good if I'm going to be working with her. Everything is starting to come together, like little pieces of a jigsaw puzzle.

*With the exception of a small corner of my heart that won't let me forget the past.*

That black thought drains any positivity I've gained throughout the day. How am I going to deal with this and move on? I can't keep going back and forth in my mind. The directional changes have me feeling dizzy. I've grown to be a pro at detaching from reality, but if I retreat back into my own head it will be the end to all the new starts I've made. I want to feel the passion and desire I've recently discovered.

I want to *feel*.

"Wait up!" A voice snaps me out of my daydream and I turn to find Lottie bouncing toward me. When she reaches me, she bends and puts her hands on her knees, panting for breath. "Are you deaf or something, woman? I've been calling you for a couple blocks!"

"Sorry. Looks like someone needs to hit the gym. Unfit, much?"

"Don't you start. Spike is always nagging me about keeping fit. Whose side are you on?" she retorts sharply, now with her hands on her hips.

"Hey, merely making a statement."

Her face turns curious. "What'cha got there? Had a little retail therapy?" She tries to peek in one of the bags. "Arianna Fraser, are you a bloody millionaire and just haven't told me yet, or did Denham give you his AMEX? Because there is no way your average person could afford to even look in the direction of the Chique Boutique on the Strip, let alone shop there. Yet here you are with no less than ..." she pauses while she counts, "... FIVE bags, full to the top! Spill it ..."

A grin spreads across my face. "I have a job!" I say excitedly.

"Doing what? Are you the new CEO of a multibillion dollar company?" she quips.

"No, silly. At Chique. I'm their new assistant buyer."

"You're fucking kidding me! Ari, that's awesome!" She launches herself at me in true Lottie fashion, her arms wrapped tightly around my neck so I can hardly breathe. I'm pretty sure that if she could wrap her legs around me like a baby chimp she would. "You know what this means? It means you're sticking around! And how much discount do you get to give your closest, bestest friend?" Her grin stretches the whole width of her face and her eyes are wide like a child's at Christmas. "Let's go celebrate!" Lottie chirps. "We need champagne, lots of it!"

"Whoa there, just a minute. I'm not rich, so let's not go spending my money before I've earned it."

"Arianna, I love you, but stop being so fucking sensible. Live a little. You have a millionaire boyfriend who will gladly fill us up with champagne because he will quite possibly be more happy about you staying than I am."

"He is not my boyfriend."

"No? Well, what is he then because I sure as hell know that he's something. I've never seen him so rapt. And you, missy, your eyes are starting to show that twinkling light again." Nothing gets past her. "So, what is it? Boyfriend? More?" she asks impatiently.

"I don't know, Lottie," I snap. I don't mean to bite the words out, but I'm not used to all this dating business. How many dates before you're a couple? Is he my boyfriend? Just a friend? "I don't have an answer for you ... hell, I don't even have an answer for myself," I mumble.

"Ari, stop negating everything. Positive things do happen, and you have to learn to let them." She rubs her hand up and down my arm and I nod in acknowledgement to her words. *Easier said than done.* I know she's right. I want to look ahead, but I'm afraid of disappointment if I look too far.

"You need a damn good night out, girl. The three D's." She wink s."Drinks, Dancing, and Denham." She waggles her brows. "And I'm thinking in that order. Just so you know, I'll only be doing the drinking and dancing with you. You can *do* Denham on your own." She smirks, pointing a finger at me.

"Lottie!" I say, shocked at her directness, but I know I shouldn't be, she always speaks her mind and it's part of why I love her.

"What? And why are your cheeks flushed? Have you... did you do it already?" she blurts.

"No!" I squeal. I turn and start to walk back toward the hotel. Sex has not really been something I'm comfortable doing, let alone talking about. It's never been a great experience, and certainly not all hearts, flowers and orgasms like everyone makes it out to be.

Lottie is hot on my heels and fishing for information. "Come on, Ari, give me some info. I know you haven't slept on your own for the last two nights. Did you guys even kiss yet?"

"How do you know that I haven't slept alone?"

"Duh, my boyfriend is Denham's brother. When he couldn't get hold of him at his place, he asked why. It's nothing more sinister than that. So, you cleverly avoided my question. Did you kiss yet?"

I sigh—inwardly and audibly. I want to tell her everything.

*How* he kissed me and ruined me for anyone else.

*How* his nearly naked body has been wrapped around me for the last few nights.

*How* my body went into overdrive when he pressed my hand to his crotch.

*How* I want him so badly that my whole damn body hums whenever I think about him.

"Girl, that faraway look tells me you need to get laid."

"Lottie, not everything is about sex, you know."

She links her arm in mine and giggles. "No, but it makes for a damn good time along the way. Come on, I'll call Spike and tell him we're going out tonight. In the meantime, we're going to charge a bottle of champagne to your room, raid those shopping bags of yours, and get ready to go out and party with our men."

# Chapter 14

"Will you let me see now?" I whine.

"Nearly finished. Be patient," Lottie chastises me like a child. She has insisted on 'dressing me up', and she's making me nervous with the amount of time she's taking. I know she has great taste, but I'm hoping that after the amount of time she's spent on my hair, makeup and nails, that I don't look like a two-bit hooker on a Saturday night.

"Just a little gloss, here ..." she slicks the brush across my lips. It smells of berries and I immediately want to lick it off. "Don't!" she snaps as my tongue touches my lips. "Do not undo my good work. Now ... go look," she says proudly, bouncing on the balls of her feet as I stand and walk to the full length mirror at the bottom of the bed.

I don't recognize the image looking back at me.

She has curled my hair into loose ringlets, then twisted and pinned each side up. My makeup is barely there but accentuates all my good features and hides the ugliness of my bruise. My eyes look huge framed with long mascara coated lashes and a hint of sparkle in the eye shadow.

"Lottie, you're an absolute pro. Where did you learn to do makeup like this?" I turn to face her and find an unusually shy Lottie nibbling at her nails. "Seriously, you should get a job doing makeup for photo shoots or film sets."

"Don't say stupid shit, Ari. It's just a bit of fun. You don't get to look like this…" she circles her face with her finger, "…without a lot of practice. Now, let's get you in that awesome dress of yours and go knock those boys dead."

Her sharp tongue and bravado is a mask, a protective layer. I hate how she changes the conversation so quickly and I also hate how deep down she second guesses everything she does, even though she appears to have an endless amount of confidence, I know different, and I wish she would take some of the advice that she so often dishes out to me.

"You can cut out all that deep thinking crap tonight too. We're going to have some fun," she quips before filling our glasses with the remainder of the champagne. She raises her glass. "To having my best friend back, and to moving forward." Her glass chinks against mine and I toast, "To new beginnings."

I step into my new favorite dress—a midnight-blue, knee-length, figure-hugging dress. It has long sleeves and a plunging back, so Lottie has dusted a shimmer powder across my shoulders and down my spine. I love her attention to detail and make a note to see if Beth knows anyone who would like to take her under their wing. Even though she's had no professional training, she would be great behind the scenes of a photo shoot or fashion show.

I step into gold jeweled heels and wrap the long straps around my ankles. I'm good to go. Lottie has disappeared into the bathroom and emerges not ten minutes later, completely transformed. She has on a sleeveless, emerald-green dress which sits above her knees; skater style with peep toe ankle boots. Her makeup is a heavy smoky eye with bright-red plump lips. It compliments her cropped fiery hair which she has ruffled into an orderly mess. I love her quirky, unapologetic style.

"Lottie, you look hot! How do you even do that in ten minutes flat?"

She shrugs. "Practice, I guess."

"Are you ready to hit the town?" I ask.

"Arianna, is the town ready for us? That's the real question."

We exit the bedroom and I stop in the lounge to gather my phone and some cash to put in my purse. Just as I am dropping my phone in, it dings.

*Denham: You look beautiful x*

*Me: How do you know? Do you have a secret camera watching me? ;)*

*Denham: No, but that's a good idea. I know you look beautiful. You always do x*

I smile down at the screen. He says the sweetest things.

"Let me guess ... lover boy?" Lottie quips. She checks her cell too. "Nope, nothing," she mumbles, looking disappointed.

"Come on," I encourage. "They'll be waiting for us downstairs." I have butterflies in my stomach as we ride the elevator down to the foyer, and I try to resist from picking at my fingernails as Lottie has taken so much time in painting them. I'm excited. I've never had excited butterflies before.

"Ari ..." Lottie nudges. "Step out." She gestures to the open door of the elevator with a huge grin on her face.

I step out blindly and hit that familiar wall before I have a chance to look up. I know who it is. I can smell him. The length of his index finger comes to rest under my chin and tilts my head up slowly until his golden flecked eyes meet mine. His other hand rests on the swell of my hip and his fingers tighten to hold me in place.

He looks at me intensely. "How long did it take you to get ready?" he asks.

"Long enough, why?" I question, confused by his question.

"Because I want to suck off your lip gloss and tangle my hands in your curls" he says, his voice breaking with huskiness. He watches my reaction and gently twists a lone curl around his finger. Lottie clearing her throat behind us at the same time that Spike stifles a snort. "But I have a feeling Lottie will kill me if I do that." He chuckles.

"Fuck me, you guys are too damn cute, but for Christ's sake, get a room!" Lottie interrupts.

"We have a room. Several actually," Denham retorts before leaning into me and whispering in my ear, "and I plan to make use of every available surface *very* soon."

He doesn't let me linger on that thought as he drapes an arm around my shoulder, tucking me into him. We follow Lottie and Spike out of the hotel and into a waiting Limousine.

"What's this for?" I ask curiously.

"Transport for the evening. After you, Stunner."

He gestures for me to enter. It's not easy to get into a car gracefully in such a tight dress, and certainly not when I can feel him watching my every move. Of course, Lottie and Spike are already in and Lottie is pouring more champagne by the time I get seated. Denham slides in next to me, taking the first full glass from Lottie and placing it in my hands. I try to take it from him with a smile, but he doesn't let go. Instead, he pulls our hands to the side, being careful not to spill the champagne and moves in to kiss me. He brushes his nose up my neck and along my jaw, and I can hear him gently inhaling as his free hand comes to rest at the nape of my neck. He grips firmly, pulling me in closer to him and hovering his lips over mine, taunting me, barely touching me, but causing every nerve in my body to react.

"One day soon we'll have a Limo to ourselves." He speaks in hushed tones so Lottie and Spike can't hear. "Then I'm going to show you exactly what's happening in my head right now." He smiles wickedly and licks my top lip, taking with him some of my gloss. My tongue darts out to meet his, but I'm too slow. "Nuh uh." He shakes his head gently from side to side with a sexy grin on his face and flashing that killer dimple. "I don't want an audience, and I especially don't want my brother to be that audience. Now, I'm going to have to think of something nasty before we exit the car or I'll be giving everyone a show."

My eyes can't help but move south. When I look back up, I'm being treated to the same smile as before but this time with a quirked brow. My cheeks flush; I've been caught blatantly checking out the impressive bulge in his crotch. I start to fidget and pull the champagne glass toward me, this time he lets go.

"I've told you before, "he says confidently, "look all you like because next time we're in here, we'll be doing more than looking." He shifts in the seat until he's facing the others. Lottie hands him a full glass and he rests his free hand just above my knee, drawing lazy circles with his thumb.

"Where are we going then, boys?" Lottie asks excitedly. I watch as a grin spreads across Spike's face. "Spike, does that smile mean what I think it does? Really?" Lottie hoots before launching herself at Spike and kissing him passionately.

"That doesn't really answer the question," I say, puzzled. "I'm still none the wiser."

"It's Lottie's favorite place, and I believe you'll like it too," he answers cryptically. Something tells me he doesn't want to give too much away so I don't pry. I actually like the fact that it's a surprise.

"Is it far away?" I ask, wondering how long we'll be in the Limo.

"It's just down the strip but we'll circle until we've finished our drinks." He speaks matter of factly, not looking in my direction, keeping his gaze fixed out of the window.

"Are you okay?" I probe gently.

"I'm thinking about visiting with my elderly grandmother," he says as if talking to the pane of glass in front of him, "because if I look or think about you right now, Ari, all that effort will be wasted and I'll be back to square one again."

"Denham," I whisper, and I watch as the shiver works its way down his neck and settles in the base of his spine. "You can't not look at me all night."

"Well, fuck. Apparently I only have to hear you say my name to get hard again," he says under his breath but loud enough for me to hear. The thought of him being hard at the sound of my voice sending shivers of pleasure through me. It also gives me an air of confidence I've never had before.

I lean forward and whisper over his shoulder and into his ear. "You want me to do something about that for you?" I say in the sweetest, most innocent voice I can manage. Denham and the alcohol are making me brave, but not quite brave enough that I don't feel a little embarrassed at being so brazen.

Denham snaps his head around to me in total shock, then sits up straight and announces, "Turn the fucking car around."

Lottie stops looking into Spike's eyes and snaps, "Oh no you don't, D. For fuck's sake ..." she mutters as she gets up out of her seat and making her way over to me. She swats Denham's shoulder. "Go sit over there and calm your raging hard-on, will you?" She doesn't give him a lot of choice before she wiggles her bottom in next to me and makes Denham shuffle around until he's next to Spike.

"There ..." Lottie says smugly. "That should do it!" I still can't believe how direct this girl is. I love her. "And you!" Lottie points one of her long talons at me. "You little tease, try not to raise his main sail *all* night. The poor boy will explode before you get your hands on him," she chastises before knocking back what's left in her glass. "Now drink up, you lightweights. I wanna go party!"

The Limo circles the strip one more time as we finish off the champagne and settle into friendly banter. Luckily, the sexual tension diminishes somewhat and it makes it more comfortable for Denham to relax and have a good time. It doesn't vanish completely, and I'm feeling sassy enough to have some fun with him a little later, but for now we're all out to have a good time.

We finally pull up outside a very plain looking building. I glance at Lottie for an indication that we have stopped at the wrong place, but she grins and holds out a hand to help me out. When I stand, I straighten out my dress and shake my hair out a little. There is no signage, just a roped area with a queue as long as the road. I inwardly groan. Even though the evening is warm, I don't want to stand here for what will probably take the best part of an hour to get in.

Denham and Spike exit the Limo. Denham takes my hand and kisses my cheek before steaming ahead and jumping the queue. I half walk half jog to keep up until we get to the front of the very long line of people. He greets the bouncer with a slap on the back and we walk straight in. I shouldn't have expected anything less. Denham knows everyone, everywhere.

He walks us to the back of a long hall, dipping through a door to the left and down another shorter hallway. When we reach the end, there's an elevator and he presses the button. We wait for the doors to open and he squeezes my hand while we wait, prompting me to look to him. He still looks ahead, but a sexy grin plays on his lips as he knows I'm smiling at him.

We step in when the doors open and it immediately strikes me that it's made of glass. I can see the steel and brickwork surrounding it which is bizarre when we start to move. There is no indication of how many floors we travel, but some time passes and I know that we're not traveling a couple of levels. As it starts to slow, a blue glow starts to get stronger. We emerge from the brick tunnel and the image we are presented with is fabulous.

We're on the roof. The elevator has taken us to the open air, and the doors open wide onto a spectacular platform situated six foot above the main area. I'm pleased that we went all out with the outfits this evening as it looks like the dress code is 'dress to impress'.

In LA, the people dress to make a statement. Who can wear the best designer? Who paid more for their dress or shoes? In Vegas, the people seem to want to look good regardless of the price. Don't get me wrong. I'm sure there are plenty of "moneyed" people here, but the atmosphere tells me they are all here to have a good time rather than to see who they can impress. Everyone looks awesome—quirky and unique. It's my kind of look and I love it immediately. There's a huge bar, a dance floor which is pumping out sultry R&B tunes, many tables and a couple of roped off areas around the perimeter.

Lottie comes up behind me as she exits the elevator. "Welcome to Sky lounge. Get your ass to the bar, babe!"

We weave our way through the crowds of people, Denham nods in acknowledgement to many patrons as we walk on by. They all look like they want to stop and talk, but a tight nod is all he gives and we keep moving.

"What would you like to drink, Stunner?" Denham asks, his sole focus on me.

I feel a tug on my arm and look to my left at Lottie's excited expression. She's practically bouncing. I grin back at her and we both blurt out at the same time, "Dirty martinis!"

Denham shakes his head affectionately at us and turns his voice to the bartender. "You heard the girls. Gimme the best dirty martinis you've ever made and keep them coming until I say stop, understand?" His authoritative voice is not to be messed with and the bartender gets to it instantly.

Hearing him be so bossy when I know how soft he can be, just makes me want him even more. I feel my core twinge and I know that I have to have him sooner rather than later, before I combust with lust. This is how it should be, all of it. Wanting someone, and having them want me equally. Friends, fun, and family. Living life to the fullest and having a future to look to, not living each day just to get through it. This is what being happy feels like.

Before the drinks are made, we're shown to a table in one of the elevated private areas by a very long-legged, stick thin waitress. She runs her eyes over Denham's body, and I understand why she can't look away because in his gray slacks and fitted white shirt he looks edible. With the top few buttons of his shirt undone, the definition of his chest is almost visible and she has a hard job even looking him in the eye. When she does look up, past his body, she locks her eyes to his and bats her lashes like a hooker waiting for her next lay and clearly has no shame about it. Denham is seemingly oblivious and takes no notice whatsoever, but I can't help myself.

I clear my throat rather loudly. "You seem to have a problem with your eyes? Did one of your fake lashes come unstuck?" My tone is threateningly sweet, just the way I meant for it to be. The waitress's cheeks flare red and she opens her mouth, presumably to come back with something smart to say, but catches my pointed look and struts back in the direction of the bar. I sit down to find everyone looking in my direction with very amused expressions on their faces. "What?"

"You just marked your territory, babe, that's what," Lottie announces.

"I did not! I just ... she had ..." Did I really just mark my territory? The waitress looking at Denham like she wanted him made me jealous and that's something I've never felt before. Even when I was at my happiest with Aaron, I was never jealous of anyone who flirted with him. He didn't matter to me enough.

"Get out of that head of yours, babe. That was fucking hot."

Denham is leaning into me, but his lips aren't touching me at all. His words travel up my shoulder, along my neckline and settle in my ear where the hairs stand on end and jolt my body into a chemical reaction. The whole world falls away and it's just us there for a minute. I'm looking into the depths of his eyes and I see so much passion, I don't know what to do with it and I can't tear myself away. It's so freakin' intense and powerful that I'm consumed.

Lottie's sharp elbow to my upper arm brings me back to the present. "Ow! What was that for?" I grumble, rubbing what I'm sure will now become a bruise.

"Will you two stop eye-fucking each other. You're not the only ones here, ya know. Jeez."

"I'm sorry, Lotts," I say, patting her knee.

As if on cue, the drinks arrive at the table. Lottie's eyes light up and I know what she's thinking. We've never gone out together and not downed the first drink. It's tradition. Lottie swears that it gets you warmed up, ready for the night ahead. I swear that it gets you drunk quickly so you don't remember much. I haven't done a lot of drinking in the last few years so I'm a lightweight and I have no intention of getting wasted. Just fuzzy enough around the edges to let go and have some fun.

"Ready?" Lottie asks.

"Ready as I'll ever be," I mutter, not entirely looking forward to the burn I know will come from downing the drink, but it's balanced out by the excitement of recreating happier times with my best friend.

I can feel Denham looking at me, but I don't want to risk Lottie's pointy elbow being shoved in my arm again, so I pick up my glass, chink it with Lottie's and we grin at each other before knocking it back. It takes her a very skilled four mouthfuls before it's all gone and she's banging her glass down on the table. I take a deep breath and gulp down as much as I possibly can in one mouthful. I screw my eyes shut while the liquid burns my throat and I force it to stay down.

Denham whispers huskily in my ear, "I hope you enjoyed that one, Stunner. I'm not gonna let you do any more like that." My head snaps round to meet his hooded stare. "I want you compliant, not comatose when we leave tonight."

I have mixed feelings about his statement. I don't want him to tell me what I can and can't do, but I also want what I think he's offering and I want it more than losing the use of my legs and a blinding hangover. If I'm honest, I don't think he would actually stop me if that was what he thought I wanted to do. If I thought for one minute he would dictate to me, he would be kicked to the curb in a blink. I feel a sharp stab in my chest at the thought, and I brush it off because ...well, because I just don't want to even venture to those thoughts.

"Man, that was a good warm-up," Lottie gasps. "Let's order another. Waiter!"

"I'm not downing another one, Lottie. I want to taste it this time," I grumble, still feeling the burn in the back of my throat.

"Whatever makes you happy, babe," she answers me with a dismissive wave of her hand and proceeds to try and catch the eye of the waiter.When the waiter doesn't seem to take any notice of Lottie yelling and clicking her fingers at him, Spike calls him over with a quick wave of his hand.

"How the hell did you do that?"

"Lottie, babe, you don't need to go all guns blazing just to get a drink. Keep it cool, okay?" Spike chastises her gently and Lottie sits back in the seat, pushing out her bottom lip in a pretend sulk. Her eyes are still twinkling though, so I know she secretly likes it when Spike shows his alpha side.

"We'll have two dirty martinis, two Jack and Cokes and I think me and my girl here..." he sits back with Lottie, wrapping his arm around her shoulders, "...are gonna have some fun with some flaming Sambuca chasers," Spike states. He kisses her hard and breaks away with a smile and rubs her nose with his. These guys are just too cute. Spike's cuteness balances out Lottie's crazy which makes for a perfect match.

"Are you coming next Saturday, Ari?" Lottie asks.

"Coming where?"

"To the ball. Oh for goodness' sake, D, you haven't asked her?" she grumbles irritably.

"Asked me what? What ball?"

"Well, if your big-mouthed friend had given me half a chance I would have asked you to come with me to the Summer Charity Ball next Saturday evening." He stares hard at Lottie and she shrinks into her seat, picking up the martini that has just been placed on the table.

"Eeek, sorry!" she squeaks out, looking toward Spike who affectionately shakes his head at her opening her big mouth.

"So will you come?" Denham asks tentatively.

I hear Lottie snort at his question and it's my turn to dig her in the arm with my elbow. An opportunity to turn an innocent question into something rude never escapes her.

"OW! Well, come on, Ari, that's kind of an open-ended question, don't ya think?" she squeaks at me.

"Well, I kinda think the answer depends on how good you treat her, D man ..." Spike teases. They both dissolve into fits of giggles and it's hard to even pretend to berate them.

Denham has one elbow on the table and his head in the palm of his hand. "It's like having a couple of teenagers around with you guys. Arianna, I'm sorry about the two idiots sitting next to you, but I'd really like it if you would accompany me to the charity ball next Saturday."

"I would love to come with you, but can we talk about this in the morning when I'll remember all the details?"

"Sure thing, Stunner."

"Ari!" Lottie jumps up. "This is our song!"

*Low* by Flo Rida is guaranteed to get us up and dancing wherever we are. She motions to Spike to down his shot with her, so he flicks a match and lights the clear liquid and they down it at the same time. Their faces scrunch up and I'm so pleased they didn't insist on me doing that; it would be more than I can take.

"Come on!" she shrieks. She is out of her seat and grabbing my hands before I can blink, dragging me to the illuminated glass dance floor. The lights flash in time with the music and it doesn't take long for us to be swept away with the tunes and let loose. After the champagne in the Limo and knocking back the dirty martini, I'm feeling fuzzy around the edges but not too drunk I can't feel my feet. There are happy vibes all around me and other than the bimbo waitress earlier, I don't catch a sly look or nasty vibe anywhere.

Lottie and I dance for maybe five songs before I decide that I need a drink. The dance floor is starting to get crowded and there's a small part of me that would like to go see my man.

*My* man? I don't know where that thought comes from, it's out of the blue. Or is it? Have I actually felt like that from the very second I crashed into his hard body and he flashed those wicked golden-flecked eyes at me?

Maybe I'm crazy, but I'm all right with it.

I also know that I need to revisit this thought when I'm fully sober and not under any influence.

Robin Thicke's *Blurred Lines* starts to play and Lottie mouths, "Oh my god." I follow the direction of her eye line and the crowd starts to whoop and cheer as I see two very familiar bodies getting their groove on.

What's sexier than Denham King?

Denham King dancing.

He moves as if it's as easy as breathing, and it looks like he and Spike have a little routine going on.

"Is this a party trick they do?" I question Lottie,

"Every time we come here ... they dance." She sighs dreamily. "Ari, you're in for a treat with Denham, girl. He can sing, dance, and by the sway of his hips right now, I'd say the dude can make sweeeeet music."

If it was anyone else who'd just said that I might have had to resist the urge to scratch her eyes out, but by the way she's ogling Spike, I have no doubt that she only has eyes for one of them. Lottie makes no apologies for saying what she thinks, and in this instance, I think she's rightI watch, mesmerized. Anyone would think I've never seem a man dance. I have. The main thing here is that I've never seen *my* man dance.

My man.I can't help it.I like it.I want it, him, so badly.The song finishes and Denham and Spike bow to a crowd of excited onlookers. They high five each other, then move quickly toward us, trying to avoid the party goers that want to speak with them along the way.

Denham's sexy smile finds me and I have to check that I'm not drooling over the flashing dance floor. His chest is glistening with a fine sheen of sweat after his rhythmic exertions and his shirt sticks to him a little. I have to resist the urge to peel it off him right here.

He slides his hands around my waist and nuzzles into my neck, burying his face into my hair and I feel him take a deep breath. "You smell like sunshine ... or moonlight ... I can't decide which ..."

"You sure gave Channing Tatum a run for his money up there," I quip.

"Yeah, well, I taught him everything he knows."

"Oh yeah?" I say, feeling sassy. "Wanna teach me? I'd love to see some of your moves."

"Oh, you're gonna. Every." *Kiss*. "Single." *Kiss*. "One." *Kiss*.

I grin and kiss him softly on the lips, holding there, eyes closed, drinking him in. I feel his lips twitch and his mouth open, letting his tongue snake out until it finds my bottom lip. I groan as the touch of his wet tongue sends signals between my legs. He sucks my lower lip as his hips grind against mine in time to the music and I slowly open my eyes and look up at him through a lust filled haze.

The blink of the lights and getting knocked by someone dancing vigorously behind us, prompts us to move from the dance floor. I hold one of his hands with both of mine as we weave our way toward the bar, then he picks me up under my arms and places me on a high bar stool, pushing himself in between my legs.

"Are you trying to show everyone my underwear?" I ask, pulling at the sides of my dress to cover my legs somewhat.

"No one will be seeing your underwear, I'll make sure of it. I just want to be between your legs," he says deadpan. My eyes widen at his words. The alcohol has loosened his tongue too. "Don't be surprised, Ari. I've wanted to be between your legs for days now. I've had more cold showers than I can count, and I've gotten very good at thinking of boring scenarios to get my mind off you. Nothing works."

"Nothing?"

"Nothing," he replies, shaking his head. "It's a problem, I tell ya."

"It sounds like it."

"There's only one solution."

"Mmm hmm." I humor him, pushing the conversation so he has to tell me exactly what he wants. I love how he's waited until I'm ready, until he's been able to prove to me that he's a good guy. I also love this back and forth, the tease, the anticipation.

"I need to stop thinking and start doing."

"Doing what?" My voice drops to a whisper as I play innocent.

"You, Ari, only you. All day, all night until you don't see anything but me. Everywhere you go, everything you do, I want you to feel me and want me like I want you."

My mouth drops open and I gasp to let more air into my lungs.

He grasps the back of my head and pulls me to him, kissing me hard. I try and deepen it, but he pulls away, replacing his lips with his forefinger.

"Save that thought, Arianna." I don't have time to reply before the bartender is in front of us ready to take our order. "Do I need to ask what you would like to drink?" Denham jokes.

I shake my head no. I'm still speechless. I hop off the stool while Denham is talking to the bartender. I need to pee and I need to straighten up. "I'm just going to the ladies," I utter.

Denham gives me a gentle nod and I can feel his eyes follow me across the room. After using the bathroom and washing my hands, I look into the mirror. Miraculously, everything is still intact. Makeup is still perfect, hair a little more messed up than before but knowing the reason is because Denham's fingers have been tangled in it ... well, I can live with that. I smooth down my dress and I'm good to go.

I head back out into the thrum of the main club and notice a table of men. I hadn't noticed them before and the only reason I notice them now is because they're all looking in my direction. I watch as one of them makes a joke and they all start to laugh, but their gaze doesn't leave me as I walk toward them. I look around to find an alternative route to the bar, but there isn't one.

I pull back my shoulders and look toward the bar where I can see Denham laughing and joking with Lottie and Spike. I relax knowing they're there. I start to pass the table and relax just a minute too soon. A cold strong hand with very long bony fingers shoots out to capture my wrist. I gasp and try to wriggle free which just makes him tighten his grip.

"Hey, sweetheart, you're a feisty one, huh?" I watch his eyes light up when he speaks to me. The dude is wiry, and not ugly, but not handsome either. He's dressed in jeans and a tee and I wonder how he managed to get in here looking so underdressed. He stands up from his chair, blocking my view to the bar.

"I saw you dancin'. You've got a fuckin' hot body, you know that?" he drawls with his stale cigarette breath, making my stomach churn. It's clear he's had far too much to drink, and he's even starting to sway a little.

"Excuse me, but my friends are waiting for me at the bar," I say politely, giving the man one chance to move. He glances over his shoulder, but still doesn't let me pass, and my nervous adrenaline is turning into anger by the second.

"Those your friends over there?" he says, screwing his nose up. "Hell, girl. You're slumming it this evening," he slurs, making his friends laugh. "Why ya wanna travel in economy when there's a first class seat right here, baby." He thrusts his hips forward and points at his crotch with his index finger. His scummy friends dissolve into fits of laughter at his antics, but I'm not finding this in the least bit funny.

I place my hands gently on his shoulders and he looks shocked that I seem to be responding to him. *Oh, I'm responding to him all right.* "I asked you nicely," I speak directly into his ear so he doesn't miss a word, "to move and let me pass, but you thought it would be funny to try and humiliate me in front of your friends."

It's clear that he's confused as to how to handle me. The calm, threatening voice is always the worst. I've learned that from e xperience."I don't take kindly to being laughed at or indecently propositioned by cockroaches. My man is a hundred times the man you'll ever be and after this, you won't be any kind of man for some time."

I smile, a sinister, crooked smile that feels so fucking good. I'm taking control, fighting back, reclaiming my life, and unfortunately for this man, he's bearing the brunt. My knee moves swiftly and powerfully upward. It connects with his groin at full force and he drops with a strangled moan. I watch with satisfaction as his face contorts with pain and he struggles to catch his breath. With any luck, he'll be out of action for quite some time.

His friends leap up but don't come to his aid until they're sure I'm not going to turn on them. I step over the jerk and find Denham, Spike and Lottie standing on the other side of him.

"Oh, hi guys," I chirp nonchalantly.

"Ari!" Lottie screeches. "That was badass! Did you see the way that guy dropped? Like a fucking tranquilized elephant."

"He was just in my way." I shrug.

Spike looks at me with an amused expression while Lottie bounces excitedly next to him, holding his hand. "Listen to you!" Lottie exclaims. "Remind me not to get on your bad side ..."

"You guys gonna stop staring at me like I have three heads and get me a drink, or what?"

My cool, calm exterior is the opposite of the shaking mess I am inside, but the fact that I actually stood up for myself, that I fought back, makes me feel empowered. I'm still running on adrenaline which adds to the alcohol and the intense lust from a little earlier. It's a potent, heady mixture, but one that makes me feel pretty damn good. I can't stop smiling.

Denham is still standing in front of me, silent, his brows drawn into a tight frown and his thumbs tucked into the pockets of his pants. I step into him, sliding my hands around his waist and hooking my fingers in the belt loops of his slacks, and pull him closer to me. With my heels on, there's only a few inches difference in height, and he looks down at me through those thick, dark lashes that frame his golden eyes and tilts his head questioningly.

"You're brooding," I state.

His eyes narrow and his gaze pierces the guy who's still rolling around on the floor. "I'm trying to decide if I should wait here and beat that guy's ass when he gets back up or ..."

"Or ..." I prompt.

"Whether I should take you home right now and make you scream my name until sunrise." His hard stare softens and he looks over me seductively.

My mind is made up. If there was ever any doubt, it has been permanently erased. It's not the drink talking. *It's* lust ...

*It's* happiness.

*It's* confidence.

*It's* him.

All him.

"Let's go," I say boldly, wetting my lip with my tongue and drinking in the desire oozing from him.

# Chapter 15

The Limo doesn't circle the Strip on the way home this time. The driver is instructed to take the shortest route possible and I don't know if I should be pleased about that or not.

I'm nervous.

Sex has always made me nervous. I've never really enjoyed it. Never wanted it. I just did it because that's what is expected of you when you're a wife or fiancé.

Until now.

This, whatever I have going on here with Denham King, is different.I know it's different because I feel a tingle start in my toes when he looks at me. It travels through every inch of my body, to the top of my head, every follicle, every nerve ending on high alert which thrills me as much as it frightens me.

*What if* I'm not good enough?

*What if* he doesn't like my body?

I know my nerves are unwarranted. Denham has shown me more love and compassion in the few days we've known each other than any man ever has.

A few days. Less than one week.

Is it too soon? Does this make me a slut?

I can't do it.

A large hand creeps along my collarbone and gently grips the nape of my neck. I turn to meet his compelling eyes and something in his manner soothes me.

I can do it.

I want to do it, more than I've ever wanted to do anything.

I catch a glint of the golden flecks in his eyes as he looks over me seductively.

His look.

His touch.

It calms me. Makes me feel like anything is possible. I just need to learn to reach out and grab it with both hands.

He kisses the pulsing hollow at the base of my throat and works his lips upwards.

Sucking ... Licking ... Nipping ...

Leaving a searing path until he reaches my lips, claiming me hungrily and without apology.

When the Limo slows he pulls back, leaving me breathless and wanting more.

"Arianna—"

"Shhhh." I soothe, pressing my finger to his lips, knowing what he's about to say. My eagerness this evening is reassurance enough. We've danced for days, now it's time for the main show.

He smiles and kisses my finger before jumping out of the door purposefully and extending a hand to help me out. He walks calmly through the main foyer of the hotel, his demeanor confident. But underneath the cool, calm façade he is emitting, I sense this is something deeper for him as well.

We enter the elevator, the usual crackle of electricity bouncing between us when we're in this confined, intimate space. Denham takes up his usual position by my side, holding my hand and facing the doors, trying to disguise his elevating pulse rate and fast, shallow breathing.

I drop his hand and stand in front of him, my back to the doors, and he looks to me questioningly. I want to show him that I'm ready, more than ready. I know he needs to know that I'm whole, that my mind isn't blurred. "Just so you know ..." I speak seriously, with an edge of seduction. "This isn't a snap decision." I step into him, placing both of my hands lightly on his chest. "You're not a rebound. I don't know what you are yet, but I want to find out." I move in closer, sliding my hands up his chest to his broad, muscled shoulders and continue to move forward, pushing him gently with my body so he backs up into the wall. "I want you. It's nothing more complicated than that," I state confidently.

His eyes haven't left mine. With each word, his pupils dilate further, the light smoldering in the gold flecks surrounding his eyes and he looks at me. Predatory. Passionate.

My hands follow the collar of his expensive cotton shirt and find the first button that's standing in the way of his smooth, sculpted chest. He watches me with his hands by his sides, not touching or interfering, silently giving permission to continue my exploration. I've seen his body. I know how it looks and I know how it feels. But somehow this feels different. This is a different discovery of each other. My body reacts as if this is the first time I've touched him, brimming with excitement and a desire that has so far been untapped.I undo every button and tug his shirt free from his pants. I push it open and let my eyes roam freely.

*No* inhibitions.

*No* worries.

My fingers trail over every ripple of his stomach, hard and smooth until Denham's patience snaps. His hands capture my face, his fingers holding my jaw in place while he burns into me with his hungry stare. His head dips slowly, and I take in every second, every breath, then his lips crash into mine. Fast. Feverish.

His tongue finds mine and strokes coaxingly, a mutual exploration and a discovery of something very special indeed. I faintly hear the ding of the elevator reaching the penthouse and the doors sliding open as Denham walks us backwards, not breaking our kiss.

We reach the door in a tangle of hands and clothes. I can't touch him enough, I want to feel every part of him, every inch, even if it takes me all night to do it. He pushes the door open and I've barely stepped in before he scoops me up into his arms and kicks the door shut behind him. He carries me effortlessly, his breaths coming rapidly through desire as opposed to exertion. He lets my legs down gently until I'm standing albeit shakily.

"Ari, this is your last chance to back out. I want you ... God, I want you," he says squeezing his eyes together, "but if you don't want to ... I won't ... I'll wait. I'll wait as long as it takes."

I don't answer with words.

I kiss him, every feeling poured into the sensations passing through our lips and he understands perfectly. I can't stop. I don't want to. For the first time in my life, I'm in charge of how I feel. I don't want it to be over as soon as possible so I can scrub the feeling away in the shower and hopefully not have to do it again too soon. I want it to last all night. I want to be able to touch him every day, make him mine and give myself to him in return.

"Turn around," he orders huskily.

I do as he asks without hesitation. I face away from him, but make sure I turn slowly so his eyes can drink me in. He slides the dress off my shoulders, down my arms and pushes it gently over my hips. The garment pools at my feet until I'm standing in only heels and black lace panties.

He groans and his finger lightly touches the back of my neck before he trails it down my spine. He elicits a shiver from me and his touch twinned with the exposure causes my nipples to peak. He takes his time, placing feather-light touches in the curve of my waist, the backs of my legs ...

I hear the thunk of his shoes being discarded, then the clink of his belt buckle being undone. His hands travel back up and down my body, deliciously torturous, until they come to rest on my shoulders.

He turns me toward him gently and sucks in a deep breath when I'm fully facing him. His hand cups one of my breasts, gently stroking my nipple with his thumb. Fire jolts of electricity to my core and I let out a whimper. He takes a step back and keeps me at arm's length, letting his gaze drift over my hard nipples and dropping down to my flat stomach, then traveling the length of my legs.

"Mmm, black lace," he mutters appreciatively. "And heels. I love the heels."

If it were anyone else I would feel objectified, but it's not anyone else. It's Denham King and I feel beautiful. Desired.

"I want to see you in just heels more often ... and diamonds ..." he muses. "Yes, heels and diamonds."

I can't wait any longer. I step toward him and reach for the button on his pants, his belt is hanging open and his torso is on display. He is an Adonis.

Sculpted. Bronzed. Beautiful.

I undo his zipper and slide my hands in the waistband of his pants, pulling them down to join my dress on the floor, I'm met with skin.

No boxers. No briefs. Hot, smooth skin with no more barriers between us.

I take a deep breath, knowing that this seductive undressing is about to come to an end and I need a minute to try and gather my thoughts. He's gloriously naked in front of me, so I give in to my desire to touch him, sliding my hand between us, down the channel of his 'V'. I take his length in my palm and wrap my fingers around him firmly. His chest shudders.

"Fuck ..." I mutter under my breath.

"Was that a request, Stunner?" he jokes with a smirk, flashing me that sexy dimple.

"Yes," I reply seriously. "I can't take it anymore. I want you inside me."

His eyes widen and his body stills. I've stunned him with my dire ctness.He seals my words with a hard kiss and backs me up to the bed before laying me down gently. My hair falls around my head in ringlets and Denham leans down to touch it.

"I love your hair in curls. I love your hair any way you wear it. You're perfect, Ari, you really are." I don't turn away at his words. "You're not embarrassed that I called you perfect, Arianna?" he says, his finger trailing lightly from the curl in my hair, along my collarbone and down my body between my breasts. He stops when he reaches my stomach and places the heel of his hand over my sex.

"No, I'm not embarrassed," I whisper.

"Would you be embarrassed if I did this?" He dips his head and sucks one of my tight nipples into his mouth. The pressure increases in my core and I rotate my hips against his hand, trying to find some friction. He groans against my flesh, releasing my nipple from his lips and blowing gently across the wet skin, causing it to tighten and peak.

My chest tightens and my breath is shallow. "No," I reply hoarsely.

His hands slide over my smooth skin, the rough pads of his fingers heightening the sensation as he trails my waist and hips before hooking his thumbs into the corners of my panties. The muscles in his arms bunch as he pulls, ripping the delicate fabric and exposing the last covered part of me. I gasp as he tugs me to the edge of the bed and drops to his knees. He runs his hands slowly up the inside of my legs. Torturously slow.

Then he licks. The hypersensitive nerve endings have my body jerking in response to his tongue. I've never been licked there and embarrassment washes over me. I turn my head into the mattress and my curls follow to mask my face.

"Arianna ..." his voice is low, seductive with an edge of concern. "You don't like that?"

"I ... I've never ..."

"I will not let you be embarrassed now. Look at me," he commands.

I turn my head slowly, curls still covering some of my face. His fists are buried into the mattress beside my head and his body is towering over me, stretching all his defined muscles. "I told you before, I want to cover every inch of you ... I want to explore every part of your body with my eyes, my lips and my hands. But I won't do it if you're shying away. Be bold."

I brush the curls from my face and look directly in his eyes. They're burning. "No one has ever kissed me ... there ... before ..." I feel small and inexperienced.

"Good," he replies firmly. "I don't want you to think of anyone else. Ever. I want you to remember me and only me. The way I make you feel, the way my fingers tangle in your hair, the way my tongue sets your hot little pussy on fire. Ari, we are going to make love and wipe out the past. It can't hurt you now, I won't let it. Just think about the here and now. Think how good it's going to feel when I push inside of you. Now close your eyes."

I let my eyes flutter shut, the smell of scotch washing over me as Denham breathes close to me. "When I've finished with you, you'll be begging me to let you open your eyes and watch us, but for now, keep them closed and just feel."

His hands move from beside my head and the heat of his body disappears from above me. I'm desperate to open my eyes to see where he is, but I don't. I obey his gentle command and keep them shut, waiting for his touch, waiting for him to make me feel.

He kisses my flat stomach, the gentle kisses moving south. Little trails of sensation transferring from his lips to my skin. I tense but don't give in to the urge to cover myself with my hands. I want to move past it. I want to move on.

I feel a rough fingertip gently trace my hip bone, following the top of my leg around, then slowly dragging his finger up through my opening. His touch is light, teasing, but when he reaches my clit, I jolt, this time with less emotional discomfort and more pleasure. His other hand comes up to hold my hip as his finger stills. I lift my head and I'm about to open my eyes when he starts to move in a circular motion, gently massaging and building an intense pleasure that has me panting and instinctively pushing my hips to meet his hand for more resistance.

Every muscle in my body is quivering for more as I rotate my hips and match the rhythm of his dexterous fingers. Blood whooshes through my ears as my body climbs higher. I can hear distant moans, and unfamiliar noises and I realize they are coming from me, my own body voicing immense levels of pleasure and reaching an explosive climax.

I call Denham's name, a blessing and a promise floating from my lips. My breath comes in long surrendering moans as my body rides the hypnotizing aftershocks of my orgasm. Denham leaves me momentarily, I hear foil rip and a moment later the bed dips with his weight.

I open my eyes to meet his burning stare. "More stunning every second that you breathe," he groans. He kisses me, then tilts his hips and pushes into me, inch by delicious inch.

I'm still on the high my orgasm left me with and I feel greedy that I want more. Denham has opened up a floodgate, draining my defenses and awakening my body from its sleeping sexuality.

His body shudders as he pushes as deep as I can take him. "Fu-uuuck," he hisses and I groan in response. He draws back painfully slowly and pushes in again, his thrusts beginning to come faster.

"We fit like you were made for me, just me," he states. "I can't make it slow this time, Stunner. You feel too fucking good."

"I don't want it slow," I respond, surprising myself with the words that follow. "Fuck me fast ... and hard."

"Fuck, you talk like that and I'm not gonna last long."

I lift my legs and open my pelvis, seating him deeper and triggering something carnal within him. His pace picks up and I dig my heels in his ass, pulling him closer, not wanting to let him go. Our bodies are covered in a fine sheen of sweat as we glide against each other, his rhythm increasing.

The building pressure in my core surprises me and I thrust my hips upwards to meet Denham's. The sound of our flesh slapping together mingles with the moans escaping our bodies.

"Ari, fuck, that's it ... ride it with me," Denham rasps out.

His lust filled voice is all I need to hit the peak. Denham grits his teeth and pushes into me as far as he can go, the pressure holding me at the top of my climax as I feel him swell and pulse inside of me before letting me gently over the edge to float back to earth.

He rests his head on my shoulder, his breaths matching mine and coming fast in heaving pants. He isn't allowing his full weight to rest on me, but our chests are touching and I feel his heart beating through his ribcage.

He lifts his head and brushes his lips across mine. "Arianna, you're ... that was—"

"Shhh." I press my lips into his. I don't want words. We don't need words. I'm pretty sure we could live forever without needing to talk to convey our emotions.

I know.

He knows.

Denham disposes of the condom, then lifts me onto his side of the bed.He folds my curves into the contours of his body, naked and covered in a sheen of sweat from our lovemaking. We lie flush, skin against skin, not a scrap of clothing between us. I want to stay like this forever.

"Sleep, Stunner," Denham whispers. I close my eyes and smile with the feeling of satisfaction and contentment.

My body has surrendered to him and my mind quickly follows.

# Chapter 16

I wake up draped head to toe in Denham King. Soft, full lips kiss me awake, running along my collarbone, nipping at my neck, then taking my mouth in an insistent but gentle caress. I automatically start to protest because I'm pretty sure Denham does not want to be greeted by my morning breath. After all, he's not deluded. I don't taste of vintage champagne all the time, despite what he might say.

"Nuh-uh." I shake my head and turn away from him.

"You don't want me to kiss you, Stunner?" he asks curiously and I can hear the smile in his voice.

"Morning breath," I mumble into the pillow.

"You think that would stop me from wanting to kiss you?"

"You'd want to kiss me if my breath was stinky?" I ask, frowning.

"Yes, but I might just kiss you like this ..." He starts to kiss the delicate flesh under my chin before licking my jaw line, painting a path to my ear. He takes my lobe in his mouth and sucks gently. I moan as it sends jolts to my core and I forget what I was protesting about. He has my full attention and I couldn't turn away from him now if I tried.

"I want to kiss your lips, morning breath and all. I want to suck on your tongue and hear those little noises you let go of that make my dick hard. You'll still taste like honey to me. You want me to kiss you, Ari?"

I nod as he has left me speechless with his direct words once again. "Tell me," he orders. My brows scrunch together and he rewords his demand. "You want me to kiss you? You have to ask."

My breath comes on a choked laugh. "I have to ask?"

"Yes ..." His voice drops to a husky whisper and he teasingly hovers his lips over mine; I can feel the heat coming from him. "Ask me to kiss you, Ari ..."

No matter how brave I feel, it's still hard for me to be so forward. I know what he's doing. He's not pushing me out of my comfort zone to make me uncomfortable. He's doing it to make me brave.

"I ..." I stutter, the words faltering and sticking in the back of my throat. Then I look at him, his soft eyes with those mesmerizing gold flecks, and I muster up all the confidence I own. "I want you to kiss me, Mr. King. Will you ... please?"

His eyes react before his body and his lips meet mine before I can prepare myself. He pulls back, straddling me with his long muscular legs and resting his elbows either side of my head. His breath has picked up as his lips brush softly back and forth across mine, teasing me and sending sparks flying through my whole body. I arch my neck, pushing my lips further into his, and he smiles against me.

"Oh, Arianna, what I'm going to do to you ..." he growls.

His lips leave mine and he licks and sucks his way down my neck, then he pushes up on his strong arms and sits back. Taking my breasts in his hands, he squeezes and pulls a moan from my body when his thumbs graze my nipples. My back arches involuntarily, pushing my breasts further into his touch as his hands begin an arousing exploration of my soft skin, searching for pleasure points and finding more than I knew I had. He moves downward, skimming my waist, then back up slowly over my ribcage. More sensual than I ever thought possible.

I let my gaze travel over his body as he touches mine. He's beautifully proportioned and owns masculine. His stomach muscles are taut, and his V is prominent, drawing my line of sight down to his cock. I can't help but look. It's not something I've ever felt compelled to do but now, with him, I can't stop myself. He smirks, then winks, rewarding me for not pulling back, for not withholding my desire to feast my eyes on his body. He lets his hands slide back up, and leans into me, his cock flat against my stomach as he tilts his pelvis toward me.

"I have never wanted anyone as bad as I do you," he groans. "I want in you, Ari. I want on you and I want over you."

I stroke his back with my nails, gently at first, then deeper into his skin. He grinds into me harder and I give in to the need to touch him. I leave one hand on his back, clawing gently as I wrap the other hand around his cock.

The way his body reacts to my touch has me feeling empowered. He moves his hips, pushing into my hand. He may be on top, but I now feel like I'm the one in control. Spurred on by the heady feeling, I let my fingers travel down his back and dig my nails into his ass.

"Fuck," he cusses. His teeth clamp together, wanting to enjoy it but trying not to lose control. "Too much, Stunner. I'm not gonna last," he pants. He reaches into his top drawer next to the bed, pulls out a condom and puts it on while still straddled over me.

I feel like a voyeur.

My mind still tells me that I shouldn't be looking, but it's getting easier to be brave, and the fact that I know he would like me to look, makes me want to watch him even more. He strokes himself slowly after the condom is fitted and I can feel everywhere south of my belly twitch and clench in response.

When I tear my eyes away, I meet his hooded stare. "You like watching me, Ari?" he asks throatily. I nod. "Someday soon you can watch while I come all over your beautiful skin, but right now I want to be inside your tight little pussy. I want to feel your desire grip me when I make you scream."

He slides his finger between my legs, coaxing my opening, stroking my clitoris with his thumb in rhythmic circular motions and curling his finger inside me. Heat rises through me like the hottest volcano, clouding my brain and drawing me to a height of passion that makes my whole body vibrate. I can't control the scream that slips past my lips.

"Denham, fuck ..." I pant uncontrollably as my body explodes into sharp jerks and shivers. Every nerve shakes as I ride his hand and let the waves of the most powerful orgasm I've ever had ripple through me.

Denham's hand leaves me, and I feel suddenly empty but not for long. He pumps his cock twice with his hand, takes a deep breath, and then thrusts into me hard. He fills me completely, not allowing my sensitive body enough time to come back to earth.

"I can't go slow, I want you too bad," he pants into my ear. "So fucking stunning when you come ... so fucking stunning."

Each thrust builds the tension through my body again. "Holy shit!" I cry. "I'm gonna come, you're gonna make me come again."

I bring my heels up to dig in his ass, wanting him deeper, pulling him into me. "Yes, Ari," he pants breathlessly. "Ride it, Stunner. Come with me." His voice is strained and I feel his body tighten along with mine.

He moans as he thrusts hard, driving into me, reaching as far as he can go and taking my body with him. He swells and pulses as he comes and my muscles grip and pull him in. The pleasure is pure and explosive as we both come fast, peaking together and letting our bodies experience a deep carnal connection. He seals my mouth with his, swallowing my cries and letting his tongue lave mine until our bodies start to come down from the crescendo.

We lie entangled with a sheen of sweat covering our bodies and a haze of bliss settling around us as we let our breathing regulate. "Never been so good," Denham mumbles. He places a lingering kiss on my lips and carefully rolls off me to dispose of the condom, then joins me back in the bed, pulling me tight to him. "You amaze me, you're amazing."

I can't speak. I feel my bottom lip start to quiver and I know that the minute I open my mouth to say something I'm going to cry. I'm not sad or unhappy. I'm overwhelmed, consumed by the feelings running through me, the experiences I'm having and the fact that I'm so damn happy for the first time in forever.

I shift in my seat and feel the tender ache between my legs from the previous night and this morning's activities. Memories invade my senses as I recall things that were firsts for me in so many ways.

I'm opening my heart; I can actually feel it moving, swelling and breaking free of the bonds I had imposed.

I'm also opening my mind, no longer shut off to the possibility of being happy, fulfilled and sexually awakened. I have discovered a wild side that I like, and I want more.

I feel the blood start to move a little faster through my veins, heating me up, when I recall the way I was awoken this morning.

*I hear his moans in my ear, feel his breath on my skin and his fingers on my ...*

"Earth to Arianna ..."

I'm at a restaurant having lunch with my mom, thinking about being in bed with the king of my castle. My skin is flush with the thoughts of us getting hot and sweaty this morning and I'm sure my breathing has accelerated.

Mom waves a hand in front of my eyes. "Arianna, sweetheart, where did your mind wander off to?" she asks in an amused voice.

"I'm sorry, Mom, what were you saying?"

"Never mind what I was saying, you want to tell me what or who has you in a dreamy trance?"

"I was just ... ugh, is it that obvious?" I cover my face with my hands. I'm so embarrassed.

"When you haven't heard what I've said for the last five minutes, then yes, it's fairly obvious I would say. Were you thinking about Denham?" she asks tentatively.

"Yes."

"You want to talk about him?"

"Oh, I don't know, Mom." I sigh. "I just don't understand how I'm feeling. I don't understand what's going on between us. It's hard to figure out everything else that's going on in my life, but when I'm with him, it all ... it just ... it feels right and I don't know why. I shouldn't even be letting anyone else near me. Last week I would have been happy to become a nun, live in solitary and never set eyes on another man again. And now he's come along and ruined everything, except it's not ruined, I feel ... I don't know, I just don't know." I take a deep breath and dramatically throw my head down into my folded arms on the table. I hear my mom trying to contain her laughter. "Mom! This isn't funny!"

"Darling, I'm sorry. It's not a bad dilemma to have ... all you need to do is let him l—"

"Don't even finish that sentence. I don't want to hear the L word. It corrupts people's minds and makes them think they can own you," I scold bitterly.

"No, my girl," she says softly. "Love doesn't do that to someone, don't confuse it with greed. Love makes you a better person. It doesn't make you greedy, in fact, it makes you think less about yourself and more about the person you are in love with. It opens your heart to a world of possibilities."

"It also opens your heart to a lifetime of heartbreak if that feeling isn't reciprocated." I sound so cynical even to my own ears, but I can only draw on what life has taught me so far. "All I know is that Denham can make me feel like no one ever has. He makes me want to let him in, let him be there for me, but I don't know how to convince myself to allow him to do that. I have to try and protect myself. I let my guard down with Aaron, and look what happened. How do I know it's not going to happen again?"

"Did you love Aaron?"

"No."

"Do you think you could love Denham?"

I pause and look her in the eye. "I've only known him a week, how is that even possible? I'm not sure I even know how. Maybe I'm not capable ..."

"Of course you're capable. Look at me. How many frogs did I kiss before I found my prince? It felt different from the very first minute with Brent, but I had to kiss a lot of slimy toads to find him. Maybe you've kissed enough frogs and instead of a prince, you've found a King ..." She lets her thoughts linger in the air quietly while she gets up to go to the restroom.

Maybe it is my turn. Maybe it's my time to grab at my chance of happiness. I admit to myself for the first time that I do feel something surprisingly deep for Denham, something I never knew existed. I don't know if it's love, but it's different from anything I've ever felt for anyone. I've given him my unwavering trust and I don't regret it one bit. I've let my heart's guard down further than I have with anyone and he hasn't used it to his advantage. I've let him in and I think the thing that scares me the most is that I want it. I want it all. He makes me push away everything that I've ever believed true because he's rewriting my trust. There's just something stopping me from letting go completely. I can't lose control. I need to keep hold of the reins for self-preservation.

"Excuse me, ma'am."

I look up from my thoughts to see the waiter standing by the table with a single, long-stemmed red rose between his fingers. He offers it to me with an outstretched hand and I take it reluctantly.

"I am told to tell you, that you will know who it is from and he just wanted to let you know he was thinking about you," the waiter offers cryptically.

"I ... uh, thank you," I stutter. I haven't spoken to Denham since he left to go to work this morning, so I'm not entirely sure he knows where to find me, although, we are eating in one of the restaurants in his hotel.

I don't know how to tell him that I hate roses. I'm used to them being a way of an apology, making up for a misdemeanor of some sort. The flower itself means nothing to me, I don't take it as a loving symbol, but I love the thought behind it. It makes me smile big to know that he thought enough of me to send it.

I pull my cell out of my purse and bring his name up to send a thank you text.

"Ooh, darling, where did the rose come from? It's very beautiful." My mom seats herself back at the table and my phone rings before I can compose a message to say thank you to Denham.

It's Lottie calling.

"Well, if it isn't the queen of Sambuca ..." I answer and chuckle to myself.

"Ugh ... tell me you feel like shit too," she groans.

"Nope, fresh as a daisy!" I gloat. I fail to add that I'm exhausted but not through alcohol intake. I'm tired to the bone for reasons far more worthwhile, but I don't have a hangover.

"You're so lucky. I feel like someone swapped my head for something loud and heavy."

"Well, that's because you knocked back a ton of shooters and drank champagne like it was water."

"Where are you anyway?" she asks, changing the subject. "I called your room ..."

"I'm having lunch with my mom in La Casa."

"HI MOM!" she yells, nearly bursting my eardrums. I hold the phone away from my ear in Mom's direction.

"Hi, Lottie," my mom replies, not quite as loud as Lottie but loud enough that neighboring tables turn to look at us.

"What time will you be back? You have details to fill me in on."

"I do?"

"Yes, don't even try to deny it. You know exactly what I'm talking about."

I do know exactly what she's talking about, but I don't want to share details like a teenage girl who just lost her virginity. I selfishly want to keep every detail to myself. Every last little kiss. The small kisses have as much of an effect on me as the big kisses, maybe more.

*The little tingles that fire through my skin when his lips skim mine ...*

"ARI!"

"What?"

"You weren't listening ..."

"Sorry." I mumble. Oh god, I've got it bad. I could try to play my lack of concentration off as not nearly enough sleep, but I'd only be fooling myself. "I don't know how I possibly thought I could ignore you," I retort sarcastically.

"Ha-ha. What time will you get back then?"

"I'm not sure, can I call you?"

"You better! Oh, we have outfits to plan too for the ball, and how much discount do you get at your new job?"

"Lottie, I haven't even started yet. I can't go asking for a discount already."

"Sure you can. Do you have enough money to pay full price?"

"That's not the point. Can't we rent something?"

"Oh maybe, we need a whole day to try things on. There's a theme, you know?"

"What? Why are you only telling me this after I've agreed to go?"

"Chill, chica. It's a James Bond theme. They think it makes it more exciting to be 007 rather than calling it black tie. But that's really what it is."

"Okay, fine. Look, I have to go. Mom only has a few hours and I've already devoted ten minutes of this precious time to you."

"Yeah, well that's ten minutes you'll never get back." I hear her snigger. "Call me," she orders, then hangs up.

God, I love that girl.

I toss the phone in my purse and look at the food that arrived while I was talking to Lottie. "Wow, this looks great." I dig in, suddenly realizing how hungry I am. I stop chewing and look up at my mom who hasn't even picked up her knife and fork yet. She has tears pooling in her eyes, making them look glossy.

"Mom?" I question.

She smiles. It reaches right up through her cheekbones and creases her eyes, and the movement allows a tear to escape and fall down her cheek."I never thought I'd be able to do this." She gestures around the table. "Just having lunch with my very grown-up daughter, talking about normal stuff and being able to look forward." She wipes the tear away with the back of her hand. "Oh, look at me getting all silly. Take no notice."

I cover her hand with mine. "I know, Mom. I never thought we would be able to do this together either. It's perfect."

"Arianna, I can't tell you how happy it makes me to think that for once in your adult life you seem to have doors opening all around you."

I smile and nod, scared that if I open my mouth to speak, I'm going to let go of the sob that's pushing its way to the surface. There have been too many tears shed already.

She straightens in her chair and smoothes the napkin in her lap. "So tell me what Lottie was getting all excited about."

We chat for a few hours, normal conversations about normal things. It's everything I have dreamed about for a long time. I find out that Mom and Brent have a new house, one that I promise to visit in the next couple of weeks to see the renovations they have going on. For now, they are staying in an apartment just outside of the main town so it's still central for Brent to get to work. His job is obviously going great and I'm so happy that things aren't just falling in place for me, they are falling in place for her too.

I tell her all about my new job and don't miss the excitement in her eyes. I must get some of my passion for clothes from her. Even when we had little money, she liked to look good and would rummage in the local goodwill store to find little hidden treasures. She had an old sewing machine that she would customize things with. It used to drive me mad to hear the constant drone in the background when I wanted to watch one of my favorite programs, but the look on her face when she has finished one of her masterpieces was worth every minute.We argue about who gets to pay the bill. Not because neither of us wants to, it's because both of us try to do it. I leave her at the front of the hotel, where she gets in a cab with a promise to call her within the next couple of days.

I head to my apartment, rose in hand and a smile on my face.

I drop my purse on the couch and stand the rose in the vase that holds the other rose Denham gave me on our first date. My aversion to roses diminishes the more I look at this one. This is prettier than others I've seen; more pinkish-red, and fuller petals. I know it's the person behind the gift that I see every time I look at it, and that alone stands as a lesson. Not all roses have to signify something bad or regretful, just like not all men will treat me like shit.

I sort some of my clothes, hanging things I hadn't gotten around to yesterday and killing time, until ... well, I'm not really sure. I haven't had a chance to develop a routine. My down time has been filled with different people, mostly Denham admittedly. I will have a definite routine next week when I start work, which I'm looking forward to, but I'm missing things that I used to do for myself. I crave independence that I used to have, but at least over the last few days I feel like I'm gaining more control and direction.

I'm eating far more than I usually would with everyone taking me out to lunch and dinner and drinking far more than I usually would under Lottie's influence, so I grab my phone and text Denham.

*Me: Can I please use the gym? Where's the best place to buy some gym clothes?*

I have a quick flick through my wardrobe, knowing I don't really have anything suitable other than a couple of tanks, but looking anyway just in case something magically appears.

My phone dings a couple of minutes later.

*Denham: The gymnasium has a sports outlet, you will find everything you need in there. Take what you need and tell them who you are. xx*

I appreciate the gesture, but I'll just pay for it myself and not tell them who I am.

*Me: Thank you! See you this evening? x*

*Denham: You can bank on it xx*

I throw my cell on the bed while I hunt around for a hair band. It dings again and I snatch it up.

*Denham: You're going to be getting all hot and sweaty without me. How am I supposed to concentrate? I'm sulking.*

His text makes me laugh. I can just picture those full lips forming a pout. God, he even looks sexy in my mind when he's pouting.

*Me: You can make me hot and sweaty all over again later ;) xx*

I love being flirtatious with him, and I have no doubt that he will hold me to my words later this evening.

I grab up my belongings and head downstairs. After picking up some shorts, a sports tank, running shoes and a set of headphones, I head into the gym. I pass one gentleman who is leaving as I enter. He smiles a tight smile and heads off. The gym is now empty. No one at all in sight and although this is great as I can work my way around the machines as I please, there was a part of me that wanted to train in a buzzed, busy room and feel the atmosphere that surrounds it.

I glance around and survey the equipment. I thought I had top of the range gym equipment at Aaron's house, but seeing this room, I'm not so sure. Every piece of machinery is pristine. The metal gleams and there is not a fingerprint in sight on the touch screen consoles.

Mirrors line one wall and cross trainers, treadmills and rowing machines line the other. There is a free weights section on the far side, and other resistance machines dotted around the free spaces. A regular beat pushes through the built-in speakers around the ceiling ensuring you have music and a rhythm to work out to wherever you are positioned and all the cardio machines have a headphone jack.

I always work out to music. I'm disappointed that I left my music player behind when I left Aaron. I could store music on my new cell, but I haven't had it long enough to think about it. I love music. I love how it can stir such deep responses just by tempo or beat.

I warm up on one of the cross trainers, and it takes me nearly five minutes to figure out how the damn thing works but once it gets going it's great. The action is smooth and uninterrupted and I'm soon in the zone and enjoying the stretch of my muscles.

I haven't exercised since leaving Aaron's and after being so used to doing it every day, I've missed it. I come to a halt after twenty minutes and make my way to the soft matted area to stretch before using the free weights. The music is feeding through the speakers in the ceiling so I still feel buzzed and ready to push my muscles a little harder.

I stretch my back out by bending forward fully and placing my hands flat on the floor. I've always been very flexible. I learned to keep supple as a young girl when I went to ballet lessons and even though I haven't danced since I was eleven years old, I have kept up the exercises that keep your muscles strong and flexible. I lift my heel and hold it tight to my body, regulating my breathing and keeping my balance without a wobble. I hold like this until I feel the stretch ease and repeat with the other leg. I lie flat on the matting and pull one knee up to my chest, holding for a count of ten then releasing and doing the same with the other one.

When I sit upright, ready to stand, I gasp.

Standing in front of me is Denham, wearing the smirk to end all smirks. His dimple is in full force and he looks hot as hell in gym pants and a racer back tank that shows off his broad shoulder muscles and wide back.

"Hi," I say.

"Hi, yourself."

"What are you doing here?"

"I'm watching you," he answers unapologetically.

"How long have you been standing there?"

"Here? Oh, not long. I was standing in the doorway long enough to see your tight ass pointing north when you started stretching though."

I shake my head at him. "You're cute, you know that?"

He moves fast gripping the back of my head with one hand and my waist with the other. "I've told you before Arianna, I am not fucking cute," he speaks against my lips before stealing a kiss and releasing me. It leaves me breathless and I breathe deep to regain my control.

"You can continue if you like ..." he offers, taking up residence on the closest weight bench. He sits comfortably with one ankle resting on his knee.

"You come here to watch or you actually gonna work out with me?"

"I don't know what I'd take more pleasure in, watching you get all hot and sweaty or actually get hot and sweaty with you." He rubs his chin with his thumb and forefinger while he thinks about his own statement. I don't miss the gold glint in his eyes, and I know his mind is veering away from actually working out with me.

"Train with me on the punch bag."

"You want to throw some punches, Stunner? I already know you have a pretty mean right knee," he jokes.

"Come on, I've never done it, pleeeeeeease ..." I bounce in front of him from one foot to the other, side to side and he laughs.

"Fine, come with me but don't blame me if you hurt tomorrow."

"Why would I hurt tomorrow?"

"You wanna work out? Let's work out ..." He punches a fist into the flat of his hand, making a slapping noise that reverberates around the room and I know he means business.

Eeek, now I'm a little nervous.

We gear up in the segregated area of the gym room. I have on padded gloves and he's holding up a pad in each hand. "Okay, hold your hands up like this," he demonstrates before continuing, "then strike the pad. Try to catch me off guard."

I nod and guard up. I don't know which direction to go first but I figure I'm right handed so he would expect me to lead with that one, but I don't know how to throw a punch with my left and it feels awkward when I lift it."Well ... are we going to be here all day? Talk about fighting like a girl ..." he teases.

Fine, he wants to see what I'm made of, then I plan to show him. My right hand flies up, striking the pad with such force it sends his arm flying backwards. His grin tells me that's exactly what he wanted.

"Good. Another."

I punch left then right, repeating over and over in different patterns to try and catch him out. The thud of the gloves hitting the pads is exhilarating and I find myself trying to hit with more force and more determination each time. I throw my whole shoulder into each strike and each time he just nods, encouraging me to continue.

A slight pause between sets and I fake wiping my brow with my forearm. He does exactly as I suspect and drops his guard, just a little, and I strike hard and fast. It not only catches him off guard, it knocks him off balance. I see the shock register on his face as he struggles to compose himself, but it's too late. He hits the mat with a crash.

I nearly fall over with laughter, laughing so hard that my sides start to hurt and I buckle to my knees. I can't talk. Every time I think I have it under control, another bout of laughter hits me.

He looks at me in disbelief. He either can't believe that I decked him, or he's pissed that I find it so funny. I fall back on the mat, my stomach tight from the physical exertion as well as the belly laughter. "I'm sorry," I manage to offer.

He moves from sitting where he landed on his ass, to straddling me in a blink. I gasp as he surprises me and pins me with his hard stare. "You're not sorry, that was premeditated."

"I am sorry!" I try to convince him.

"Not only was it premeditated ..." His hard façade slips and his eyes fill with lust. "It was fucking hot." His lips crush mine and his tongue pushes past my teeth. He's unapologetic with his assault, claiming my mouth.

Claiming me.

I'm a willing participant and it surprises me that I not only want to be claimed, I want to claim him too.

My tongue fights against his, a battle of who wants who the most. My hands tangle in his tank, pulling it up past his waist so I can feel all the hard planes that have been taunting me for the last twenty minutes. I trail a hand to the waistband of his track pants and push my way in. His erection is hard, hot and pushing into my palm. He hisses in a breath when I make contact and he glances up at the mirrors lining the wall. It's only then that I remember that this is not a private gymnasium. It's a public facility, one of which anyone could walk into at any time.

"Shit," I murmur, pulling my hand out of his pants. "We can't do this here!" I say before trying to wriggle out from underneath him.

"Why not?"

"Because anyone could come in at any time. I don't know about you, but I'm not into exhibitionism," I bite.

Amusement flickers in those mesmerizing eyes of his "The only person I want to watch is you, Ari. No one will be walking in until I've finished with you."

"But it's a public place. How do you know that?"

His lips seal mine, trapping my words and almost making me forget what I was protesting about. He breaks the kiss to drag his tongue along my jaw, upwards until he reaches my earlobe. "I've locked the world out, Stunner. Those shorts of yours are far too scant for the eyes of anyone else," he growls softly. "The only person who will be watching when I'm inside you is me." He pauses to pinch my earlobe with his teeth "And you."

The only part that registers is the fact that we're locked in, and everyone else is locked out.

Nothing is standing in my way.

He rolls to his side, then onto his back, pulling me with him so I'm now straddling his hips. His hands push up the side of my waist, taking with them my tank, pushing it up over the curve of my breasts and forcing me to raise my arms. He pulls it off completely and tosses it aside. With a flick of his wrist, he has my bra unhooked and removed, disposing of it the same way he did my tank.

"Stunning ... simply stunning ..." he mutters, running his hands over my chest and cupping my breasts with his hands, trapping my nipples with his thumbs. He squeezes gently at first then harder and I feel a jolt to my core. "Does that make you wet, Ari?" he asks. I nod. "Tell me. Does it make you wet for me, Stunner?"

"Yes, I'm wet for you ..." I admit.

"Take off your shorts." It's a straight out order.

I stand over him, still astride his hips and slide my shorts down kicking them off one leg at a time. He pushes down his pants just far enough to let his erection spring free before I lower myself back down to him, placing my hands aside his head and hovering my body over his. I kiss him gently, teasingly, before becoming more insistent and feeling more empowered by the second. I take his length in my hand and stroke him from base to tip. He groans into my mouth and I feel his cock harden under my touch. I am in control and I like it.

My lips leave his and I miss them instantly but I know that where I'm about to go next will be just as rewarding. I shock myself at the level of desire I have to taste him. It's not something that has ever interested me before, but my mouth is watering at the very thought of it. I kiss my way down his chest, following the light dusting of hair down his stomach and coming to the V that tempts my eyes every time it is bared. My tongue snakes out involuntarily and I lick my path to his erection before taking him in my mouth. I open my throat and take him as far as I can go in one move.

He tastes of sweet and salt, all man and no apologies.

"Fuck ... Ari, that's ... fuck ..." he rasps, his head hitting the matting as he lets it fall back.

I lick and suck, feeling his muscles bunching and releasing all through his body while he's trying to hold on to some kind of self-control. Only, he's not in control here. I am. I know he's close. I keep an insistent pace until he grasps my shoulders and drops his hips, leaving my mouth momentarily empty.

"I'm gonna come soon, Stunner, and I want to do it inside of you, please." His voice is strained.

I look into his eyes. Soft sincerity mixed with a hungry passion looks back and me, and I know I can't deny him anything.

He reaches down into the pocket of his pants which are still around his ankles, and pulls out a condom, handing it to me. I look between the wrapper and him. "I've never ... I don't know how ..." I admit.

"Like this ..." he says softly.

He rolls it halfway and I feel my pulse accelerate faster watching him touch himself before he gestures for me to complete the action. He screws his eyes up tight when I stroke him gently at first then harder and faster.

"As much as I hate to stop you, I want inside you, like now, Ari ..." he orders desperately.

I rise up on my knees, positioning him at my entrance before lowering myself slowly and taking him in all the way. We both let out a groan and I gasp as waves of pleasure radiate to every part of my body and he begins to move inside me, stretching me as far as I can take it and filling me completely with every thrust of his powerful hips. I rise and fall, matching his relentless pace. Our breathing increases until it's erratic and coupled with moans of pleasure. I flick my head up and catch a glimpse of us in the mirror right in front of me.

I'm mesmerized.

I watch him move inside me. Grinding his hips and pushing as far as he can push. "You like watching us, Ari?" he grates out.

It's one of the sexiest things I've ever seen and I feel myself get wetter with every thrust that I watch in our reflection. I dip my head to kiss him and he moves his head to the side.

"Watch. I want you to see what I see when I make you come. You're close aren't you, Arianna? I can feel you starting to twitch around my cock."

He takes both of my hands in his and I place them either side of his head, pinning him and steadying myself as he pushes into me hard. "Look in the mirror and see how sexy you are," he orders. He drives into me with a force that lifts my knees off the ground, and it triggers tremors through my body.

I watch in the mirror as my jaw drops, letting strangled cries escape as he pounds into me, drawing out, teasing, then pushing back in, balls deep. My muscles start to contract and I know there's no going back. Where I felt powerful just a few minutes ago, I now feel powerless to Denham and the fierce orgasm that's building. He's taken back the control and I'm too far gone to care. I let my eyes close as sensations threaten to overwhelm my body.

"So fucking close, so fucking beautiful ... open your eyes now, Stunner."

Every muscle in my body draws tight for what seems like an eternity, then he thrusts once, twice, and I'm beyond the point of return. Sensations burst through every nerve ending in my body and I throw my head back as my whole body goes into spasm, contracting around him.

"Fuuuuck," he hisses as I feel him swell before he comes too, his muscles tightening in spasms as he lets out a groan. I let my head rest on his shoulder and he strokes my hair as we both come back down to earth, small tremors making us both shudder in delicious aftershocks. We stay like that until I start to shiver, our bodies sticky with sweat.

I reluctantly peel myself off Denham's chest, then stand up and extend my hand to help him up. He takes it and tugs, pulling me forward so I land back on his hard glistening body. "You're really something else, Ari," he mumbles, kissing me hard on the lips and rolling me over so I'm underneath him.

He hops up quickly, holding out his hand and pulling me up. We move about the room, sorting ourselves out and collecting our clothing that have been strewn around the place, stealing glances at one another and sharing contented grins. I unhook my bra from the handgrips on one of the weight machines and hear Denham snigger.

"No fair, I have more to get dressed into than you," I pout.

"No, Ari. You have more garments, however, the amount of fabric is certainly less. You know that if you work out in here again, you're going to have to wear something a little less revealing."

"Excuse me?"

"Well, look how short those shorts are, and that tank ... it shows your cute belly button. I don't want the world to see ..." he scuffs at the ground with his foot as his voice trails off.

"Denham ... you can't tell me what to wear," I say gently.

"I know, but I also don't want to have to beat the crap out of someone for looking at you the wrong way," he huffs. "I don't want to tell you what to wear, but I will ask you to please not torment me."

He stands with his hands on his hips, looking at the ground and I can tell this is hard for him to ask. He's done nothing but push me to find myself, do what makes me happy, so asking me not to do something is a contradiction.

But I understand.

I understand because I don't want anyone ogling him the way I do. The thought of another woman having thoughts about touching his body makes me feel rage from the pit of my stomach. I walk toward him, push my hands through the loop in his arms and wrap around him tight. "I won't torment you ..." I say, looking up into his eyes. "Not in public anyway."

"Good, because it caused me a shitload of trouble to shut this place for the last hour ..." He looks sheepish the moment the words escape from his lips.

"You closed it ... that's why the last person left when I was entering and why no one came in," I say, more to myself than him.

"I didn't know what else to do. I saw you walk out of the changing rooms looking like that, all pert and sexy and I didn't know how I was going to cope knowing that there would be a truck load of guys turning up to work out any minute with their eyes burning into your ass."

"How did you see me?"

"There are cameras everywhere in this place Ari. Well, not everywhere. Not in the changing rooms, of course, but most entrances and exits are covered by CCTV, plus everywhere that they are legally allowed."

"You're a pinnacle of safety, huh?"

"This place is my baby, Arianna. Got to keep her running smooth."

# CHAPTER 17

I've showered and dressed in comfortable jeans and a tee. I've done away with any makeup I had on and I've let my hair fall freely after having it knotted on the top of my head for the most part of the day. Denham surprises me with a steak dinner he has cooked for us. We sit at the table in Denham's apartment surrounded by candles and gentle music in the background, creating a soft light and a mood to match.

"So, what will you do tomorrow?" Denham asks.

"I'm not sure. I only have a few days before I start working and there are lots of things I need to do while I still have time to do them."

"Like what?"

"I ..." I hesitate before I speak, knowing that what I'm about to say might change the relaxed mood. "I think I'd like to see my mom and ..."

"And what?" he asks curiously, placing his knife and fork down on his plate and giving me his full attention, making it a little harder for me to speak.

"I'm going to see if I can get in touch with Aaron ..."

He picks up his napkin, wipes his mouth, then places it carefully back down. "I don't want you to," he says flatly.

"Please don't be like that. We've talked about this before. I know you don't want me to, but you know I need to. I just don't understand everything. I've been going over and over it in my head, trying to piece it all together, and I can't. It all seems so unlike him.""There's obviously things that you don't know about your so-called husband. Maybe he's put on a front all this time and he's not the person you think he is," he states. I don't miss the clipped way he speaks. "After all, you fooled him pretty well. Don't you think he could have done the same to you?"

I get up from the table, my chair scraping on the hardwood floor as I stand. I go to the kitchen, drop my plate in the sink and fumble around in the cabinet to find a glass, then pour a large neat vodka, knocking it back in one. It slides down my throat then burns, making my eyes water. I don't know why his words have angered me so much, he's only speaking the truth, but Aaron and I are not the same. I lied to him to protect myself. I had to. I didn't have a choice. But it seems he lied to me for his own personal gain. It makes me question all the good things I thought about him in the time that I spent with him. It makes me question everything. So much so that I'm not sure if I feel dizzy from the quick vodka I've just tossed down my throat or the ball of conflicting thoughts whizzing around my head.

Denham comes to stand next to me and takes the glass from my hand. He places it gently on the countertop, then turns me into him. His touch calms my racing mind, and I bury my head into his chest as he strokes my hair. "I'm sorry, that was insensitive," he admits. "I know you didn't have a choice."

"I couldn't tell him. He wouldn't have understood. It was too big a secret to let out."

"I know," he soothes.

"I'm fed up feeling like I've been the bad one in all of this. I feel like I'm the one in the wrong because I lied to him about who I was, when the truth is that he has lied too." I break away from Denham and pace the expanse of the room while things start to slot into place in my head. "But he's a good person, deep down, you know? He must be in trouble. I knew something wasn't right."

I'm talking aloud but more to myself than Denham. "He was moody. I knew it wasn't right, and I didn't do anything. I could have done something. Everything could have been different. Why does he need the money so badly? What kind of trouble could he possibly have gotten himself into?"

Denham is sitting on the couch, with his elbows propped on his knees, chin resting in his hands as he lets me rant, giving me time. It's the first time he's let my mouth run away with me without trying to stop it with a kiss.

"You're not kissing me."

"No." His simple answer sends a twinge of pain through my heart.

"Why?"

He shrugs. "You need to work things through in your head, and getting it all out seems the best way on this occasion," he says sadly. He's still thinking about what's best for me but his tone is flat and I can tell he's unhappy.

"What's going on in *your* head?" I lower my voice. "You seem distant all of a sudden."

He stands and closes the distance between us, wrapping me in the comfort and safety of his arms. I feel my body melt into his. It would seem that he radiates a potent feeling of calm which washes over me and renders me unable to think of anything else. "I think that's enough talking for one night, don't you?"

"Oh no, you don't," I say, poking him in the chest. "Out with it ..."

"I'm glad that things have happened this way," he states. I stiffen, not understanding why anyone would be glad of the situation I've been in. "I mean, I'm not glad about any of the pain you have suffered, but if all of this hadn't happened, I would never have known you existed and you would still be living as a girl called Natalie with no family and no identity other than the one you created. Were you really happy?"

I think about his answer. I'm happy that my path brought me to Denham's door, and no, I wasn't truly happy. And after experiencing happiness in its purest form over the last few days, and having a glimpse of my future, I know that I would never have been truly happy. I might have some things to sort out, a few obstacles to overcome, but I feel more alive than I ever have and a big chunk of that is down to Denham King.

"No," I sigh. "No, I wasn't. It's been a long time since I remember being happy and carefree."

"We are going to rectify that, Stunner. I want to fill your head with so many happy memories there won't be any room for the bad ones. Every time you recall a moment or an event, I want you to remember good times ... great times. I want all of them to be with me."

"Denham, I ..."

"Look, I know you can't give me words to explain how you feel. I know you're scared that if you say them aloud that it will be set in stone and there will be no going back, but I don't need you to say anything."

He brushes my hair from my face and runs his thumb along my marked cheekbone. "I feel you, Arianna. There is no explanation for it. I feel when you're happy and I feel when you're sad. That faraway look that you had in your eyes is nearly gone. I've watched you come to life." He speaks on a whisper and I feel his breath on my face; I feel every word in my heart.

The background music changes and Paul Weller begins to sing about feelings deep inside. "Dance with me," Denham says.

"Dance? Here?"

"Yes. Shhh, just close your eyes and feel, Ari." He pulls my hands up around his neck and closes both of his arms around my waist. His hips rock us gently and we move together, cheeks touching and feeling our heartbeats synchronize through our chests. He's right. We have a connection, and there is no explanation. It just is what it is.

He hums the gravelly notes to me and I feel them through my body. The sound of him makes my hairs stand on end and I'm overcome. My eyes fill with tears and I'm not sure why.

Who am I kidding? I know why.

I'm falling for him. It is ridiculous to be falling in love after a week, but I know how I felt before and I know how I feel now. Denying it is futile. My glass heart is exposed, and it terrifies me more than anything, but I can't stop it. I also can't admit it out loud, it's too soon. There may never be a right time to bare my heart so openly to someone. It's my secret, to keep, to cherish, and to hold on tight to. "You're going too deep in your head again, Stunner."

"I know," I reply sadly, I wish I didn't do it but I can't stop.

"Tell me ..."

"I'm too scared."

"Look at me," he demands. "Tell me."

"Don't you think this is all crazy? You and me … this … whatever this is …" I trail off at the end, a little frightened at what his response may be.

"What's crazy about it?"

"We've barely known each other a week."

"And there's a time limit on these kind of things? Huh, let me see …" he muses, comically rubbing his chin with his thumb and forefinger. "The rule book says no sex until after the third date, you must not fall in love before spending at least two months together, marriage is out of the question until you have at least been dating for a year, and after that children may be planned …"

"I'm being serious!" I say, smacking his chest playfully with the flat of my hand.

"Okay," he replies, continuing to rock us to the beat of the music. "Yes, I do think this is crazy, but not in a bad way. So what if it's only been a week? Who says it has to be more? Who says there isn't such a thing as love at first sight? I've told you, Ari, I can't pretend how I feel. I am sorry if that frightens you, but at least you know I'm being honest with you, right?"

I nod into his chest. "Then just let it be. I don't expect a declaration of undying love from you. In fact, I don't expect anything from you. Just don't keep trying to find reasons why this shouldn't work." He tilts my chin so I'm looking up at him, looking into those twinkling eyes and seeing nothing but honesty. "When you learn that you can let go and trust me, I'll be able to show you that I'm here to catch you."

Our lips find each other. Gently at first, butterfly soft kisses that set my skin alight. I push my fingers up into his hair and pull him closer. Our tongues dance a sensual tango that has me breathless and needy. Denham's hands slide up my waist, his thumbs rolling in circles along the way until he's holding my ribs and grazing the underside of my breasts.

"Well, fuck me if Denham King hasn't gone and got himself a woman to finally get laid."

We jump apart at the very unwelcome intrusion and our heads snap in the direction of the voice. It takes a second to register that I'm not imagining my perfect moment being totally ruined by a young, pretty, foul-mouthed woman.

I can feel my hackles rising.

"Um, do you want to tell me who this unexpected visitor is or do I need to go a little crazy on the pair of you?" I bite with my hands on my hips. I'm still trying to take control of my body which is living in the feeling of two minutes ago as I take in the young girl in front of me, all legs in a pair of short shorts, a sleeveless white shirt tied at her waist, showing her belly button and a mass of blonde curls that tumble around her in all directions.

"Oooh, you got a sharp one here, big bro." She laughs.

"Tara, what the hell are you doing here and how the fuck did you get in?"

Of course. Tara, Denham's sister. I breathe out a sigh of relief.

"Just thought I'd stop in, maybe tap you up for a little cash to tide me over."

"You wanna tell me how you got in here?" Denham asks sharply, ignoring her plea.

"I walked through the fucking door, how do you think? Jeez, I thought you were smarter than that," she jokes. Regardless that I'm still very pissed off at being interrupted, the way she speaks to Denham makes me laugh. Tara walks toward me and smiles. "It seems my brother has lost his manners. I'm Tara, his favorite sister." She winks.

"Tara, you're my only sister." Denham chuckles.

"Yeah, and therefore, your favorite." She grins.

I hold out my hand to her. "Pleased to meet you. I'm Arianna."

She pushes my outstretched hand out of the way and pulls me into a tight hug. "Bro, I like her." Tara releases me and goes to the kitchen, helping herself to a beer from the fridge.

"I'm so sorry," Denham whispers into my ear. "I'm gonna get rid of her and then we're going to pick back up where we left off."

"I'm loving the soft music and candles, D. Very smoooooooth," she says before popping the cap on a bottle.

"Um, what exactly are you here for, T?"

"I just wanted to see my favorite brother. Is that such a crime?"

"You want cash," he states.

"Well, if you're offering, just until payday. Oh, by the way, the door is open to the other penthouse. You should really be more careful," she casually says, taking a swig from the beer she has helped herself to.

Denham reacts instantly, not even asking her what she means. His reaction worries me and I follow him out of his door and into my apartment, watching as he switches on all the lights as he goes, frantically checking every corner, behind all the curtains and doors, even flinging the doors to the wardrobe open and slamming them with a bang that rattle right through me.

"Denham, stop ... you're worrying me."

He stops instantly, not even realizing I was behind him. His chest is heaving with concern and his face full of worry.

"What is it?" I ask.

"I'm sorry, Ari, I didn't mean to worry you, I just ..."

"What? Please, tell me."

"Your door was locked. And no one can get up here without the code."

"What aren't you telling me?" I ask, knowing there's an underlying reason for his frantic behavior.

"Nothing, there's nothing to tell, it's just ..."

"What?" I insist.

"You make me not think straight! I don't process anything rationally, and the thought of someone being in your apartment ... it scares me, Ari. You could have been in there on your own."

I know exactly what he means as I feel it too. I'm also sure the doors were shut, but we've been so carefree, so caught up in each other ... it was an easy thing to overlook. "Think about it, Denham, do you *actually* remember closing the door? We've been kinda ... preoccupied." I pull him to me, turning the tables and reassuring him for once.

"You're staying with me tonight," he states.

"I was planning on staying with you anyway," I reply confidently.

Denham raises his brow at me, flashing the golden twinkle in his eye. "Oh, you were?"

"Yes. Come on." I tug him by the arms and turn off the lights as we move through the apartment. Denham is still on edge and scans every corner, but doesn't argue. His unease makes me nervous and I think there may be something he's not telling me. But it's just a feeling and I convince myself that I'm looking for shadows in the darkness because I don't truly expect life to let me be happy.

I close the door and Denham rattles the handle to make sure it's shut properly, then hugs me tightly, exhaling deeply and kissing me on the forehead.

We enter his apartment to find Tara has made herself very comfortable on the couch. "What is up with you guys? Panic much? Relax, you probably just forgot to close it in your haste to get each other's clothes off."

"Don't you have somewhere to be, sis?" Denham grumbles through gritted teeth.

"Nope," she says, checking her watch. "Not for, like, an hour." She smiles smugly. "Anyway, I want to get to know the woman that you deemed good enough to bring up here."

"Tara ..." he warns.

"Ah, don't give me your big brother warning tone, D. You don't scare me. Do me a favor and grab me another beer while you're there, get Ari one too. Us girls can get to know one another while you make yourself busy with the washing up or something."

Oh, she has him wrapped around her little finger. She's so straight talking, and I instantly like her. She reminds me very much of Lottie—shoots straight from the hip and makes no apologies for it. She winks in my direction but keeps a straight face.

"Tara," Denham says exasperatedly. "You come in here, interrupt us, then order me to get you beer. And how do you know that Arianna even likes beer?"

"Because, sweet brother, any woman who has good enough taste to spend time with my brother will happily drink beer with me." She smiles sweetly. I see from the twinkle in her eye that she loves to wind him up, and I also think if she hadn't walked in at the exact moment that she did, he would be enjoying the banter. But right now he's a little tense. She does have a carefree, calming effect on him though and regardless of the panic that moved through both of us, I can see that he's starting to relax. He grabs two beers from the fridge and pops the caps. I take them from him and whisper a thank you, kissing him on the cheek.

"You don't have to drink that if you don't want to," he reassures me.

"It's fine, just go do the washing up or something," I quip, turning before he can say something back. I start to walk away, but he catches me on the ass with the flick of a hand towel before I can move very far which makes me yelp. Tara laughs so hard she almost falls off the couch and Denham's laugh rumbles around the apartment. Just like that, the earlier atmosphere is lifted.

Laughter really is a great cure for anything.

# CHAPTER 18

It's been a long day emotionally and physically and I've been lying awake for ages, even though Denham has drifted off to sleep. He sleeps like your typical man—two seconds and he's out for the count.I find myself chuckling about the stories Tara thought would be funny to tell me. Denham, of course, did not find it amusing and pretty much walked her out the door when she started to tell me about the time Denham let her play dress up with him, makeup and all. She never got to finish the story, but I would really like to spend some more time to find out what happened and get to know her a little better. She made sure we exchanged numbers so maybe I'll grab lunch with her sometime.

The situation with the open door also runs through my mind. Would we have been careless enough to leave it unlocked? Quite possibly. It seems that the rest of the world falls away when we're together and all that matters is each other. What we feel in that particular moment consumes every part of my being, Denham's too if I am to believe what he tells me. And I do believe him. It's crazy given the amount of time we have known each other.

No matter which way I puzzle and try to analyze things, I always come back to the same conclusion. Whatever happens, I'm powerless to the draw, to him and to how he makes me feel. I'm not sure how long I can accept this explanation for the intensity we have, or how long I will just let it happen before my cynical mind tries to find a hidden meaning or agenda, I just have to savor every minute of goodness and forget about the rest.

I study Denham's profile in the moonlight. Until I slept here, with him, I had always shut out the light, shut out the rest of the world in an attempt to block out reality and pretend, for whatever small amount of time I was allowed, that my dream world was real because, for the most part, it was better than the cold light of reality. But now, as everything else around me is changing, so is this. I'm grateful for the subtle light. I don't feel the need to shut out the rest of the world as I'm content where I am.

The light touches Denham's face on all his handsome edges; it highlights his sharp cheekbones and I instinctively trace them with the very tip of my finger, gently so as not to wake him and disturb the very peaceful sleep that he has found. His stubble prickles my finger and I stroke his face along his jaw until I reach his lips, his smooth, soft, full lips that I so badly want to kiss, but I don't as it would be selfish to wake him no matter how much he would protest to that thought. I could sit and watch him sleeping peacefully all night, but my eyes feel heavy and I figure I'll have many more nights to watch him sleep.

Instead of running from that thought, I embrace it.

When my mind finally stops racing so fast, and I'm content to just let myself be in a happy place, I lose myself to sleep. Sleep is less than kind to me though, and I'm plagued with dreams and scenarios that have me clutching at the sheets and wondering if I am in my own personal Hell or an imaginary world. Whichever it is, it's not somewhere I would willingly venture.

*My back hits the rough concrete wall and the breath leaves my body with a whoosh. His fingers grip tightly around my throat, so tight that I try and gasp for air but with each breath his fingers grip tighter and my lungs get smaller. He's yelling so loudly that the sound hurts my ears and the words blur together as the blood flow slows around my body.*

*"You stupid bitch! Look at what you made me do! You're a slut, nothing but a fucking slut!" He spits putrid, stale saliva at me as he throws the vile tirade in my direction. The only part of my body that is functioning properly is my vision, so I see it all. It's all happening in slow motion, drawing out the agony, making the fear last long enough so that he knows I won't forget it.*

*I see the rage ... the pure evil in his black eyes.*

*"You're gonna learn the hard way. How many times do I have to do this, eh? Do you like being punished, Arianna baby?" Every one of his loaded words stabs me, and my vision narrows as realization hits me that he is going too far.*

*He's going to cross the line.*

*I'm being hurtled toward a black tunnel that's closing in fast as his fingers pinch tighter with every second that passes. I try to call out one last time, and every last ounce of strength I have in my body is used in this last ditch attempt to make him stop.*

*But it's too late.*

*The darkness takes me ...*

"It's okay, Arianna ..."

The voice doesn't belong to the face in my nightmares. It doesn't match.But I'm in too deep. It won't stop.

I throw my head from side to side and push him away as hard as I can. I can't do it again. I can't.

I'm sweating, hurting, terrified.

No longer able to detach and block it out, I feel every hateful word, every threat, every nerve ending that's protesting against the pain.His hands tighten around the tops of my arms, pushing me into the mattress and rendering me unable to move.

Then he kisses me. Hard and insistent at first, and my instinct is to pull away, but I can't. He's too firm.

What's happening?

He tastes familiar. Then his lips are gentle and coaxing, encouraging me to respond and willing me back to him. I gasp, realizing where I am and who I'm with.

Denham releases my arms, breaking our kiss and pulling me onto his lap, holding me tight with his arms and shielding me from everything until I start to shiver.

"Shit," Denham curses under his breath. He shifts us to the edge of the bed, repositioning me so he can carry me in his arms. I wrap my arms around his neck as he carries me effortlessly to the bathroom, flicking on the shower without putting me down, and stepping in with me still in his arms.

I turn my head into his shoulder, shielding my face from the water as he just stands there, letting the warmth work through me. The shivers eventually subside and I pull my head out of the crook of Denham's shoulder.

"Are you okay, Stunner?"

I nod, and wriggle my legs to indicate that I can stand. I'm sure the muscles in his arms are burning after holding on to me for so long.He reluctantly puts me down but doesn't let me go. He takes off my soaked tank and panties and tosses them into the corner, then his boxers join them.

I'm stripped bare, and after that vivid nightmare I'm feeling vulnerable. I'm desperate to shake off the indecision, the doubt that fights with me in my head about what I want and what I can actually have.

*I want* to be able to move on.

*I want* to be able to love freely and not worry that it'll all be snatched away from me cruelly.

*I want* to be free from the burden of looking over my shoulder.

*I want* to stop running.

I'm tired.

The thoughts have a choke hold on me and I struggle to breathe.

"I know ... I know," his soft, gravely voice soothes. He strokes my wet hair and holds me tight.

My words weren't just running through my head. I was whispering them out loud. "It's not fair," I cry. "I want to let go of it all, but it's holding on so tight and I can't ..."

"Shh, just breathe, Arianna. You're safe with me ... just breathe." He continues to stroke my hair until my breathing starts to regulate and I start to feel self-conscious that I've just had another breakdown with him. I'm trying so hard to keep it all together and show him that I'm not damaged or broken, but deep down I know that I am. I can't hide it; it's part of who I am and if that sends him running for the hills it will break my heart.

But I can't pretend to be strong anymore.

His front is pressed to my back, so I reach for the hand wrapped around my waist and curl my fingers with his. My other arm reaches up and pulls his head into my shoulder. His lips press against the sensitive spot where my neck curves, and his stubble brushes my soft skin. "Make me forget," I whisper. "Please, make me yours."

He kisses a path up my neck and stops when he reaches my ear. His tongue darts out, licking my lobe and sucking it in between his teeth. "I won't let you be anyone else's, Stunner," he growls, taking my hands in his and pressing them against the cold tiles. The entire front of my body is exposed and the cold air reaches me, hardening my nipples and heightening my senses. His body is still pressed to my back, his erection resting between my ass cheeks, his hard chest pressing against my shoulder blades and his mouth on my neck.

"You were mine the moment our eyes locked. You know it. I know it," he states between kisses. I know he's right. His golden eyes hit me and have had me addicted ever since.

He's kryptonite to my intentions.

The exception to all my self-imposed rules.

The one to have stolen my heart and the man who I willingly give my body.

My hands slide up the tiled wall, stretching my body and allowing Denham to push harder against me. His hips rock gently, his length sliding between my legs and eliciting a groan from deep in his chest.

I'm desperate for more friction.

I'm needy for him to be inside me.

I want him to claim me, make me his, tell me he's mine.

He presses against my entrance, holding still, teasing me. I try to push my hips back into him, but he stays at just the right distance to continue to tease me.

"Please ..." I whimper.

"What do you want, Ari? Tell me ..."

"I want you ... only you ... inside me ... please ..."

"You're mine, Arianna, understand?"

"Yes ..."

"Mine to touch, mine to protect, mine to love ..." He enters me on his last word, sealing it into my mind, associating the word that terrifies me so much with a feeling so exhilarating.

His hands slide upwards across my belly, continuing until he reaches my breasts. His grip tightens with every thrust and it sends waves of pleasure bouncing over my entire body. I start to think I'm becoming delirious. My breaths falter unevenly, ragged as desire mixed with the heady feeling of letting him love me rushes through my body.

One hand leaves my breasts and touches between my legs. I jolt as the sensation is electrifying. He moves in circles, massaging me with the same rhythm as his thrusts, and I feel the tension start to build in my stomach. I clutch at the slippery wall for stability as my body moves in time with his.

"I feel you, Arianna, pulling me in. You want me?" he rasps, his heaving breaths taking over his voice.

"Yes, I want you."

"I'm yours, Ari, all yours," he grates out before clamping his teeth firmly on my neck and sucking the same spot. It sends the jolt that, along with his words, pushes me over the edge. His release comes fast, too. Our bodies in harmony and our minds making a connection far deeper than before. The pleasure is pure and explosive. Our bodies have spoken the words that my mouth was unable to do and I sigh with a pleasant exhaustion.

My hands are still braced against the wall when Denham withdraws from me, my legs quivering. I feel weak without him there to hold me up, but he's back in a flash, wrapping me in a robe and lifting me onto the countertop in front of the mirror, drying my hair gently with a towel.

"Are you warmer now?" he asks seriously.

I giggle. "Yes."

"What's so funny?"

I pull him closer to me and kiss his nose. "Will you warm me up that way every time I'm cold?"

"Every time you so much as shiver, I will be on you so fast, you won't have time to think about it," he whispers into my ear. I shudder and he looks at me wide-eyed. "Again? Now?" he asks, surprised.

"I'm not cold, Denham. Your breath tickled my ear," I state, although I would be happy for him to warm me up again. In fact, seeing him standing in front of me, wrapped only in a white towel from the waist down, has my mouth watering and my mind wandering.

"Good, because you need to rest. It's four in the morning."

"I'm sorry. I know you have to work in just a few hours and I've disturbed your night ... again."

He places his hands on my bare thighs. "No need to be sorry, Stunner, I like your kind of interruptions, but no more nightmares, okay? I'm here anytime you need me. You're not on your own anymore, so don't try to fight battles single handed."

"Okay," I agree quietly.

"Kiss me," he demands.

I look into his sparkling eyes and take his face in my hands. I kiss him with every ounce of emotion that I can muster and his response sings through my veins. I have someone on my side. Someone not only willing to fight for me, but able to fight as well.

I am not alone and neither is he.

An army of two.

I wake to the dawn light shining through the floor-to-ceiling windows. After getting dried off, we settled on the couch, curling together under a blanket and falling into a deep contented sleep. The warmth from the early morning sun shines in my eyes and I grumble, pulling the blanket up over my head and trying to disappear from the world. It doesn't escape me that I am alone, but it doesn't worry me either. I am completely aware of where I am and I think for the first time in a week, I wake without feeling disoriented. I can hear the shower running in the bathroom and I smile to myself as I recall last night. I pull the soft fleece blanket around me then go and stand on the balcony. The view from Denham's balcony is more amazing than mine. I turn my face up into the warmth of the sunlight and close my eyes. I'm not sure exactly what time it is but the roads are quiet and there is very little noise. It's peaceful and I'm at peace. In my head and my heart.

It is just then that I realize just what Denham King has done to me, for me. He has given me wings to fly. No longer trapped or restricted. But more than that, he's given me roots to come back to. A chance to love and be loved in equal measures. I still have no explanation. All I know is that it feels right. Nothing has ever felt so right. I'm aware of how things feel when they're wrong, and this isn't one of those times. It is what it is. Allow it to happen. Embrace it. Live it. Because life doesn't always give you second chances.

"Good morning, Stunner."

I turn to find Denham standing in the doorway holding two mugs of coffee. "Morning," I reply with a smile.

He kisses me before handing me a mug of coffee and standing next to me. "It's beautiful, isn't it?"

"Yes, very."

"The view wasn't bad from the doorway either." He grins down at me and I nudge him with my shoulder. "You know your phone has been buzzing off the hook this morning?"

"Mine?" I say, surprised as only a few people have my number. I frown "Maybe Lottie or my mom."

"Well, you'll find out when you look at it, won't you?" Denham says sarcastically.

"You're a bit chirpy for someone who had such a little amount of sleep, aren't you?"

He chuckles. "Yes, I should be exhausted, but it's the nature of the sleep deprivation that has me feeling great."

"Oh really?"

"Yes, you see, I had this hot little stunner in my bed last night." He pauses, looking for my reaction out of the corner of my eye.

"You did?"

"Yeah, she rocked my world," he says, trying to keep a straight face.

"Jeez, she sounds pretty awesome," I say, playing along.

"She is. She's smart, funny, amazingly talented and more stunning than the most beautiful sunrise."

I take up the usual position that I do when I'm nervous. I look down at my shuffling feet and my fingers fidget around my coffee mug. Denham lifts my chin with his index finger so I have no choice but to look at him.

"I can't get enough of her," he says softly. "I want to spend every waking minute beside her, inside of her. She's my drug."

I smile and turn my cheek into his hand. He takes my coffee mug and places it down, giving me just a second to look into the beautiful depths of sincerity in his eyes before his mouth covers mine hungrily. I wrap my arms around his neck and he lifts me by my waist, encouraging me to twist my legs around him, all the while not breaking the contact of our lips. He walks us back inside, only just holding onto the blanket that is now barely covering me.

"D, I'm sorry man, but ..."

The voice comes from the doorway and we break apart fast. Denham drops my feet to the floor and stands in front of me protectively. His chest is puffed out and his shoulders pulled back so wide I have to bend at the waist to see past him. My heart races as I gather the blanket up and peek around him to see who it is.

"For fuck's sake ... get out before I fucking knock you out, Spike!" Denham barks.

Spike holds up his hands in mock surrender. "I'm sorry, man, but you don't answer your fucking phone and there's a problem downstairs." He nervously rubs his hands on his jeans.

"What is up with my fucking family?" Denham seethes, turning to me and throwing his hands up while trying to reign in his temper. "That's it, I'm taking away all of your keys. Where's the fucking fire, Spike?"

I can't help but glance down across his body. The only thing covering him is a small towel wrapped around his waist and even that doesn't cover his very obvious erection.

"Um, you might want to ... uh ..." I motion to his crotch with my eyes.

"Shit ..." he hisses. "Fine, I'll let this go for now, but I'm saving it for later." He smirks before turning me in the direction of the bedroom, continuously covering as much of my body as he can with his, even though Spike is looking anywhere but in our direction.

"Um, D? Jack is doing his nut, down there," Spike insists anxiously.

"You gonna tell me why?" Denham retorts.

"I ... I can't ..."

I don't miss the look that passes between them. It's something he doesn't want me to know about.

"Fine. Piss off, Spike. Wait outside and I'll be five minutes." His tone is short and clipped, clearly pissed at being interrupted for the second time in as many days.

Denham gently directs me into the bedroom and I check my phone while he's getting dressed. "Gee, I have like five missed calls."

"That's what I told you ... Who wants you so urgently?" he enquires.

"Beth called," I say excitedly. I omit to tell him that I have several missed calls from an unknown number which is probably Beth trying to get a hold of me from the boutique's line.

"Well, I needn't ask what you'll be doing today."

"Is it too early to call her back?"

"No, she'll be at the boutique, give her a call." He smiles. "I don't know how long I'm going to be sorting whatever mess they've managed to get themselves into down there. I'm sorry, Ari, I would much rather be spending the day with you," he muses thoughtfully.

"And I would love to be spending the day with you, but we have tomorrow and the day after that, aaaaand the day after that too." I smooth down the front of his tee, feeling his muscles under my fingers and immediately regretting the fact that we don't have more time together this morning. "We also have this evening ..." I suggestively raise my brows.

"Yes, I have plans for you, missy."

"You do? Well, I'll look forward to them, Mr. King."

"I like when you call me that ..."

"I'll make sure to do it more often." I kiss him sweetly on the cheek. "Now go and run your empire, then you can come home to me."

"Home to you." He tests the words on his lips.

"Yes," I say confidently.

His finger gently brushes my cheek. "I think they're the most perfect words that have come out of your pretty little lips so far."

"So far today? Or just so far?"

"So far. Of course, I much prefer hearing you cry out my name over and over as your body gives in to me." His eyes darken as he speaks and our hips grind against each other instinctively. "Fuck Spike and his problems," he hisses, pulling away.

I clutch at the blanket that is still draped around me as he reluctantly lets me go. He grabs his cell and keys and kisses me hard before heading for the door. "Call me if you need *anything,* okay?"

"Okay."

"And if you need to go anywhere, Jack will take you. He'll be on standby all day. All you need to do is stop by the front desk and they'll fetch him."

"I don't need a babysitter, Denham."

"Don't argue. You're my woman, let me look after you," he insists. "Just close the door when you leave, it'll lock automatically. I'll have Tara's key from her later so you can come and go as you please."

"I don't—"

He presses a finger to my lips "I said don't argue."

"Fine." I mock grumpiness with him, but he smirks and sees the smile creep across my face. Although I don't need babysitting, I like that he wants to look after me. "Have a good day, dear!" I call out after him.

His chuckle moves through the apartment before the door closes and he's gone. I feel a little weird being in his apartment on my own, but there is something about it that is nicer than mine. It feels lived in.

Although nothing is messy, there are personal belongings around the place which makes it feel more homey. It smells of Denham too.

When I glance around the bedroom, I see his guitar and remember hearing him play. Two of the strings are broken and it reminds me that there are still so many things we don't know about each other, still so much to find out.

My phone blips as a message comes through. It breaks me out of my reverie and I read the text.

*Beth: Put that hunk of a man down and get your ass to the shop! 11am. Bring your designs.*

I laugh at her directness, but I'm also nervous about showing her my designs. I just hope they're good enough and she's not disappointed.

I hop off the bed, grab all of my clothes and as an impulse thought, I pick up his guitar. I head out, still clutching the blanket around me, but I'm only moving across the hall and there's no one around to see me anyway. I juggle everything that I'm holding to slip the card in the door and push it open. I place the guitar down by the doorway as I'll be picking it back up when I leave. I need Beth's help with something.

I click the door shut and I freeze. Something feels off. Something's not right. Ice moves through my veins, inch by inch, and I'm frozen to the spot. A breath touches my neck and the pungent smell of stale cigarettes invades my nose and infects the air around me.

It's him.

"Hello, baby ..." he leers.

It's Jonny.

Fear creeps upward from my toes and settles in every recess of my body. I knew this time would come. I've been hoping and praying with every ounce of my being that he would forget me and leave me to live as I please. I wanted him to vanish. Disappear like he never existed.

But deep down I knew. I knew he wouldn't let me go. It was a major dent to his pride if nothing else, and his compulsion to own me will always override any logical thought.

Stupid girl.

I should have stayed away.

Now the last few years have all been for nothing. I have achieved absolutely zero by being away other than a bigger mistrust and a deeper cavern in my heart made by the fact that I actually had hope and now it's gone.

He stands behind me, his index finger gently brushing my tousled hair from my bare back. The act makes me shiver. Not a shiver of pleasure that Denham gives me; a shiver of repulsion. A shiver that actually works its way down through my stomach and back up my spine. I think I'm going to throw up. I clamp my mouth tight shut and will the fear to go away. I will be strong. He will not break me again.

But I know the power he has over me.

The power to turn me to dust.

"Did you really think I was going to let you go?" he says, his voice resonating a dangerous undertone. "Did you?" He moves closer still, but doesn't touch me. "My stupid, beautiful girl ..."

His nose touches my shoulder and he draws it upwards along my neck, inhaling as he goes. It makes me want to retch.

"I can smell another man's scent, Arianna." He pauses and I hold my breath, bracing myself for what might come next. "Sex ... it reeks."

It might have been years since I saw him in the flesh, but I can remember the expressions his face holds and I can picture his curled lip and the wild look in his eye. He grabs the hair on the back of my head roughly and I cry out. Every follicle screams as I feel his grip tighten.

"How did you ever think I wouldn't find you? How did you ever think you would be free?" He almost sings the words, a torturous lullaby, barely a whisper, but loud enough to ring around my head. "Money talks, Arianna. And in your case, the talk was cheap."

The ringing in my head gets louder. Echoes further. My eyes lose focus. The pain pulling at my head takes over. "Please ..." I manage to whimper. I hate how desperate I sound, but I don't know another way out.

"My. Stupid. Beautiful. Girl." Every word is punctuated with an exhale of stale breath across my skin.

He wraps an arm around my neck from behind and applies just enough pressure that my intake of breath is affected. I can feel myself react and start to panic, but my body stays paralyzed out of fear. I search my mind for ways to get out of this, ways to make it stop, then sharp pain pierces the top of my leg, followed by a burning sensation. The mixture of his tightening grip and the realization that he just pushed a needle into me sends me into a spin.

Is he going to kill me? I pull every ounce of strength that I can from my body and claw at his hand with my nails. He drops his grip, letting me go with a snigger and I run. I run as fast and as far away from him as I can. I make it to the bedroom when the edges of my vision blur and start to tunnel. The adrenaline pushes the substance he has injected me with through my body at top speed. It acts fast and my legs lose strength and buckle underneath me.

The ground seems to rise up toward me, and my head hits the ground with such force that it steals my vision and the world turns black. The last of my senses to leave me is my hearing. Everything echoes like I have my head underwater. I hear him approach, heavy footsteps stopping next to me. An evil laugh comes from deep within him, and I try to fight my body. I try to muster up any last piece of consciousness that I can, but it's futile.

"Still trying to run, Arianna. You'll never learn."

My body is jerked to the side and my last conscious breath leaves my body forcefully as his boot hits my ribs. My muscles contort. Old injuries protest. I'm aware that it's happening, but I don't feel a thing.

No freedom. No escape. No feeling in my body, just the sound around me eventually fading to nothingness.

## To Be Continued ...

## This Story Is Concluded In 'King of My Fears'

# BONUS MATERIAL

## Denham King Alternate POV

## Elevator Meeting

That damn woman drives me mad. Why she can't leave me alone is beyond me.

Yes, I've made my bed and now I'm fully aware that I'm lying in it. The problem is that it feels old and uncomfortable, it doesn't do anything for me anymore. In fact, I think the whole thing with Amy is starting to make me feel ill. She has trouble taking no for an answer, and I know she's going to be relentless until I make it clear that we've reached the end of our ... our ... well, whatever it is we have.

I jab my finger into the button to take me down to the ground floor and my foot taps with impatience. I have stacks of paperwork, which has to be done this week, meetings with investors to potentially expand The Kingdom as a brand and open more establishments, but all of this takes time. It's something I'm desperately short of and that woman ... geez, she ruffles my feathers and not in a good way. If I can get the investments and move forward, I can buy her out and then I might just be able to breathe again. My chest squeezes as I recall the events that led me to depend on Amy for comfort. It's not often I reminisce. Delving too deeply opens wounds that have never fully healed, will never fully heal. A fucking great big cavern in my chest.

The elevator door opens and a body slams into me. I open my mouth to berate the person that has carelessly plastered herself across my body. I am not in the mood for this today.

Then I look down.

Dainty hands press against my chest as the culprit struggles to right herself. I grip both of her shoulders to steady her and watch as her gaze travels from the floor, slowly upwards along my body. I don't miss the subtle flair of her nostrils as her senses force her body to explore what's right in front of her. Her fingers tighten against my chest and I feel her nails pushing in my skin. The small gesture makes my dick twitch.

*Fucking hell, King.*

Her blue eyes meet mine and my heart slams into my ribs. She's fucking beautiful and sexy and ... bruised. Her creamy flesh is broken and blackened and I want to reach down and stroke it.

I'm torn. I'm hit by her natural beauty and drawn in by the way she fits just right in my hands, against my body, but I'm sickened by the vicious black and purple bruising that marks her defined cheekbone. And there's no light in her eyes. She has beautiful eyes, they could be captivating with a sparkle. What would it take to make them spark? I bet they glisten when she comes.

Realizing I've been staring at her far too long, I quickly mask my thoughts and try out a smile on her. It works.

"My apologies, Miss ...?"

I watch as she reacts to a shiver that looks like it travels the length of her spine before she stutters.

"Uh, Jamesson. Miss Jamesson," she answers, her voice small and breathy.

She shifts around nervously and her eyes dart to the door of the elevator. She wants to leave, but I don't want to let go of her just yet. She has me magnetized.

Then she smiles.

It's a nervous smile, but it touches the corners of her eyes and I get a glimpse of her honest beauty. I slide my hands down her bare arms, letting my thumbs skim over her inner elbows and down the underside of her forearm. I don't miss her sharp intake of breath and the way she looks up at me with her full lips parted just slightly so I can see the wet of her tongue.

My hands continue to slide until I reach the very tips of her fingers and her pads touch mine.

She breaks. Her nervousness gets the better of her and she steps to the side, scurrying into the elevator and staring at the back wall. It's just as well. If she turned and looked back at me, I'm not sure what I'd do.

Yes, I do.

I'd kiss her. I'd claim her, right here, right now.

*Then she'd probably run for the hills, you dumbass.*

*For fuck's sake, get a grip, man.*

Sure, she's pretty, actually, she's more than pretty. She's probably the most captivating woman I've ever seen, and yes, that's definitely the fastest reaction I've ever had to anyone. I want more. Fuck me, do I want more.

*I want* my name to roll from her tongue in both a whisper and a scream.

*I want* to light a fire in her wounded eyes.

I need a fucking cold shower and a strong coffee ... and some looser fitting slacks before I suffer from acute zipper strain.